Opening his e
temper, Kel g
kiss.

"I want to do it again. ~~~ ~~~ like I said, let's take it slow."

"Because of me?"

Damn. Was he messing this up? "Because I want it to be perfect and right for both of us. Okay?"

Desi nodded, then let her head fall against his shoulder. Relieved, he snuggled her in, astonished that this self-assured woman had exposed so much vulnerability to him. Vulnerability he had never imagined could be part of a woman who presented such a confident face to the world.

He felt a little shiver run through her, then she softened completely. Staring at nothing, he held her and wondered what he was walking into. What he might be dragging her into.

* * *

Be sure to check out the rest of the
Conard County: The Next Generation series!

UNDERCOVER IN CONARD COUNTY

BY
RACHEL LEE

First Published in Great Britain 2016
By Mills & Boon, an imprint of HarperCollins*Publishers*
1 London Bridge Street, London, SE1 9GF

© 2017 Susan Civil Brown

ISBN: 978-0-263-93030-6

18-0117

Our policy is to use papers that are natural, renewable and recyclable products and made from wood grown in sustainable forests. The logging and manufacturing processes conform to the legal environmental regulations of the country of origin.

Printed and bound in Spain
by CPI, Barcelona

Rachel Lee was hooked on writing by the age of twelve and practiced her craft as she moved from place to place all over the United States. This *New York Times* bestselling author now resides in Florida and has the joy of writing full-time.

Dedicated to my daughter,
an urban and regional planner,
who is on the side of preserving nature, too.

Prologue

Six men sat around a poker table in the back room of an historic hotel somewhere in Wyoming. They were only vaguely aware of its history, but the bullet holes that pockmarked the expansive wood bar out front hinted at it. The place was supposedly haunted, too, but they didn't care and didn't believe.

They had business to discuss.

A new outfitter had shown up late last spring, and from what they could tell, he was unlicensed. The men at the table were unlicensed as well, lying to clients from out of state, telling the nonresidents that they could legally hunt under the outfitter's license. Not true, but they didn't care.

No, they led the hunts into public lands as far away from possible observation as they could get, wined and dined the hunters to make them feel like big deals, then got them their damn trophies, knowing these guys would leave the state immediately.

Babied them, is what they did, sometimes even setting up the shot and aiming the rifle.

It was good money, all of it carefully laundered out of state.

But now some new guy was horning in, and he could be big trouble. Losing a few trophies to the hunters he guided wasn't as much of a concern as his lower charges. He could force them all to charge less, especially if he got enough people to work for him.

The bigger concern was that if he screwed up he'd bring a lot more scrutiny to bear and could cause their operations to cut way back until the heat went away. Also, they couldn't afford to take this fight public by reporting him. Not when they'd spent so long carefully burying themselves below the state's radar.

The burly guy with the ponytail slapped his cards facedown on the table. "We gotta eliminate him. As in dead."

The other men nodded. If this interloper had just played nice with them, they might have let him in, but instead he'd started a solo operation. No respect. Dangerous.

"Okay," said a man whose face was nearly as grooved as the mountainous landscape. "Accidents happen, people disappear out there. Find out where his base is."

"I'm hearing Conard County," said the ponytail man. He knew a lot more, but he wasn't about to share or reveal his sources to anyone. They had to be well protected. But this guy he wanted dead? He wasn't what he pretended to be, a fact that ponytail kept to himself. Knowledge was power and he had it. The last thing he wanted was for his partners to wet their pants and run.

"Well, hell," said the man with mountain terrain for a face. "He hasn't set up shop, that I've heard."

"Just about to," said ponytail. "And that's one of our most profitable areas."

"Yeah," said one of the other men, his voice gravelly from cigarettes, his face weathered until it looked like a map. "He dies. Just make it look like an accident."

The ponytailed man nodded and never mentioned that they had a second target: that nuisance of a warden, Desi Jenks. One favor for another. If they guessed that they'd probably all turn into frightened grannies.

Then they went back to playing cards, unaware of all the past times when just such murderous plans had been laid here.

Chapter 1

Senior Game Warden Desiree Jenks, or Desi as she preferred to be known, arrived at the ranch belonging to Jake Madison, just in the foothills of Thunder Mountain in Conard County, Wyoming. She knew what she was going to see. By the sound of things, Jake, who was also the Conard City police chief, was mad enough to shoot someone.

She couldn't blame him, and yet, it was her job to stay calm and maintain a good relationship with the local people, most especially the ranchers. She relied on them probably more than they guessed. Like this. Only because of Jake would she have ever known about it.

She parked her official truck near the front of the house and climbed out. The early October air had a chilly bite so she pulled on her dark green insulated vest over the long-sleeved red shirt that was part of her uniform—and the reason Wyoming wardens were called "redshirts."

She retrieved her shotgun out of the rack in the back and loaded a few shells, turning in time to see Jake coming out of the house. A tall, well-built man, he was dressed in his own insulated vest and jeans, and carrying an orange hunting vest.

"Damn it, Desi," he said as he strode up to her. "This has got to stop. My land is posted. Nobody asked for permission."

She nodded. "I get it, Jake. And it's getting worse by the year." She laid the shotgun down on the seat after making sure the safety was on, and reached for her other equipment.

"No kidding. I suggest we ride if you don't mind. It's a distance and pretty bumpy."

"Fine by me." She pulled out her orange hunting cap and crammed it on, then hung the strap of her camera around her neck. Next, she tugged out a pack carrying her evidence collection kit and slipped it onto her back. Jake had donned his orange vest. The man ought not to have to worry about such things on his own land, Desi thought. Posting it should have been enough to keep people away, not that it always was. And he had a small child to worry about, even worse. After pulling on her gloves, she followed him across the dry, hard ground of the yard.

Jake had already saddled two horses that waited patiently in the barn. Desi shoved her shotgun into the saddle holster, then mounted the big pinto easily. The ranch hand just outside waved as they passed by, clearly about to climb into a battered pickup.

Riding side by side, they moved quickly. "Did you find it?" she called to Jake.

"Larry did. He came riding back to tell me, so I went out and...well, the air turned kinda blue. Crap, I hate poachers, but my cattle are out there, too. The hunters must have chased that bighorn down the mountain."

"Maybe." It was still a little too early for the bighorn to be migrating to much lower altitudes. Later in the month or early next month, as the weather got colder and mating season drove them, they'd come down lower, seeking a safe valley for rutting. But that didn't fit this place or this time. Yeah, some hunters with dogs might have driven him down. Or maybe he was sick. She'd have to find out.

Twenty minutes later they approached the site of the kill. She could smell it. Must be two days old. Rain the last two nights. No footprints of any kind to help her investigation.

But there was no question about what she saw in the tall yellowed grass. "Damn," she swore.

"Yeah," said Jake. "And double damn."

The remains of a large ram's body lay headless in the trampled grass. Trophy hunting. God, it sickened Desi. The meat left to rot, which was a crime unto itself, the animal expertly skinned for its pelt...and the carrion eaters had already started their job.

The horses didn't like the smell, and began to sidle and nicker. Hanging onto her reins, Desi swung down and passed them to Jake. "You take the horses back a way. I need photos and samples."

The wolves had already been here, along with the hawks and vultures and ravens. Not good about the wolves. Desi hated to see any of them get killed, but if they menaced Jake's herd, he was going to do exactly that.

Half an hour later, she'd retrieved all the evidence she thought she'd find, including a single bullet. Straightening, she walked over to Jake. "We gotta get it out of here. Wolves found it only recently. Maybe they didn't catch the scent right off because of the rain. Anyway, they haven't finished feeding yet, maybe scared off by Larry, but they're probably watching right now, waiting for a chance to finish it."

Jake nodded as he passed the reins back to her. "Larry's bringing the truck out. I guess I can't take the carcass up the mountains? And it's no good for anyone to eat now."

Desi stared at a mess she felt bordered on some kind of desecration. Leaving it here would attract the wolves. Moving the remains...depending on where it was dumped there could be some legal issues. Mess though it was, it was still evidence.

She sighed. "You know you can't dump the meat, Jake. It's probably useless at this point, especially since I have tissue samples, but I should take it in for evidence anyway. Nor would burying it keep the wolves away."

"Got my herd to worry about."

"I know. Help me get it into the back of my truck. I'll cart it to an evidence freezer, not that I expect we'll locate whoever did this. But we can't leave it here."

"Guess we're going to be keeping a sharp eye out the next few days."

Desi just shook her head, her stomach roiling with anger. "It stinks, Jake. I can't tell you how mad this poaching makes me. Bad enough in the mountains, but worse on private property. So I guess I need to go back for my truck."

"Larry's coming. He's taking the longer way around. I knew I was going to have to do something about this one way or another. I don't want any wolves eyeing my herd."

"No, you don't," she agreed. Then she offered some

casual conversation, seeking a way to avoid erupting. "How's Nora?" His wife.

"The doc says she still has a month to six weeks, but if you ask me, that woman is about to pop."

Desi managed a laugh. "She must be miserable."

"She's getting there. The nursery's all ready, James seems to understand he's about to have a baby sister, and Nora...well, she's at the point where I have to stop her from moving the furniture. Nesting, one of her friends calls it, but would you believe I caught her trying to move a sofa bed? Must weigh damn near two hundred pounds."

"Um...wow."

Jake chuckled, though he didn't appear at all happy at the moment. "Yeah. An understated version of my reaction."

Fifteen minutes later, she heard the unmistakable approach of a truck. Turning, she saw Larry in the battered red pickup jolting his way over uneven ground. Between the three of them, it didn't take long to get the remains wrapped in the plastic Larry had brought along, and soon Jake was dousing the bloody ground with gallons of vinegar from the back of Larry's truck.

She rode the pinto back to her truck, taking her time because she'd have to wait for Larry. Jake stayed behind because he was concerned about where his fence had been broken, allowing this ram to get through.

No point calling anyone, she thought as she rode. Even if this hunter had a valid permit, he'd have to keep at least the horns attached to the skullcap to prove what he'd killed. No, this guy wasn't going to tell anyone around here about the kill, especially when he'd wasted the meat. Permit or no, the sheep had been killed on posted land, making it poaching. No truly legit hunter would do that.

Legally, however, the hunter had fifteen days to report the kill. Two down and counting. She wasn't holding her breath.

She had to remain calm and collected. It was her job. Much as the anger churned in her stomach, she had to keep her head clear. It wasn't always easy. She'd been businesslike with Jake because she had to be, but she shared his fury.

This was happening too often. In her five years at this station, she'd seen the increase, and she had little doubt that the trophy hunters were coming from outside the state.

Yeah, locals poached. It happened often enough, but the main difference was, while they might exceed the limits of their licenses, or even hunt without one, they kept the meat. They wanted the meat.

Trophy hunters were something else altogether. A big, beautiful ram had been killed just so some idiot could put its head on a wall and its skin on the floor. Wasting the meat was against the law, too, so even if this jerk was licensed to take that ram, he'd committed a crime.

Not to mention the little bit of trespass that was involved. Now Jake would have to spend days looking for where they'd broken through his fence, while guarding his herd from wolves who might now think they could find easy pickings there. Bad for Jake. Bad for the wolves. Bad for the whole darn ecosystem.

Desi enjoyed a lot about her job. She loved keeping an eye on the migratory animals, making sure they were able to trek and that they were healthy. She loved everything about protecting the wildlife around here, even when it meant giving someone a hard time for fishing without a license, or exceeding the catch limit. And she loved it when she caught a poacher.

But this…these guys weren't going to be easy to catch. They came and went like ghosts, clearing out as soon as they had their trophy. They didn't hang around waiting for a neighbor to become suspicious or someone to catch sight of what they were doing and call the wardens. Nope. Ghosts.

As she drove through town on her way back, she waved to people she recognized, and pulled over once to share a few words with Julie Archer, who kept wanting her to join "the gals" for lunch. Except Desi's job didn't often leave a lot of regular time for socializing. She liked the group of women, though, and kept telling herself she was going to make time for lunch with them some weekend. After hunting season.

When she got back to the office, the closed sign still hung in the window. That didn't surprise her. Five wardens worked out of this station, covering thousands of square miles. Most of them only checked in by phone except when there was a big meeting or they needed to coordinate on something.

Being senior warden, she was based here.

The two-story office was on the edge of town, just a small distance from a quiet neighborhood. They kept it up pretty well so it looked good, all stained wood with sturdy shutters for the windows. Her living quarters were upstairs, a leftover from days long gone. It also had a small dirt and gravel parking lot, and a blue truck with a shell was waiting there as she pulled in.

Seeing the truck, she pulled up near it instead of driving around back to the shed with the evidence lockers.

Curiosity punched her anger down a little bit, then when the guy immediately climbed out, her anger deserted her completely. An instant attraction hit her as if by magic.

He wore a plain blue shirt under a blue quilted vest, tight jeans. Every inch of him bespoke a fit, well-muscled body. As he walked toward her on hiking boots, she felt another burst of attraction. He moved easily and his dress spoke woodsman, not cowboy. Ah, cut it out, she told herself. No time for this. She had a problem to deal with.

She climbed out to face him and got another surprise when she realized how tall he was, and she wasn't short herself. Smiling gray eyes set in a square face looked at her from beneath a camouflage ball cap.

"Can I help you?" she asked.

"You must be Warden Jenks."

"Yes, sir."

He offered his hand. "Kel Westin, WIU."

Wildlife Investigative Unit? Surprised, she shook his hand, feeling an electric jolt at the contact, and summoned a smile. "Come on inside."

"Thanks."

As he followed her inside, Desi wondered if something had gone wrong. What was he investigating? Her? One of her wardens? But no, they didn't investigate that stuff, did they? Her heart rate picked up a little bit. Whatever this was about, it wasn't casual.

"Coffee?" she asked. She sure wanted some.

"Thanks. It's been a long day. And you look like you've had one, too."

"Poachers," she said succinctly as she readied the pot to brew. "Worse, trophy hunters."

"Would you believe that's exactly why I'm here?"

She hit the start button on the coffeepot and faced him. He looked to be in his late thirties, eyes the color of a storm-heavy sky, his skin pleasantly weathered by the elements. A lean face. "ID?" she asked. If this was going any further, she had to be sure she wasn't talking to her poacher.

Without comment, he reached into his hip pocket and slipped out a leather case. Flipping it open, he showed his badge and photo ID.

"Thanks," she said.

"No problem. Thing is, I'd like it if you'd keep that under your hat. Don't even tell your other wardens."

Her attention sharpened even more. "Why?"

"Because I'm here to investigate the poaching and I'm going to do it undercover by starting my own outfitting business. The less people know, the better."

"Hallelujah," she said quietly, and finally pulled out her chair to sit at her desk. "I didn't think anyone was listening."

"Oh, we've been listening. It's just this isn't the only place where this is happening and we've got limited manpower. Thing is, we just recently got intelligence that all this trophy hunting might be linked to a single very active ring. But we need evidence, so here I am."

She thought about what he'd just said and felt her heart quicken. A ring? It suggested huge problems. She came out of her thoughts about how big this could be with a start as she heard the coffee finish brewing.

"Grab a chair," she said, pivoting her own to reach for two mugs on the counter behind her and pour them full of coffee. She passed him one. "Let's talk about today, then you tell me what you need."

He picked up the mug and drank deeply, then rose immediately to refill it. At least he didn't ask her to. She was a little prickly about her gender because women were so rare in the service, and some of the men didn't hold them in very high regard. But she supposed that wasn't fair. Most of the trouble she got about her gender came from miscreants she was about to cite. Men who said things like, "They let women have guns, too?"

Then Kel Westin sat across from her again. "So, about today?"

Kel waited patiently for her to speak. Her reputation had preceded her. She was young for a senior warden, which spoke highly of her skills and service. But he hadn't expected blue eyes and curly dark hair like a tousled nimbus around her head, or the curves he could see when she pulled off her insulated vest and tossed it onto another chair. Her red shirt was beginning to show some wrinkles from a long day.

"Today," she repeated, standing to pull off her utility belt and place her gun in a locker. "A local rancher, who's also the city police chief, found a bighorn sheep decapitated and skinned on his property. Looked to be around two days old, maybe a little less because the wolves hadn't finished it. Anyway, his property is fenced and posted, so the poacher must have broken down part of his fence as well. The meat was wasted."

"Damn," Kel said, watching her as she paced to the window and back, discovering that it was suddenly easier to think about how attractive she was. He shook his head and stared down into his coffee. "What do you think brought the sheep down from the mountains?"

"They might have used dogs. Or maybe the animal was sick. I have samples to send to the lab and a carcass in my truck that I need to get into an evidence freezer, but in the meantime…" She put her camera on her desk and turned it around so he could see the screen. With a punch of the button, a slideshow started. "Have a look. Too bad it rained the last two nights."

"Maybe that's all that kept the wolves from scenting it sooner."

She nodded, then settled onto her chair again. "I hate to think of that sheep being driven down the mountain like that. Terrified by bush beaters or dogs…it doesn't matter. Out of his element, on the run, all so somebody could decorate his wall." She slapped her palm on the desk. "We only issued twenty-two permits in this area for bighorns this year. We don't have a big enough population to sustain this kind of hunting."

That was the struggle for which Wyoming Game and Fish had been created. Back in the 1880s, Wyoming's streams had become sterile of edible fish. So fisheries were their first step. Then in 1921 Game and Fish had been created and in 1929 had been given the power to limit the harvesting of game and fish both. Since then healthy populations had rebounded, but it was a never-ending battle.

Desi Jenks was right: they couldn't afford this poaching. Not of bighorns. Some other populations were large enough to withstand some of it, like antelope, but the bighorn? There was a reason they'd permitted only twenty-two to be harvested this year in her area, and that was a larger number than in some areas that were being poached.

"No clues, I suppose?" he finally asked as he scanned her photos of the scene.

"I wish. I pulled another bullet but you know they're

useless without a gun to match them to. Standard round for a thirty-thirty hunting rifle, and you wouldn't want too big a hole in your sheepskin rug."

"The skinning was expert," he remarked. "The decap appears to have been done by some kind of butcher's saw." He sat back. "They didn't want to damage the skin or head. To hell with the rest."

She nodded and picked up her own coffee, leaning back in her chair. "Experienced."

"Yeah." He tried to ignore the loveliness of the woman who sat across from him, just a normal male response that *should* be ignored, focusing instead on what this piece added to the puzzle. Not much, he decided. It was more of the same.

"What about you?" she asked.

"I'm going into competition with them. See if I can draw them out by threatening their cash stream."

She frowned. "That could be dangerous."

"It could, but we're getting nowhere otherwise. They pop up under different names every season. New phone number every week, then no phone number once they've got enough customers. All payments made by cash. Absolutely nothing we've been able to trace, including their internet postings. In fact, all that stuff has started diminishing and we suspect they're getting most of their business by word-of-mouth now. And you know darn well that with only limited bighorn ram permits, they're not in the market for a permit. They couldn't promise anyone that they'd get one at the drawing. Same for other big game."

"And it's all going out of state?"

"Of course it is. First off, a resident permit isn't that expensive, even if it's hard to get one for big game through the drawing. Nonresident permits run in the thousands. Then you've got the problem of where you're going to display that trophy. Desi, you know people around here. How many of them wouldn't mention the sudden appearance of a trophy head to you?"

She smiled faintly. "A few. There are a few everywhere. But someone, eventually, would run it by me. I have pretty good contacts around here, and despite what some people may think, most of the ranchers have a great respect for the land and the wildlife."

"Unless it's wolves," he said.

She laughed. "Unless it's wolves," she agreed. "Unfortunately."

"I hear you got some here?"

"A pack of maybe seven up on Thunder Mountain. So far there's been a détente going on, but today..." She shook her head. "Fresh kill on Jake's ranch. He'll mend his fence as soon as he finds out where it was damaged, probably by the bighorn on the run...but then he's got to keep an eye out. Right now his place may be looking like a wolf smorgasbord."

"I could go out and give him a hand."

She arched her brows at him. "What was that about undercover?"

"I'll go out as an outfitter trying to get the lay of the land. I'll just say I thought I could lend a hand while I learn the area."

She shook her head, and he realized he wasn't going to run this show singlehandedly. Oh, well. She knew the area and he had only one purpose: to gather intelligence on a ring of poachers. She spoke. "Jake's the chief of police. I told you. He's not stupid. That'll smell and he won't like it. One word of advice to you, Kel. Tell Jake what you're really doing. He might be helpful and he sure knows how to keep a secret." She paused. "He also knows Thunder Mountain as well as I do."

"I'll think about it."

But then she questioned him again. "Isn't it a little late to start your masquerade? The season's already underway for a week now."

"I'm not doing this solo." He saw her stiffen, and guessed she was wondering if she was going to be totally shoved to the side in this operation. He hastened to reassure her. "I'm solo out here," he offered quickly. "But the unit has been making postings for me on the web and social media since late last spring. In the meantime, once the snow was gone, I've been hiking all over the terrain to familiarize myself. Anyway, word about me has been out there, just not where I was going to set myself up. A few shills have already indicated their interest in a hunt publicly, so once I surface, I'll appear to have business already."

She nodded, leaning forward to rest her elbows on the desk. "What about others who call?"

He half smiled. "Well, now that's interesting. We sound them out, mentioning they have to have their own license because they can't hunt under mine, and they usually bail pretty quickly. Then we try like hell to find out where they go next. We're coordinating with other states, but so far none of these calls have been productive. Apparently, the mere question about licensing makes them too cautious to continue. Two birds, one stone."

She clearly appreciated that. "But some won't care if it's illegal."

He nodded. "Of course not. But if they're calling me, they obviously don't know about this ring yet. If we find that they've contacted someone else, we can probably persuade the hunter to deal with us rather than face charges. But the ring is getting hard to find unless you have some kind of contact. Plus, we need evidence for court. Hearsay ain't gonna do it."

He stood. "Now, don't you have a carcass to get out of your truck?" From the photos she'd showed him, he'd guess there were well over a hundred pounds left of a nearly three-hundred-pound sheep.

"Yeah. Help appreciated. I'll roll around back to the freezer building."

Behind the front offices in a steel building about fifty yards away were a series of chest freezers, all of them with serious padlocks. In them they kept evidence until a case was completed, whether dressed meat or an entire carcass. Desi tagged the bighorn in its plastic wrapping, then Kel helped her lift it into the building and put it in an empty freezer. Desi slapped a note on top of it, making it clear this meat was unsafe to eat. From time to time during the year, the wardens donated any good meat they no longer needed as evidence to a soup kitchen, or a church or even to individuals living on the edge who could use it well.

Not everything was wasted, Desi thought with satisfaction as she locked up the freezer shed. Not nearly.

"I guess we shouldn't hang much," Desi remarked as they walked back to the station. For some reason that disappointed her. She wanted to be part of his operation, was thirsty for it, but she was also kind of thirsty for the man himself. No good. "You being undercover and all."

"Hey, wouldn't I cozy up to the local wardens? Try to seem innocuous?"

"Brown nose?" She looked at him and laughed. "I'm not very susceptible, Kel."

"Didn't think you were," he answered in good humor, "but that's what people can think and I'll hurry that notion along when I can."

She stepped inside and faced him. "Why?"

He grew instantly serious. "Because I'm going to need your help, Warden. I can't possibly do this alone. So I cozy up to you, make it look like I'm trying to get on your good side, maybe romance you a bit, and no one will even guess what I'm really here to do."

She felt an unexpected sense of displeasure that he could so casually offer to romance her as part of his cover. Shaking her head at herself, she quashed the feeling. "Just don't take it too far," she said. "I'm not known for dating around here."

He nodded, accepting the warning. Sometimes, things happened at exactly the wrong time. Well, this was wrong for more reasons than timing. She couldn't let herself want this guy. That kind of stuff could only get in the way.

But she felt a little slammed by her reaction. Not in years had she reacted so strongly to a guy just because of how he looked. Right now she didn't know anything about Kel, so who needed this reaction? He might turn out to be a jackass.

She could have laughed at herself if this situation weren't in danger of affecting her peace of mind. But there was one good thing she could say about it: instant sexual attraction had taken her mind off that bighorn.

But now she needed to come back to earth and set about reporting the kill. While Kel got himself some coffee, she pulled her notebook out of the pocket in her vest and flipped it open. Her sample case was still in the truck, and she'd have to package that up in a cooler to send to forensics.

In the meanwhile…paperwork. On the computer.

As she called up the forms, Kel spoke again.

"Desi? You take this all very personally, don't you?"

She looked at him, wondering if that was a compliment or an insult. It could be either. After all, he was a man.

He sat across from her. "Good for you for taking it personally. Some get so used to it they forget. But the word *warden* has an honorable history. It means protector, caretaker, guardian."

She felt a crooked smile forming on her face. "I got the same training you did, Kel."

At that he laughed. "Of course you knew that. I'm just trying to say, I'm glad you take this stuff personally. I've met a few who don't. Just another job to them. They don't do it very well."

She guessed it must have been written all over her face how she was taking it when she pulled in. She didn't remember having said much about it except the basic facts.

Her phone rang and she reached for it. "Hey, Lex, what's up?" She listened. "I'm on my way."

When she hung up, she rose. "I'm outta here, and I guess you should leave, too, to preserve your cover."

"What's up?"

"An antelope didn't quite make it over a barbed wire fence. I guess this day's going to end on a really sour note."

Kel stood in the parking lot and watched her get into her truck. Cute bottom, he thought, then yanked his mind back into line. No messing with a colleague, he reminded himself.

He had plenty to do anyway. He already knew the terrain around here, although he hadn't introduced himself to Desi before. He'd spent all summer hiking around those mountains until he could talk about them like he knew them intimately. He'd studied the migratory maps, as well, and figured that if he ever needed to he could lead someone to a good hunting spot for big game.

But those were the routes he had to keep an eye on if he was going to pretend to be a guide, and more important, catch anyone in the act. So it wouldn't seem at all strange for him to be hiking around.

But he was going to seriously annoy any illegal outfitters. He'd known that when he volunteered, but he was no stranger to threats. In the meantime, while he waited for his hook to set itself, he could do plenty of hiking in those mountains.

He was looking forward to that. He just kind of wished he could do it under better circumstances, and maybe with Desi. She probably mapped a lot of those migrations, probably counted the herds assiduously and judged their health.

It was by going up into those mountains that she'd found most of the trophy kills she had reported. She'd make a great right-hand man if they could work it out.

In the meantime, he knew those bighorn were unlikely to come down to below five thousand feet at this time of year. Most would probably be up closer to eight thousand. So what the hell was that sheep doing on a ranch?

Driving the ten miles to Alex Thornton's place, Desi prepared for the worst and tried not to think about Kel

Westin. Her immediate female reaction to him almost soured her. She'd put that aside when she'd decided to live without men and there was no place for it on the job.

She was also worried about this plan of his. They clearly had an active poaching operation in this area. The better the herds thrived, the more big game she found had been killed for trophies. Apparently, her mapped migration corridors were providing plenty of opportunities for the poachers. Enough to sicken her.

At the same time, she understood hunting. She had no problem with the people who wanted meat to get them through the winter. If they were hunting for food, fine. Some culling of the herds was necessary, hence the harvest limits the service worked up every year.

If she hadn't been dealing with these issues for years, she'd have been overwhelmed by the system.

Now there was Kel, a big question mark. His credentials were valid, but this whole idea sounded dangerous to her. Men who were willing to risk huge fines, forfeiting their guns and their right to hunt, all to make a little money by taking a trophy? And now such a crime was a felony, so prison, not just a slap on the wrist and a fine. Men like that might be willing to kill anyone who appeared to get in the way of their money stream.

She just had to trust WIU knew what they were doing. She couldn't deny that putting a halt to this trophy hunting was a good thing. And sure as she was sitting here in her truck, she was willing to bet no one showed up in the next thirteen days with horns attached to the skull plate of that sheep. Or even just the horns. Nope. Not when they'd left everything behind but the skin.

Lex Thornton was waiting for her in a turnout beside his fence line along the county road. As she pulled up, she could see he'd cut the top of the barbed wire. Maybe a hundred feet away, an antelope hunkered down.

"Got her loose, Desi," Lex said as she climbed out of her truck. "Think her hind leg is broken from fighting against the wire. Cut all the way to the bone, she is."

This was the worst part of the job for Desi. She never got used to it. She pulled out her rifle and loaded a few bullets. Alex didn't say another thing, just swung open a ramshackle gate and let her through.

He was probably right about the broken leg, or that antelope wouldn't still be here.

When they got closer, she could see the mess of the antelope's back leg.

"They usually get over," Lex said.

"I know. How many dozens have we had to chase off your grazing land?"

"A few. Elk, too."

The antelope tried to pull itself through the grass as they approached. Then it shoved itself up on three legs, no weight on the fourth. It didn't get very far before collapsing again.

"She's worn out," Desi said. God, she hated this. That animal could not survive, however, and leaving it to suffer was the worst option. It had to be in pain and terrified, and as it became weaker and less able to move, it might be tormented by hawks and other predators. No.

So she raised her rifle and did what was necessary.

She turned to Lex, keeping her expression businesslike. Knowing it had been necessary didn't make it easy, though. "You want the meat?"

"Always."

She nodded. "I'll fill out the forms and give you what you need."

Lex stood looking at the antelope for a few seconds. "Damn shame," he said finally, then turned to follow her back to her truck. "Thanks for coming so fast, Desi. I have no idea how long she'd been stuck in that wire, but when I cut her loose...well, it was too long I guess."

After Desi filled out the paperwork and gave him the slip that granted him legal ownership of the meat, she headed back toward town, thinking that some days being a warden was absolutely no fun at all. Days like today, it sometimes got hard to remember why she'd wanted to do this job.

But there were much better days, she reminded herself. Lots of them. And now there was Kel Westin who, one way or another, was going to provide a change of pace. They needed to talk more, she decided. Somehow they were going to have to coordinate. And he *had* said he'd need her assistance.

Ah, cut it out. Her thoughts were running along the lines of a smitten kid. By now she should have outgrown it. But the simple fact was, it was easier to think about Kel than about the rest of her day. Maybe too easy.

Chapter 2

Three days later, just after dark, Desi returned to the station exhausted. She threw her paperwork and citation book on the desk in the office, locked up her pistol, then sagged in exhaustion. Paperwork could wait, she decided. There was enough in her summons book and other notes for now.

She climbed her outside stairs to her apartment over the station. Nothing grandiose about it. Once upon a time it had been a bunkhouse for wardens, but as wardens settled in this area and bought homes and raised families, it had become a leftover from another era. So part of it had been transformed into an efficiency apartment. The rest...well, it was still kind of a bunkhouse, but one with only two mattresses on cots. Once in a while, one of her fellow wardens would camp out there for a night. At least they'd given the apartment its own bathroom.

She hopped into the shower, cleaning the day off herself, then dressed in jeans and a green sweater. If she got called out for any reason, she was halfway ready to go.

There was no time of year when her life was totally quiet, but things heated up during hunting season. All kinds of people out there, even with licenses and permits, still shaded their way around the law. Easy enough, usually, when they were blending in with so many other hunters.

Three long days, she thought, but at least no blatant trophy kills. Hunting season seemed to bring the not-entirely-lawful out of the woodwork, apparently thinking they'd pass unnoticed when hunters were everywhere.

Uh, no, she thought as she toweled her hair a little more then headed for her kitchenette. It got to be ridiculous sometimes. She'd had to escort four hunters off posted property. She'd come up on more than one group where people were firing from the road. In those cases, when they killed game, she not only had to cite them for the infraction, she had to recover the carcass. Lots of heavy work, not always aided by hunters who were angry with her because they had to pay a fine and had lost the meat, license or no license.

A tip had kept her out later last night, and sure enough, after hunting hours closed for the night, two hunters were busy ignoring the time. At least they hadn't gotten nasty about it.

On the other hand, she'd talked to a lot of nice folks, some of whom she knew. And Jos Webber, another warden assigned to this area, had agreed they ought to team up even if it expanded their usual patrol areas. Something about this hunting season seemed off and she and Jos agreed a little extra caution wouldn't hurt.

The phone rang while she was reheating some left-over stew, and she answered it. "Game and Fish, Warden Jenks here."

"Hey, Desi," said the familiar voice of Craig Stone. He was a lawman and biologist for the US Forest Service, and sometimes their jobs overlapped. "I hear you lost a bighorn."

"That's putting it mildly, Craig. Have you been seeing any poaching?" His forest abutted her area, and reached further back into some of the mountains.

"Not yet. We decided to close ourselves to hunting this year, though. You must have gotten the memo."

"Yeah. And all I could think was, great, it's going to be my problem."

Craig laughed. "Look at it this way. We find any hunters on our land, they'll go immediately to jail. Maybe that'll help you."

"Jail for how long?" she snorted. "Trespass doesn't put anyone away for long."

He didn't laugh this time. "I know. And I know how thinly spread you all are. So basically I'm saying, if you need help, call. I realize I can't legally do much on your land, but I *can* help."

"Thanks, Craig. It's appreciated." Then she thought of Kel. "I have someone I'd like you to meet." As soon as she said it, she winced. She was supposed to be protecting the guy's cover, not bandying it about.

"Sure. When?"

"I'll let you know." And maybe that would get her off the hook. She could just let it drop. She asked after his wife, Sky, and their toddler, then said good-night to Craig, realizing this day had managed to sap her. She'd barely eaten, she was tired and she probably wasn't at her best mentally, to judge by her slipup just now.

"Food," she said aloud. "Then rest." With the phone right beside her head. Such a glamorous job.

A laugh escaped her as she began to scoop hot stew from the pot into a bowl. Really, all she had to do was remind herself of springtime, when she'd be out looking for newborns in the wild populations, when she'd be counting herds and checking to make sure nothing impeded their necessary migrations.

And after that was summertime when the biggest problem she usually dealt with was fishermen who were either unlicensed or who took more than their catch limit. That was rare enough around here because there weren't a lot of good fishing holes. But there were a few. Conard City hadn't been built without an eye to a nearby water source. And of course, there was always some game poaching going on.

She sat with her feet up on a battered coffee table, trying to decide if she wanted to watch television or just enjoy the peace and quiet when there was a knock on her door.

Aw, man, she thought, putting her hot stew aside and going to answer it. There, in the dark of early autumn, stood Kel Westin.

She blinked at him as he said, "Hi."

"What are you doing here?" she asked. "This is hardly undercover."

"No one saw me. No one who matters anyway. I walked and you're a little outside town."

"A little." Slowly she stepped back. "Well, I guess you're more interesting than TV. Come in."

He grinned. "Better than TV? I don't know whether that's a compliment or not."

"Keep wondering," she retorted as she closed the door behind him. "Want me to heat you some stew? I was just about to eat."

"I ate at the diner. Go ahead and dig in."

So she returned to the battered sofa and picked up her bowl and spoon. She watched as he wandered around familiarizing himself with the layout.

Something about the way he was looking, moving... she'd seen it before. "Military background?" she asked.

He faced her, hands in his pockets. "Yeah. Rangers."

"It shows. When you've got the place memorized, have a seat."

He looked almost rueful. "That obvious?"

"Only to someone who's seen it other times. We have a lot of vets in this county, a lot of special-ops types. So yeah, I know how they get the lay of the land."

So she waited while he finished scoping the place. He probably wouldn't be comfortable until he knew the exits and windows, and whatever else might concern him. But eventually he sat in the armchair across from her.

"To what do I owe this honor?" she prodded.

"We really didn't get a chance to talk before you got called out."

She arched a brow, spoonful of stew halfway to her mouth. "There's more?"

He half smiled. "Isn't there always? You know the guys with the forest service?"

"Most of them."

"They're working with us."

She nodded slowly. "So that's why Craig Stone called to remind me they were closing to hunting."

"The state public land abuts the forest. But you know that. Anyway, we're hoping by closing that area, we can create a bit of a funnel effect. Nobody wants their hunt blown up on a trespassing charge."

"Of course not." She forgot her dinner. "Do you have any idea how much difficulty those rangers have patrolling the forest service land? Talk about porous. Barring hunting there is going to make about as much difference as no poaching is making."

He shook his head a little. "You know you have to have road access on all public lands. No off-roading. Craig said they even shut down their ATV trails two years ago. Anyway, since you can't drive willy-nilly over open ground and have to stick with the roads, then you've got to ask yourself how far a trek can you manage to get your trophy out of there. Craig's got enough manpower to close the forestry roads over there. Anybody coming that way with hunting gear is heading for trouble. So they gotta stay on the state land and the public access roads."

She thought it over as her stomach rumbled and reminded her that she needed to eat. She picked up her bowl again. "I could use a hundred more people at least."

"Sorry, we don't have them."

"I know." Far too few wardens for the land area they needed to cover. And when you got up into those mountains, it wasn't like there were houses scattered around with people who were willing to call and complain about suspected poaching. There was nothing up there except a couple of park service shacks, and most of them would be closed for the winter.

She glanced at Kel again, liking the lean toughness of his face. Liking his lead-gray eyes. Ah well. Finally she acknowledged there was only one way to go at this, much as she didn't like it. "Your idea is probably the best."

"To get the outfitters ring? Yeah. Won't stop any other poaching, though."

"I know, but since we can't staple a warden to every animal or herd, let's get the most egregious offenders. I can't tell you how angry it makes me, Kel. Furious to think that people are profiting this way off these animals. Poach to feed your family? I get that. But these guys, dangling bait in the water and charging lots of money for guiding someone who only wants a trophy and doesn't care if it's illegal? There's something about that..."

She trailed off and tried to continue eating. She couldn't really explain the difference in so many words.

"I get what you're saying," he said while she ate some more stew. "It's in no way excusable. Charging thousands to bring in people from out of state and lead them illegally to an animal when all they want is a trophy? I can understand the hunters better than I can understand the outfitters."

"I can't," she admitted after she swallowed. "I hate trophy hunting above all. The guys helping are after the money. Greed is a motivator for a lot of people. But the hunters? All they want is bragging rights hanging on their walls."

He nodded. "And we've got a little quirk in Wyoming law that hinders us finding these guys."

She swallowed some more stew and looked at him. "You mean that anyone can guide two other licensed people with him on a hunt as long as he doesn't get paid? Yeah. Hard to prove the *no pay* part."

"Regardless, the licensed professional outfitters are

working with us. They're no more happy about the poaching than we are."

"Cuts into their business?"

He nodded. "When the illicit guys offer the hunts for a lower price because they're not licensed and because their clients don't have to get through a drawing to get one and pay for it...they have an advantage, money-wise. Plus, they're reducing the number of trophy animals available. The pros are out there all year scouting."

"No kidding." She finished her stew and carried her bowl to the sink to rinse it out. Then she got them both some fresh coffee. "I run into some of the nearer outfitters when I'm out tracking the herds. I have to admit, they help by sharing information."

He looked at her over his mug. "But you don't like them."

She flushed faintly. "I don't *dislike* them, but I was raised to hunt for myself. My dad went out every year to bring home venison for the family larder, usually with a buddy or two because packing that animal out required more than one pair of shoulders. But it wasn't the clambake method with a bunch of guides, cooks, tents, horses..."

"I get it," he said when she trailed off. "You don't like lazy hunting."

"It's not really sporting, to my way of thinking. What animal stands a chance when it's been tracked by spotters for months, when there are people there to find it again, help the hunter aim his rifle and take his shot? And the outfitters aren't supplying hunts to those who need the meat to eat. But...they exist, they're legal, and my personal opinion can't matter."

"I hear you," he said. "But the law allows it, so..."

"And as long as the hunters have the right permits and don't break the law, I can't really complain about their methods, can I? At least baiting big game is illegal."

He rose from the chair and paced her small apartment slowly. "You're interesting, Desi. I'm guessing you became a warden for the protection part."

"Meaning?"

He halted and faced her. "You want to save the wildlife."

"Absolutely. But I also understand the importance of harvesting. As long as we manage it so the populations don't shrink, or don't get so large they're starving, I have no problems with the system."

He laughed quietly. "Do you hunt yourself?"

"Only poachers." But then she joined his laughter. "I don't have time during hunting season, Kel. I'd need to take time off, and there just aren't enough of us."

The phone rang, and she gave thanks that she'd at least had time to eat. "Warden Jenks."

"Jim Cashford," said a voice she knew well. "Desi, there's a fire and some lights up on the mountain near the old Cranbrook road."

"I'll look into it."

When she hung up, she found Kel already pulling on his vest. "You think you're going?"

"Hey, I'm your new best friend. What's going on?"

"A fire, which is illegal, and lights bright enough to be seen from Jim Cashford's ranch."

Downstairs she got on the radio and raised another warden. "I need backup," she told Jos Webber. "Fire and lights near old Cranbrook Road."

"On my way," came his crackling answer.

She picked up her satellite phone, slipped on an armored vest and donned her olive-green jacket over her sweater. No red shirt tonight. Just a lot of protection.

"You got any armor?" she asked Kel.

"Not with me."

She hesitated, then went to a locker and tossed him a vest. "Mind yourself now," she said. "Or stay here."

He didn't stay behind.

Kel was amused. Desi was quite an interesting character. She didn't approve of sport hunting, but accepted that some of it was allowed by law, and could even summon a good reason or two, like the herds needed to be harvested to a reasonable extent, and the outfitters offered her information from their scouting trips. She liked eating game but didn't have time to hunt.

And she told him to mind himself. As if he wouldn't know how. He'd been an army Ranger before he'd come to this job, and had walked into a lot more dangerous situations than this. Which was not to say a warden couldn't get shot, but it didn't happen that often. Though people might cuss them when they got a citation or lost their hunting privileges, they weren't inclined to murder. But it was still dangerous. Careless hunters were always dangerous.

They drove through the night toward the mountain. He already knew Cranbrook Road. It was hardly more than a cart track that was occasionally graded mainly because it provided access to the state lands hunters and fishermen wanted to get to. By keeping Cranbrook basically functional, it reduced the likelihood that hunters would travel over posted private property to go hunting.

He watched her drive with calm competence over back roads she probably knew as well as her own hand and sensed the distance in her. He wondered if he had put her that much on guard, or if the job had. She could laugh and smile, but she avoided getting personal about anything except being a warden. And she hadn't even questioned him about his background. Pure business.

He wondered if those walls ever fell. She was appealing, and he'd really like to get to know what lay behind the warden's facade. She couldn't possibly be nothing but a warden. People had lives, had problems, had hopes and dreams. But Desi…always back to business.

He admitted he'd been guilty of some of that himself for a long time. When you lost buddies, you stopped making close friends. War had carved something out of him.

But what had carved Desi? Something sure had.

He forced his attention back to the job at hand. The darkness of the night was consuming. No stars, no moon. No wonder that rancher had seen the lights and fire on the side of the mountain. There was no light anywhere else.

He caught a glimpse of it as they climbed in the truck, but only a glimpse. It was a camp, not a city, and vanished in the trees almost as soon as he saw it.

"Any idea where it is?" he asked.

"Some, but I hope you're ready to hike. You can stay with the vehicle if you want. Jos is coming to back me up."

"I'm not staying with the car," he said firmly. No way was he going to stand back when there might be danger.

"What do you want me to tell Jos about you?"

"That I insisted on coming, that I just got out of the Rangers."

"I don't like lying to my fellow wardens."

No real surprise there. Not only did they have to work

together, but they had to trust each other. He sighed. "Can they keep secrets?"

"As far as I know."

"Then I guess I can let them all know what I'm here for. Might as well. There's just so far undercover I can go, I guess."

"You might need backup," she pointed out. "You can't run a one-man operation. If these guys come after you…" She paused. "You know, interfering with one of their hunts might be the most dangerous thing you can do. If you come across one, you're going to need backup."

"Maybe so. But if coming across one of their hunts were likely, you and your wardens would have already done it. No, I need to draw them out. So I ask again, do you trust all your wardens?"

This time she didn't answer as they jolted their way up the track. When she finally pulled over onto a small patch of flat, open ground and turned off her engine, she finally spoke. "You're a friend of mine, you just got out of the army and came to visit. End of story."

"Fair enough."

"And I guess that means you ought to move into the bunkhouse." Then she slipped out of the truck and opened the crew door to pull out her rifle. Because tonight was potentially dangerous. He didn't need a map to know that.

"How are we going to put out the fire?" he asked.

She passed him a shovel and a jerry can full of water from the bed of the truck. "The usual way."

He could have laughed. He put the can down beside his feet and leaned on the shovel. Before long he heard another truck approaching. It turned off its headlights before it reached them.

Soon a young game warden joined them and was introduced to him as Jos Webber. He almost looked wet behind the ears, but his bearing pegged him as confident and experienced.

"Kel Westin," Desi said as she introduced him. "Old friend. He just got out of the army rangers."

Jos stuck out his hand. "We can probably use you, sir."

"Well, I don't intend to get in the way."

Jos looked him over in the dim glow of his flashlight. "Somehow I don't think you're the type. Interested in what it takes to be a warden?"

"Very," he answered. But he was wondering why Desi had decided to use a cover story for him after saying she didn't like lying to her fellow wardens. Did something not feel right to her? Or did she think they'd tell someone outside the service, like a family member? Or maybe this whole idea of illegal outfitters had her wondering just how far this stuff went?

He hoped after this she'd talk to him some more. He kinda felt like he was dangling by a thin rope here. He might have learned the terrain over the summer, but he hadn't learned any of the people. He was going to need to rely on Desi for that.

Jos got his long gun and soon the three of them were heading into the forest where it impossibly grew even darker. As his eyes adapted more, however, the single red-lensed flashlight in Jos's hand gave him ample light to avoid obstacles. After a half mile or so they didn't really even need that as the flickering of firelight began to reach them through the scattered trees. A soft bed of pine needles silenced their feet.

"Spread out," Desi said quietly. "I'll approach."

"Got you covered," Jos answered. "Kel?"

"I can bash heads. Should've brought my pistol."

"Stay behind one of us," Desi said. "And put that water where you can find it again. I hope we won't need it."

Much as he hated it, Kel hung back just beyond the light cast by the campfire. He narrowed his eyes to prevent eyeshine from showing, set the heavy can down and waited half behind a tree. Easy from here to make out three tents and six men sitting around a fire. A fire in the tinder-dry autumn woods. Idiots. One spark on some dead pine needles and this place would go up fast.

Desi approached them, no longer moving quietly, with her rifle slung casually over her arm and pointing to the ground.

"Evening, gentlemen," she called out. "Game warden."

The men who'd already turned their heads her way and started to rise immediately sat back down on their folding camp chairs. "Howdy, Warden," one of them answered.

"You guys out here hunting?" she asked pleasantly.

"In the morning," the same man answered. "Half hour before dawn, right?"

"Right. Appreciate you paying attention to that." She switched on her own flashlight. "Mind if I see your licenses?"

This caused all the men to stand to pull wallets out of their pockets. Kel felt uneasy as six men nearly surrounded Desi, but so far nobody was acting hostile. As each handed over his license, she studied it. "A moose permit?" she asked one of them. "You're lucky."

The guy laughed. "Been trying for ten years."

"I hope you bag a nice one. And if you do, I guess you'll be glad your buddies can help you carry it out."

"You bet. That's one of the reasons they're here."

"Just remember, gut it where you kill it, and tag it for transport. Wouldn't want you to lose it."

"Me neither," the guy answered.

"Well," said Desi, "you're all square. Just a couple of things."

"Yeah?"

Her voice tightened a shade. "Bright lights were seen here from below. You aren't hunting with them, are you?"

"Hell no," came a chorus of answers.

"Then don't turn them on again tonight or I'll have to come back and cite you. And I *am* going to have to cite you for that fire. You know you're not allowed to have one out here. But first let's put it out."

"Just trying to stay warm," someone grumbled.

"I understand that, sir, but it's against the law. You wanna put it out right now, I could let you off with a warning. If you do it right."

Still grumbling, but quietly, the men doused the fire with water.

"Guess we'll have to go get more water tomorrow," one said. "Dang."

Desi squatted and felt the wet fire pit. "Turn it over, would you?"

One of the men got a small shovel and turned the ground over. Desi felt again. "A little more water to be safe. It's still warm."

A few minutes later, she stood, brushing her hand on her jeans. "Okay. No fire, no bright lights. What were you using them for anyway?"

"Setting up camp."

Her voice turned a little sarcastic. "Really? I'm not saying you're lying, but we both know you were probably doing more than that. Too bright and on too long.

Don't let me see them again. And if I get another call from down below about them, you won't be hunting here for a while, okay?"

One of the men raised his arm. Kel acted instinctively and in a few strides was standing next to Desi. Jos had the same reaction, and he was on her other side just as fast.

"What?" said the guy who'd raised his arm. "I was just frustrated."

"No reason to get frustrated," Desi said mildly. "If you took your hunting classes, you don't need me to explain the law. What's more, we fly a plane over here at night sometimes, so you could get caught again. Since you already have a warning, nobody's going to give you a second chance. Clear?"

Desi pulled out her book, and taking each hunter's license and ID, wrote him a warning, then passed him a copy. When she was done, she wished the man well with his moose hunt, reminding the group that the national forest was closed to hunting this year.

A half hour later, they were hiking back through the woods to the road, this time with the aid of two flashlights.

"I'm thinking," said Jos, "that they were pushing the law."

"It occurred to me," Desi said drily. "I hope they got the message. But when you wait ten years for a moose permit, maybe it's a little harder to follow the rules."

Kel thought that was pretty generous considering the men had been committing two serious violations. If he had the time and opportunity, he hoped he could figure this woman out a little better. In some ways she appeared to be a bundle of contradictions.

Lugging the big can of water and the shovel, he studied what he could see of the back of her head, and decided this was a good view, too.

Back at the trucks, they all shook hands, then Jos took off into the night. Kel helped Desi load the water can and shovel into the bed of her truck, and stood by while she removed the ammo from her gun and put it in the rack in the back.

"This place will be crowded before dawn tomorrow," she remarked as they jolted down the road. "Well, as crowded as can be in the middle of nowhere."

"Will you come back then?"

"Depends on how the rest of this night goes."

He waited a moment, then asked, "What did you mean about me staying in the bunkhouse?"

"I've got a couple of cots upstairs off my apartment. They mostly get used by wardens staying overnight, but you're welcome to one if you want it. Didn't I just announce you were visiting me? Like that won't get around." She laughed quietly. "I don't date. Everyone's going to hear. Anyway, if it won't interfere with your plans, help yourself."

"But won't I get in your way?"

"Not likely. This is the time of year when having a flexible schedule often means I have trouble finding time to put my head on a pillow."

In his end of the business, as an investigator, he never really got into the ins and outs of a warden's life. He supposed with so many people hunting in the fall, she probably had a full plate between patrolling for violations and the calls she received from people reporting them. He wondered about other times of the year, but didn't ask.

He *did* know how much the wardens relied on people to inform them of possible violations. Some ninety wardens couldn't be everywhere in a state this size. For every square mile of public land, there must be a helluva lot more private lands where game caused problems, where hunters went even when they shouldn't. Impossible to keep an eye on everything.

"I'm going to introduce you to some people," she said unexpectedly. "Some of the ranchers who border the public lands. They can be eyes and ears, if you want."

"You trust them?"

"Most of them are cops, special-forces types or married to them."

He smiled into the dark. A fascinating list.

"Like you," she added, surprising him by teasing. "Do you trust yourself?"

"Of course. But this undercover op may be getting awfully big."

"Well, I can talk to them myself, but you'd be safer out there if they knew what you were doing."

He should probably think about it. "Let's not tell anyone just yet. I'll give it some thought, but for now I'm just an old friend visiting. Anyone who would doubt that?"

"Not really. I know people around here, but I've only been in this area for five years. There's a lot about my past no one would know in any detail."

That was an advantage he supposed. "Regardless, I need to know some of that past and how I fit in because somebody's going to ask questions."

She hesitated. "You going to take up the offer of the bunkhouse?"

"Now that you've announced me, I suppose I should." He'd come out here with one plan only, to keep his eyes peeled for questionable activity and to try to draw a threat his way. Somehow, everything was changing.

His plan about appearing to be trying to get close to her hadn't involved sharing quarters. He'd better get on it before it all went sideways.

Chapter 3

Kel went back to the motel to gather his personal gear. Desi wondered if she were busy losing her mind. The guy had come out here to try to stick his head in a noose, and she was inviting him to stay with her?

She paced her small apartment, reminding herself that he'd suggested that looking like he was cozying up to her would fit the role he was playing. Well, this was going to get really cozy now.

She knew that some of these illegal outfitters could net upward of fifty thousand dollars in a hunting season. Because they stayed small to avoid trouble and notice, they didn't guide as many hunts, and didn't provide all the comforts. Two or three guys, a tent, trail food and bring your own gun. But still cheaper because they took hunters who weren't licensed, which was a big savings for the nonresident hunter, and a savings for them because they didn't do the big production method.

They might have a few horses to pack into the wilderness, but they could run only one hunt at a time and didn't have the cost of a large stable. On the one hand, on the other hand. Trade-offs. She remembered one outfit that kept operating long after their license had expired…and got caught only because somebody who was considering hiring them actually checked out their outfitters license listed on the webpage.

But Kel was after something that was apparently breaking itself into small pieces to avoid notice. A group steadily sinking below the radar. A group taking game it held no permits for.

Kel was running a big risk. The loss of money, the possible jail time, the fines…yeah, it could get dangerous going after people who faced that.

But first they had to be found. She wondered if any other officers with the WIU were in other locations doing the exact same thing. Probably.

Sighing, tired of thinking about the job all the time, she put some music on her stereo, something quiet but upbeat, started some coffee, then hopped in her shower for a quick wash.

She realized she didn't have much of a life anymore, outside her work. Maybe she'd become obsessed? She promised herself that after this season was over, she would find something to do with her time that in no way resembled her job. Maybe hang out with the girls as Julie and Connie kept suggesting. She'd worked awfully hard to become a senior warden so early in her career, and she guessed she'd become a little distorted in the process.

Work all the time? That had to stop.

She was wearing some casual sweats when she heard Kel rap on her door. Yep, he was taking her up on the bunk. She went to let him in, saying, "Straight back, the door at the end of the hall."

"Thanks." He smiled at her and carried his duffel over his shoulder, marching away.

It was, she thought sourly, a sign of her fatigue that she'd made this offer, especially to a man she found so attractive. She could almost smell trouble in the air, like smoke in the breeze.

Oh, well. She plopped on her sofa, put her sock-covered feet up and worked on a mug of coffee. She was lucky that caffeine never kept her up.

Kel returned a few minutes later.

"There's coffee if you want any."

"Thanks. Think you're done for the night?"

"Who knows? Flexible hours sometimes means all of them."

He laughed. "Yeah, I'm familiar with that."

She watched him stride around the edge of the couch and sit in the chair on the other side of the coffee table. "Get-acquainted time," she said. "When did you leave the Rangers?"

His dark gray eyes studied her. "Three years ago, after I tore up my knees so bad they gave me a medical discharge."

She sat up a little straighter. "Did they fix them for you?"

"I can still walk. The pain doesn't count, so the answer is no."

"That stinks."

"I'm not so sure I want artificial knees just yet. These are still working."

She sipped some more coffee, aware that emotions were trying to edge into this picture. She wasn't sure she should let them. Keeping a reasonable distance from entanglements had so far served her well. "That's tough."

"That's what they make ibuprofen for. I'm okay."

"And then?"

"After the Rangers?" He smiled and sipped coffee. "I decided I wanted to do something constructive from there on out. I was lucky to get hired by Game and Fish, took all the training, and then for reasons known only to the Fates, I was assigned to WIU."

She smiled faintly. "Do you wish they'd made you a warden?"

"I did at first," he admitted, then looked a bit rueful. "I think I had a romanticized view of what you do."

"Hah!" She slapped her thigh. "I did, too, once upon a time. But even if it's not romantic, it's important. Like last spring when I rescued an orphaned mountain lion cub. That made up for a whole lot."

"I bet it did."

She hopped up and went to her small personal desk to open a drawer. Pulling out a photo, she walked over and handed it to him. "That's me and the cub."

"My God, it's cute." He stared and smiled, before passing it back.

She tossed it on the coffee table and resumed sprawling on the sofa. "They're going to be endangered before long, at least in these mountains. Sport hunting is putting them near critical."

"Think we'll protect them?"

Again she laughed. "Well, that depends, doesn't it? They're mostly seen as a threat to livestock or as a trophy. But like everything else, they're an important part of the ecosystem. So I imagine we'll have a knock-down, drag-out fight over protecting them when the time comes. In the meantime…well, I can rescue cubs."

"Like wolves," he mused. "There's been a lot of upset since the court put them back on the endangered list."

"I love the wolves," she said truthfully. "I understand why so many ranchers think they're a threat, but I still love them. Two summers ago I got to see most of the pack when I was up in the mountains. Unfortunately we feed the elk because of loss of habitat, and no one wants to see the end of elk, or elk hunting. But those feeding areas are like ringing the dinner bell for the wolves. They usually only kill what they need. Usually. But I guess some people don't want to share."

"It's been my experience that wolves are pretty shy of people. But I suppose the ranchers can't afford full-time range riders or shepherds."

"Not anymore," Desi admitted. "Raising livestock is a difficult job under the best of circumstances, so I understand the concerns the ranchers express." Then she caught herself. "But why don't we talk about something besides the job. I was thinking earlier that I'm almost obsessive. I need some fresh air in my brain."

He chuckled. "Well, the job brought us together, so it makes sense we'd talk about it. But on to other subjects. Let me think."

She was content to let him do the thinking as she rose again to get more coffee. As she returned to the couch, she saw it with fresh eyes for the first time since she'd moved in. She wasn't even sure what color it was, it was so old and faded. Somewhere between brown and gray? She was fairly fastidious about keeping things clean, but as she stared at that couch she wondered if cleaning it would help.

Seated again, she watched Kel sip his coffee, his gaze distant.

"I know," he said finally. "Would you believe I actually saw a snow leopard when I was in Afghanistan? In the wild."

"For real?" She sat up a little straighter. "Aren't they rare?"

"Exceedingly. There are only about 250 left."

"So how did you manage it?"

"I was on a mission to train Afghani forces in mountain fighting. Early one morning I was scanning the mountains around us through some high-power binoculars and there it was. I didn't tell anyone about it because their pelts are highly prized and the last thing I wanted to do was let anyone know it was there."

She felt herself smiling broadly. The story made her heart lift. Now, this was a change from her usual rut. "I think I'm going to die of envy."

He laughed. "Don't do that. I just wished I could take a photo, but it was too far away. Warming itself on a high ledge in the first sunbeams of the day. It was stunning, Desi. Just stunning."

"That's something I'll only ever see in a photo," she remarked. "But I'm glad you kept it secret."

"I didn't tell a soul. Everyone knows there are snow leopards in the Kush, but they're hard to find, they range large territories and…well, I wasn't going to pinpoint one. Afghanistan wants to protect them, but given how rough things are over there…" He let it hang, evidently feeling a long explanation wasn't necessary. "Anyway, I'd seen one of their pelts in a market in Kabul. I wasn't going to add to the count."

She nodded, understanding completely. "You must have seen a lot of exotic things."

"Depends on what you mean. I saw an awful lot of ugly things, some beautiful things. I made friends but I'm sure I made more enemies. I had about as much idea of what it would mean to be a soldier as you probably had about being a game warden."

She nodded slowly, feeling an unexpected ache for him. This man bore burdens she couldn't begin to imagine. He seemed to bear them well. So far, anyway.

He appeared to hesitate. "I think it's only fair to tell you that I was married once. It blew up when I came back from my first tour in Iraq. I was fairly messed up, explosive temper, flashbacks. It settled down, but too late."

"And what about now?" she asked, her heart accelerating.

"It's under control. That's probably the best I'll ever be able to say about it. But I can't complain. Plenty of guys have it worse."

She bit her lower lip, wondering. "Why did you tell me this, Kel? Is it something I need to worry about?"

He shook his head. "You might see me get a little edgy on occasion, but like I said, I have a handle on it now. Which makes me luckier than most. I just wanted you to know in case I got snappish or withdrawn for no apparent reason."

That was a whole mouthful, she thought. He might have a handle on it, but that didn't mean he wasn't being tormented anyway. She could have sighed. So many young men and women, haunted forever. But she sought a more helpful attitude. "That's okay. I get the same way sometimes. Maybe not to the same degree. I don't know, but I have my moods, too."

He smiled. Such a warm expression, and it charmed her. "Thanks. Mine can be worse I suppose, but like I said I've got it pretty much under control."

"How much time did you spend over there?" she asked. "If that's not prying."

He looked away for a moment. "Since we invaded Afghanistan? A lot. There were breaks, of course. Time to land for a while. Then back again. Maybe seven years or so?"

She couldn't imagine it. Simply couldn't. Bouncing back and forth between peace and war like that? It seemed to her that that alone would cause problems. "That must have been rough," she said after a moment.

"It was what it was."

Such a casual answer. But she was emerging from her self-imposed preoccupation with her job, a way of avoiding everything else she sometimes thought, and began to see Kel. Really see him, beyond his sexual pull for her. He was treating all this so casually. *Had it under control.*

That casualness, she thought with gut-deep certainty, was a mask hiding some real suffering. Maybe he'd managed to bury that pain so deep that it didn't drive him all the time. Maybe he'd even grown accustomed to it.

But she didn't know how to ask him. Didn't want to pry, and from the vets she knew around here she thought that prying would be bad anyway. None of them seemed to want to talk about that stuff, not with people who'd never been there.

She could comprehend that. She'd met people who couldn't fathom why she was able to shoot an injured antelope as she had. Not because she was hunting but because it was the only help she could offer it. They talked about veterinarians, about rehab places, all without knowing that with an injury like that there was no help. And she had to make that decision with a quick inspection. Did she feel nothing? If only.

So she kept her heart locked away on the job as necessary, avoiding thinking too hard about the parts she didn't like, focusing on the parts she loved. Kel was doing that with a whole big chunk of his life, she guessed.

All of a sudden she felt closer to him. Felt the early stirrings of understanding. There was no real comparison in their experiences, but enough of one to create the first thread between them, on her side at least.

She rose and got the coffeepot, warming both their cups.

"You okay, Desi?" he asked suddenly.

"I'm fine. Maybe a little burnt out," she added honestly.

He half smiled. "Early in the season for that, isn't it?"

She shook her head as she settled on the couch again. "It's year-round, one way or another. Think we don't get poaching in July?"

"I know you do."

"Exactly. There's a lot of other crap, too, like offroaders driving on posted range land, mudders tearing up sensitive ecology in the spring. Frankly, I'll never understand the thrill of driving through deep mud. All it does is make a mess."

His smile widened a bit. "Do it because you can?"

"Seems like." She offered a smile in return. "There are good things, too. I know a lot of good people, for one thing. For another, there's nothing like rescuing a baby critter that's lost its mom."

"Like the mountain lion cub."

"Or a bear cub. Or a mess of raccoons. Even injured

birds. There's also fun, like the time a bunch of us had to drive a huge herd of elk off a rancher's grazing land. They'd pushed their way right though the fence."

His interest perked. "How many?"

"Seven, eight hundred. A regular roundup."

"Sounds dangerous."

"It could have been but mostly they wanted to get away from us, so we were able to convince them to go back through the fence. We had a lot of local help with that one, and we didn't lose a single elk."

He nodded and sipped more coffee. "Bet it felt good."

She laughed, feeling as if a spring inside her were uncoiling a bit. "It felt like a triumph. Nobody wanted to see that herd hurt, but the rancher needed the land for his own stock."

His face shadowed a bit. "Not enough room anymore."

"Not anymore." She stifled a sigh. "It's a constant battle, Kel. You must have figured that out. Not enough open land anymore, not for the way it used to be. We keep migration corridors open, we have feeding areas for the big game because otherwise they'd starve and guess what happens?" And here she was, talking the job again. A one-trick pony.

"What?"

"Brucellosis. Everybody wanted to blame it on the buffalo coming out of Yellowstone, but the truth turned out to be the elk were passing it along at the feeding sites, and when the elk ran into buffalo or free-range cattle... well. Not the buffalo at all, really."

Then she sat up. "I believe I said I didn't want to talk about the job tonight."

"You did. I'm sorry."

"I'm the one who keeps bringing it up like a broken record." She shook her head.

"Well, it can be a 24/7 job. But right now you're relaxing, so let me think of something else to talk about. I was trying to do that earlier, and not so successfully it seems."

It was true, she thought. She gave him points for being helpful in more ways than one. She must sound like a whiner. Or maybe a bore. Either one was bad.

"Got any family?" he asked.

"You mean the deserters?" She smiled. "My parents headed for sunnier climes as soon as they could manage. My mother never liked the cold, and as she got older her dislike grew. My dad swore he couldn't take the complaining anymore. So off to Texas, where he's working construction and Mom is selling real estate."

"Do you go visit them?"

"Christmas, if I can get away for a few days. Mostly in the summer. Yeah, it's warmer. I don't like it."

He laughed outright, drawing an answering laugh from her. "I'm not keen on hot climates. Any delusions I had about that ended in Iraq. I'll take cool and cold any day."

"So you weren't just in Afghanistan?"

"Not always." He paused, his gaze growing distant. Then he shook his head, as if a gnat were annoying him. "As to family…there's just me."

"I'm sorry."

He shrugged. "I was adopted. I don't remember my real parents, and my adoptive parents were older people, more like grandparents, and childless. I guess I'm weird, but I never had any urge to hunt up my biological mother or father. My adoptive parents were good to me. I loved them and they loved me. That's all I need to know."

Never having been adopted, Desi didn't know how to evaluate that, but she suspected this was a man who was good at compartmentalizing his life. Then it occurred to her that in her own way so was she. The Job. All the time, the Job.

"Didn't anyone ever sweep you off your feet?" he teased.

Well, there was nothing like a spot of truth, she decided. "One guy tried."

"And?"

"I kicked him in the nuts."

His face suddenly went stony, as if he were refusing to react to the range of possibilities inherent in her statement. Good choice, she thought sourly.

"Exactly why?" he asked after a minute.

"What seemed like a date turned into a rape." There, that was bold. But she didn't see any reason to pretty it up. It had been ugly and she'd cried for two days afterward. Then she'd vowed to never be a fool again. So how was it possible she could feel attraction to Kel? To any man? Dangerous waters.

He swore, then said, "I'm sorry. I'm surprised you're lending me a bunk."

"That's different. Colleagues use that bunkhouse all the time. Just don't try to snow me." With that she stood and went to her own bedroom and locked the door behind her.

God, it was all swimming up again. Why the hell had she ever pulled the cork out of that bottle?

She settled into her rocking chair and just rocked. What else could she do? It'd settle again. It always had before.

* * *

Left to his own devices in her small front room with the remains of a pot of coffee, Kel thought about what she'd just revealed. It had been a stunner, all right. And maybe self-protective.

A few times he'd caught female interest in her gaze, the same kind of attraction he felt for her. Maybe she was afraid of her own feelings. Or maybe she'd sensed his. So she'd put up one great big warning flag.

Just don't try to snow me. That was a revealing statement. It might explain why she lived for the job, why it was so much of her life that she talked about little else. If so, he felt really sorry for her.

But not just because of her job preoccupation. Because someone had raped her, and the assault had cut so deep that she let nothing else into her life.

If there was one thing he'd learned during his long road of dealing with post-traumatic stress, it was that the world was full of walking wounded, people who'd never been in an official battle zone, but who'd fought their own desperate wars of one kind or another.

So many people. Life didn't leave many unscathed. Everyone dealt with their scars in their own way, and like a bunch of phoenixes, they tried to rise from the ashes and build on them.

Knowing that, however, didn't change Desi's situation one bit. She chose to let her job consume her, and she did a damn fine job to judge by the way she'd risen so rapidly in the service. But she left room for little else, and he'd threatened her just by entering her space.

Maybe he should move back to the motel. But wouldn't that look odd, and by the size of this town he imagined gossip got around. Checked out, checked in again the same night? That'd make for some speculation, all right.

He sure didn't want to draw unwanted attention her way. Perhaps that was inevitable now, no matter what he did.

He'd wedged himself into her life and he needed to do some serious thinking about why. Yeah, he'd had to let her know what he was doing here. The point of his operation was not to keep such a low profile that nobody knew where he was. No, he had to draw the bad guys out. Couldn't do that if he buried himself in a hole, and Desi needed to know what was coming down because he'd be operating in her territory.

But he could have left it at that. Why hadn't he?

Pouring another coffee, he sat and stared into the places inside him, places he often hated to visit, seeking an answer.

All he found was a deepening concern for Desi. He'd awakened that buried memory in her, brought it out of the dark place she hid it. And then she'd warned him.

Not good. Not good at all. But he didn't know what to do about it.

It was late, but Desi was in no mood to sleep. When she heard a vehicle pull up out front, she went on immediate alert. Looking out, she saw a sheriff's car. What now?

She jammed her feet into her boots and headed out to the front room. Kel was still sitting there, mug in hand, but he'd heard the vehicle, too.

"Trouble?" he asked.

"No idea. Sheriff's vehicle." She grabbed her jacket and stepped outside to take the stairs down. She was forestalled by Deputy Sarah Ironheart at the foot of them. A middle-aged woman with raven-black hair, Sarah was of Native American descent and one hell of a nice person.

"Hey, Desi," Sarah said.

"Sarah. What's up?"

"Well, you have a guest. Everything okay?"

In spite of herself, Desi colored. So…she had a guest and it was so unusual that the sheriff was going to check up on her? Man, she must have some reputation. "I'm fine, Sarah."

"I can see that."

Desi relented even though she felt people might be getting too far into her private business. "Come on up. I'll make some coffee."

"I never turn down coffee when I have night patrol. Thanks." Sarah climbed the stairs and followed Desi into the front room. Kel was still sitting in the chair with a mug on the coffee table. He stood up immediately.

"Sarah, this is Kel Westin, an old friend. Kel, Deputy Sarah Ironheart."

"Sarah will do," she said as she shook hands with Kel. "Old friend, huh?"

Kel glanced at Desi. "Yeah. Recently discharged. That's why you haven't seen me before."

Smooth lie, Desi thought, rounding the bar into her teeny kitchen to start a fresh pot of coffee. She didn't know if it was wise to mislead the local law. As a rule, she avoided it at all costs. But maybe Kel feared blowing his cover. After all, he didn't know if Sarah was trustworthy. How could he? He didn't know Sarah.

Sarah took one edge of the ancient couch. "So where'd you two meet?"

Ah, hell, Desi thought. They hadn't worked that out, and the smallest detail would give it away.

"When I was at Fort Hood in Texas," Kel answered easily. "Desi was down that way visiting her parents and...well..." He gave a charming grin. "There was this bar, and then there was this summer romance. Followed by a lot of me being away and us chatting by email and Skype. I thought it might be time to meet up again, now that I'm not being sent away all the time."

Well, that covered all bases. Desi felt relieved that he'd apparently thought about what he'd say. And boy, how much he'd accomplished with one little tidbit about her.

That was when something gripped her. Pain or anger, she couldn't tell. She'd just watched that man snow Sarah. He wasn't trustworthy, badge or no badge. He lied like a pro. Later she was going to have some words for him, but right now she couldn't. She just had to play along.

She brought Sarah a mug of coffee and heated up Kel's cup. "Sarah, you want me to fill a thermos for you?"

"I have one," Sarah answered lightly. "It's just downstairs, and was I going to turn down a neighborly cup and chat?" She glanced at her watch. "Fifteen minutes, then I'm back on patrol." She looked at Kel. "Desi's a special woman. She can hand out a citation without making the violator furious."

Desi managed a laugh. "They just don't let me see it."

Sarah smiled over her cup. "Yeah, that's often wise. So Kel, you just got out? Any idea what you want to do now?"

"Trying to settle into a different way of life," he answered.

Sarah nodded. "It can be difficult." Then she winked. "Now you even have to decide what to put on in the morning." She patted her leg. "Something to be said for uniforms."

At that, Kel laughed. "You've got a point there. Maybe I should just buy seven days' worth of clothing that all look alike."

"Well, that's one way," Sarah agreed. She drained her cup and stood. "Desi, you look tired, so I'll just be on my way." She paused. "I heard about that trophy kill. Any leads?"

"Zip," said Desi. "Absolutely nothing. And the meat was wasted."

"I'll keep my ear to the ground. Nice to meet you, Kel." Then Sarah let herself out.

Alone, Desi and Kel exchanged stares. Then she rose without a word and went back to her bedroom, locking the door. He lied too easily. Maybe it was required for working undercover, but it didn't mean she could trust him.

So just don't trust him, she told herself as she readied for bed. If she didn't trust him, he couldn't hurt her. And to hell with the simmering attraction she felt. She'd lived without men for a while now.

Kel was no reason to break her rule.

Chapter 4

In the morning, Kel didn't need a neon sign to tell him that Desi was angry about something. The tension in the air was incredibly thick, her answers or statements about anything, even coffee, were short and abrupt.

He hardly knew the woman, and maybe this was her morning mood. But from the way her gaze kept sliding away from him, he was quite sure it was more than that. Namely, it was something he'd said or done.

But what? They hadn't had that much interaction last night. The deputy had stopped by, it seemed like a pleasant visit, then Desi had gone back to her room for the night.

Somewhere in there he had seriously screwed something up. Or maybe it didn't take much with her. How the hell would he know?

So he let it ride, figuring that if she had a problem with him she'd spit it out sooner or later. She didn't seem particularly reluctant to express herself.

"Time to go," she said when the kitchen had been tidied. She pushed a key across the counter. "This will get you in my door and the bunkhouse door."

"Thanks."

Then she was pulling on her belt and jacket over her red shirt, and striding toward the door. Feeling off-kilter, he followed, wishing he knew what the hell was going on.

"You have your work and I have mine," she said when they reached the foot of the stairs. "See you whenever."

He knew when he was dismissed. Without a word, he climbed into his own truck and watched her tear away. He had no idea where she was going, although it clearly wasn't to the ground-floor office.

Nor did he really have any idea what he was supposed to do himself that day. Waiting for roaches to crawl out of the woodwork might take a while. He was here only because so much of the recent trophy hunting had happened up in those mountains over the last two years. No reason to assume it would continue this year, not in large numbers.

But they were taking the chance that it would, and hearing a bighorn had already been killed illegally up there seemed to confirm it.

Another couple of weeks. The ring would get some time to locate him, then he was taking two guys up into the mountains on a hunt. That they'd be undercover, too, would only increase the likelihood that the ring would believe there was competition.

And that he might have other guides working with him, because the nature of his ads were changing a little at a time, hinting he could provide guides anywhere in the state.

A bigger threat. Much bigger. But for now, time hung

heavy on his hands, leaving him too much opportunity to wonder about Desi.

Not knowing what else to do, he drove into town to make himself visible. He had to be found to get the game on.

God, that had been tense, Desi thought as she drove away from the office. The trouble was, she wasn't good at hiding her genuine feelings except when in her role as a warden. Somehow those barriers didn't cover times when things got personal. A failing? Probably.

How much time did she spend cultivating light but friendly relationships? A whole bunch. But now she couldn't even bring herself to talk to Kel. He was a colleague. She ought to be able to deal with this, so what was wrong with her?

Pulling out her cell phone before she got out of range of a tower, she called the office and checked her voice mail. Nothing. She hadn't expected anything, though, because there was an extension line upstairs in her apartment so she wouldn't miss night calls. She hadn't even really thought about it, though, because she was in such a hurry to get away from Kel.

Because he had lied to Sarah. Because he had lied easily. Maybe it had been necessary, but how could she trust him now?

Aw, hell, she told herself. Forget it. Bury the attraction she'd been feeling and keep it all on a business level. That was where it belonged. After all, the guy had come out here to dangle himself as bait in hopes of shutting down an illegal operation, one that might have been responsible for that trophy bighorn. Nothing else mattered but getting the job done and protecting the wildlife.

Right. She'd been slipping off course. Time now for a correction. What's more, she needed to get herself sorted out before she returned later. She hadn't revoked Kel's access to the bunkhouse. No, she'd given him a key, mainly because the story making the rounds would be that he was an old friend. Her fault for starting that one.

And because he'd mentioned that it might be helpful if he appeared to by cozying up to the warden. Well, of course it would. She didn't need an explanation for that.

She was heading along the back roads that led up into the mountains, across the public lands that were so popular for hunting. There might be some licenses to check, and other activities that needed attention. Until her radio sounded, she was picking her own routes and duties.

The longer she drove, however, the more her internal argument grew. She'd told Jos yesterday that Kel was an old friend. What had he done that was so much worse? A tiny bit of embellishment, but not much. His cover had to be protected.

So why was she so angry with him? Yeah, Sarah was her friend, but so was Jos. Either one would understand the need for secrecy if the truth came out later.

Maybe she was overreacting, although she wasn't usually the overreaction type. So why react so strongly to a necessary little bit of lying?

Because she needed a reason to dislike Kel that might be stronger than her attraction to him?

Feeling suddenly gut punched, she pulled over to the side of the road and rolled down her window so she could listen to the soft sigh of the breeze in the evergreens.

She had never believed herself to be the kind who could play such mental games with herself. She didn't like the idea at all. Yet, it held a ring of truth.

God, couldn't she deal with her attraction without inventing other problems?

But lying...lying was at the top of her list of personal crimes. Little white lies were one thing. Bigger lies were something else. The question was why she wanted to put Kel's story into the bigger category. He was doing what he had to. Part of his job.

Surely she could swallow that?

Putting her truck back into gear, she pulled onto the road and started wandering again. It wasn't long before she saw two pickups pulled to the side. The sight relieved her. She needed to work, and checking some hunting licenses would be just the thing.

Kel wandered Conard City. It was much like other towns of its size in Wyoming except that it hadn't succumbed to tourism...yet. The streets weren't lined with all kinds of eateries—there was only one right now—and it had avoided the proliferation of taverns and whatnot shops that almost crushed the Western flavor of some of the towns he'd visited.

Must be too far off the beaten track, still. He liked it.

When he stopped in the diner, he fell into some conversation and let it be known he was an outfitter and was thinking of branching into this area. Nobody seemed especially bothered by the idea, and one guy said he'd love a job if the opportunity arose.

"Depends on how much business we get," Kel answered. "You do much hunting?"

Well, that encouraged a long ramble. Short take: the man was an experienced hunter and a couple of years ago had won a moose license in the drawing. Now he was after a bighorn permit, maybe next year.

Kel dutifully wrote the information in a pocket note-book and promised to keep the guy's name and number.

Drinking coffee at Maude's diner, as everyone called the City Diner, seemed to be a good way to get in touch around here. The locals weren't standoffish, and soon he was included in a discussion about the bighorn trophy that had been recently taken.

To a man, the people who were talking were appalled by the meat wastage. It was interesting to him that they were more outraged by that than the poaching that went with it.

Although none of them approved of poaching, and made it clear to him almost as if they were warning him, it was leaving the meat behind that really offended them.

Then one of them asked him point-blank, "If you take people on trophy hunts, will you take the meat as well?"

"Of course," he answered vehemently. That was en-tirely truthful. He never would waste meat. He'd seen too much real hunger to ever waste food again.

That seemed to win him some approval.

"It's the law," said a wizened man who looked almost as old as the mountains. "Never got this trophy hunting idea. When me and my dad went hunting, it was for the meat. Even before all them laws, nobody took more than they could eat. Went entire winters on venison jerky."

Kel resisted speaking, waiting for someone else to state the obvious. A guy with a long beard finally did.

"If everyone had been like you and your Dad, Ed, we wouldn't need all them laws. Folk fished the river dry, and nearly wiped out the moose and elk."

Ed grumbled. "I get it. The old days ain't never com-ing back."

Some of the men chuckled. Then Ed looked at Kel. "So why you doing it?"

"Leading hunts?"

"Hunts for trophies."

Kel shrugged one shoulder. "A man's gotta make a living, Ed. Long as they have a permit and we don't waste the meat, it's no different from anyone else."

One guy slapped his knee and chortled. "Sure enough it is. The out-of-state hunters need hand-holding and guiding. Never be able to do it without guys like you."

Kel nodded. "No argument. But it makes jobs, makes money that gets spent locally and the license fees are high, so it helps in conservation efforts."

At that point, Kel realized these men were coming to like him. Good. If they got wind of anything, they might let him know. He needed ears locally, ears besides Desi's.

"So you're staying with Desi Jenks?" one guy asked.

"Old friend. And I'm staying in the bunkhouse."

More laughs, but one man nodded, saying, "She's a good one, that woman. Makes you smile when you get caught with too many fish."

Guffaws answered that.

Desi had done her job well, Kel thought later as he resumed his stroll around town. Judging by the group he'd just talked to, she was well liked. That was important to a warden who couldn't have eyes on every acre or in the back of her head. She had to rely on people to report it when they saw something wrong.

As for him, he figured he'd set his hook. He wondered how long it would be before he started getting nibbles.

There was no such day where Desi didn't have a full plate. She got called to take care of an eagle that had been struck through the wing by a bow hunter. The bird was trying to drag itself along the ground. The hunter was probably nearly as distraught as the eagle and she talked him down a bit while she got her gear. She felt for him, but her real concern was the bird.

She donned her protective gloves and safety glasses, covered the bird's eyes, used shears to cut the ends of the arrow off, and then scooped the big angry bird into one of the large pet carriers in her truck bed.

Then she eyed the hunter. "How in the name of Mike did you manage that?"

The guy had the grace to look sheepish as well as anguished. And at least he'd called for help for the bird. "I didn't see it," he admitted. "I'm kinda rusty so I was shooting at tree trunks but one of my arrows flew too high and next thing…"

Desi shook her head. "Isn't there someplace safer to do target practice?" Of course there was.

"Yeah, but…" The man was young and looked utterly miserable. "I'm sorry. I was wrong. Give me my ticket."

She could have. Eagles were protected, but she didn't want to nail a guy who'd made a stupid mistake and had owned up to it. "Just a warning. Find a better place to practice, sir."

"I will." The young man looked toward the carrier on her truck bed. "Will it survive?"

"I hope so. But you know eagles mate for life? If we can't rehab this one, there's going to be one very lonely eagle in these woods."

"Hell." He stuffed his free hand into a pocket on his camo pants. "Where are you taking it?"

"First stop Dr. Windwalker. If he thinks it can be saved, he'll probably remove the arrow and call a rehabber to pick the bird up."

"I hope it's okay."

"Me, too," Desi agreed. She stripped off her protective gear, got the guy's bow hunting license and ID and started to write the warning.

He accepted the papers and stuffed them into a breast pocket. "I don't need to do anything?"

"No." Desi shook her head. "The warning will be on the record, though, so don't make another mistake. Find a better place to practice, one with some sight lines so you don't hit something you shouldn't."

"You're right. I never even thought about it. I just wanted to practice in the woods, like I was hunting." One corner of his mouth turned down. "Guess I learned something."

She offered her hand. "I want you to know I appreciate you calling this in. If you'd just left it…"

The young man shook his head vehemently. "I'd never do that. Even if it was dead. I know better."

Desi started to turn away, then paused. "You hear anything about the poaching of a bighorn?"

He nodded slowly. "Heard about it. Hard not to hear when some folks are really mad about it. Think you'll catch them?"

"I'm working on it. You hear anything, you got my number."

He nodded. "I'll use it."

He seemed like a nice enough guy, she thought as she drove carefully down the bumpy dirt road so as not to hurt the eagle unnecessarily. When she at last reached blacktop, she gunned it. No way to know if that bird could make it, but time was of the essence.

Mike Windwalker's vet practice just outside Conard City had grown a lot over the last few years. People had evidently swallowed any lingering prejudice they felt toward a full-blood Cheyenne. His kennels had doubled in size, he operated a pet adoption service, had a big barn for livestock that couldn't be treated on the ranches and maybe four vet techs helped him now.

He had time for the wounded eagle, however. He came out of the exam room immediately and guided Desi and the carrier into another exam room, away from the barking and meowing in his waiting room, which had to be troubling the bird.

Wearing protective gloves and a face shield, he grabbed a towel and reached into the carrier wrapping all of the bird except the wounded wing in it.

"Cover his eyes," he said to Desi. She grabbed another towel and put it over the bird's eyes. At once its attempts to struggle ceased.

Mike carefully extended the wing and examined it. "I need to do X-rays. If this hit a major blood vessel he could bleed out when I remove the arrow. And I need to see if it got any bone. Want me to call you later? This may take a while."

"Thanks, Mike." Desi gave him a wan smile. "It was an accident, by the way."

"Accidents can be as bad as on purpose."

"So it's a male?"

From behind his protective face plate he gave her an amused look. "Like I could tell? I haven't examined it yet. *His* was the default."

"You men," she said, and heard him laugh as she walked out.

A glance at her watch told her the day was far from over. She decided to extend her patrol a bit and talk to any hunters she happened across. Maybe they'd have some intel on the poacher.

Instead she spent her time hunting down the people who had set up camp just off the road and were turning beautiful public land into a trash dump full of discarded food containers and beer bottles.

She almost enjoyed making them clean it up.

Kel returned to the warden's station at dusk. He'd had an interesting time in the local gun store. Plenty of stories to share, as the owner was a former spec-ops guy from the Vietnam era, so they hung around talking about firearms, of course, but a lot of other topics as well. The owner, Les Armitage by name, didn't seem at all bothered that Kel was an outfitter.

"Some folks wanna hunt," was his philosophical answer, "but they couldn't find their way around those mountains without help." Les snorted. "GPS wouldn't even save 'em. Who has time to spend running rescue parties for idiots? Hell, most of the time they couldn't even get a cell signal up there. Who knows how long they'd be stumbling around before they were reported missing."

Kel laughed. "You need to do your research, too."

"That's the other thing," Les agreed, leaning an arm on his counter. "Scouting. Some people don't even think about it. Me, I spend all summer scouting good areas."

"Ever got a permit for big game?"

Well, it seemed Les had, and he had a few great stories to share. In the end, though, he wound up with poaching. He looked Kel straight in the eye. "I don't mind telling you that when I get wind of poaching I report it to the wardens."

Kel nodded. "Glad to hear it. They need all the eyes and ears they can get."

"Exactly. Big state, few wardens. And this last one, happening on posted ranchland? I wouldn't mind hunting those guys myself."

Finally Kel decided to go back and face whatever was wrong with Desi. Maybe it had evaporated during the day. Right now, he could only wonder. He stopped at the diner and picked up some takeout, then headed back.

He was just pulling into the parking lot when he saw Desi emerge from the office. She locked the door, then waited for him.

Maybe he was about to get his marching orders. He kinda hoped not. The woman intrigued him, and he needed to work closely with her on this.

He pulled the big paper bags out of the truck and walked toward her. "How was your day?" he asked.

"Interesting." She hesitated. "Sorry, I don't mean to sound abrupt. Let's go up. I'd like to put my feet up."

Well, that sounded more gracious. He followed her up the outside stairs and into her apartment where he deposited the diner bags onto the counter.

"I'll be right back," she said. "I need to wash up a bit."

Not a bad idea. He let himself into the bunkhouse section and used the bath there to scrub away some of the day's grime. He beat her to the front room, so he pulled the foam containers and tall coffees out of the bags. He hoped she liked steak sandwiches. Then he took one of the coffees and settled on the chair, waiting and wondering.

He'd learned a bit today, and figured there were a lot of eyes and ears that gave a damn about poaching. Desi had built some good relationships around here. And he was welcome as long as he stayed within the law. So that was good.

But the messages that had been spread around on social media under the fake name of his outfit implied something else altogether. He hoped the locals didn't make the connection because that would blow everything out of the water.

His skin was beginning to crawl a bit, though. A feeling he hadn't had since he left the army. A feeling he rarely ignored. It didn't seem possible that he'd been localized this quickly by the outfitting ring. He'd only been here a couple of days. But if locals talked, it shouldn't be too much longer.

A threat was marching his way, not a new thing, but playing bait was different. The question was whether they'd simply hunt him down and remove him, or if they'd lay a trap. Given the kind of people they were, he was betting on a trap.

Meanwhile he and Desi had to be on the lookout for more poaching, more signs that rules and laws were being ignored. Which meant he needed to start spending some time up in the public lands keeping watch. Desi had a whole list of things she needed to keep an eye on. She couldn't simply join him in a manhunt in the mountains. No way.

But he'd feel a whole lot better if he could find out what had gotten under her skin.

She emerged at last in clean clothes, half-ready to drop everything and get on her steed in minutes. Funny, he'd lived that way once, but hadn't considered that she was living that way, too.

No clock punching for a warden or a soldier.

"I brought dinner," he said, pointing to the counter. "The coffee's yours."

"Thank you."

She seemed a little cool and he wondered if he should ask what had happened. But he hadn't noticed she had any problem speaking her mind, so he guessed he'd just have to wait.

She didn't seem to mind steak sandwiches, because she took one of the containers and the coffee, then sat on the couch with the container in her lap. "Thanks," she offered.

"My pleasure. So how was your day?"

"Pretty much the usual. However…" She paused and smiled faintly. "I made a crew of eight campers miserable by ordering them to clean up their trash and watching while they did it."

"Pretty bad?"

"The place was looking like a landfill. Of course they claimed they were going to pack it all out when they were done hunting, but the astonishing absence of trash bags kind of gave lie to that."

He laughed. "It would. So you made them clean it up?"

"Every scrap. I hate to admit how much I enjoyed it." Then her face clouded. "Unfortunately, I got a call about a wounded eagle. Seems a young man, only twenty-one, decided he needed to practice with his bow in the woods instead of at a range. God knows how, but he hit a bald eagle."

Kel straightened a bit. "Oh, no. It's dead?"

"Not by the time I got it to the vet. Arrow through the wing. I give the guy credit—he called for help as soon as he realized what he'd done. He could have walked away and we'd probably never have found that bird."

Kel nodded slowly. "Good for him then."

"Except for what he admitted was stupidity, yeah. I'll call Mike Windwalker in the morning and find out how the bird is. I hope we don't lose it, but I fear we may never be able to release it."

Kel nodded, sat back sipping his coffee, waiting to see if she had more she wanted to say. With eagles it was bad. It wasn't just one bird affected; it was a pair of birds. It was breeding that would now never occur because the other bird would never again mate. He hated to think about it.

Desi had spent all day, when work gave her a moment, wondering why she felt so damn mixed up about Kel. He was here on a job, he was a colleague, and he was undercover. He hadn't done a thing his job didn't require of him, so why was she taking it so personally?

Because of her experience in college? Was that fair? Sure, she'd found it better to avoid men as a rule, especially given her job. It didn't leave her a lot of time during parts of the year for anything like a normal life... although maybe some of that was her fault. She'd joined the department with a huge chip on her shoulder, something to prove. Well, hadn't she proved it? Senior warden at such an early age. She worked with men who'd been wardens twice as long or longer and had never become seniors. So...

Her problem, she decided. Maybe one she needed to deal with. For all she knew, she was being prickly at the wrong times with her colleagues. It couldn't be too bad, or she wouldn't be here now, but...

Aw, heck, think about it later. As the steak sandwich began to fill her stomach, nothing seemed quite as bad.

At least Kel was eating now, too. Which should be some kind of social occasion, she guessed. He'd brought dinner. The least she could do was talk with him.

"What did you do today?" she asked.

"Wandered around town, talking to anyone who'd talk to me. Kinda let it be known what I was doing, got a lot of warnings about sticking to the law. Les at the gun store even warned me people around here would let you know if they saw me doing wrong. You've got a good network, Desi."

"Not nearly enough of one," she muttered, then pulled off a bit of her sandwich, holding it between index finger and thumb, looking at it. "It keeps happening. Too much wilderness out there. But I have to admit I'm grateful to all the people who really understand what Game and Fish is about and want to protect our resources."

"You do a lot of outreach?"

She half smiled, raising her gaze. "Of course. Every time I write a citation. And all of us take turns talking at schools and anywhere else we're invited. We run an antipoaching program at public gatherings, like the county fair. We even work on persuading people not to rescue baby animals but to contact us. Most of the time the young haven't been abandoned, but good people want to step in and help because Mama's away for a few hours. So yeah, as much outreach as we can fit in."

She tilted her head and looked inquisitively at him. "I guess working for the investigative unit hasn't given you much of a look at a warden's regular day."

"Unfortunately, no. I get the general gist, but seeing it on the ground?" He shook his head. "Since they assigned me to the unit, I've been pretty much…" He hesitated.

She perked. "You're kind of a secret?"

"Yeah," he agreed slowly. "I go undercover a lot. I'm not supposed to be linked to the unit."

"So here you are at my place?" The question was a little sharp, but she didn't apologize.

"Yeah. I am. Because this time I can be a friend from your past and it won't draw much attention. Because I can be here without letting anyone know what I really do. Because this one's big and I can't do it without your help."

"But what about other times?"

"It's like being a narc. I listen. I become background. Then I report what I hear. I go out when we've got something to investigate and no one wants redshirts poking around yet. I also spend a lot of time in the office."

"Well, I'm poking around."

He nodded. "That makes you even better cover."

So she was cover? At least he wasn't lying to her, but she still had trouble with the idea. He'd drawn her into this in a way that didn't make her comfortable. She'd spent a lot of time making herself into a relatively transparent person, honest sometimes to a fault. If she knew what it was, Desi spoke the truth. Maybe a reaction to Joe, her rapist, but who cared? It was who she had worked to become.

But it had started already when she told Jos that Kel was an old friend. Lie number one. How many more would there be?

"Desi?" Kel interrupted her unhappy line of thought. "Why did you tell Jos I was your old friend? Is there some reason you don't trust your wardens?"

"I told you. If four more people know, someone is apt to slip and mention it somewhere. We're not a group that's used to keeping secrets among ourselves or from our families."

He nodded slowly. "Let me ask another way. Is there anyone you wouldn't trust to know about me?"

That drew her up short. Was there? Running through four guys in her head didn't take long. Except for one, she'd known them the entire five years she'd been here. The other...she hesitated. "We've got one warden who only started here two years ago. He's young. Logan. Max Logan. But I think he's okay." Then she stiffened. "Why? Do you think this ring has inside help?"

Kel just shook his head. "Desi, I don't know. I told you. We see the results but can't get a handle on who these guys are. I have to look at every possibility. So Logan's been here only two years. That doesn't mean anything one way or the other."

"No, it doesn't. Just that he's the new guy."

"Agreed. I just wanted your sense of the situation. If using my cover story with them troubles you, go ahead and tell them what I'm here for."

Desi looked down at the half-eaten sandwich on her lap. Things were swimming to the surface from the depths of her mind. Bad things from the past. Things she tried never to remember. Joe.

God! She jumped up. She wasn't going to wallow in that again. Bad things happened to people. Big surprise there. She was hardly a special case. In fact, she'd buried it so well that it hardly rose near the surface anymore.

Somehow Kel had changed that. Why? It wasn't as if he resembled Joe in any way. Maybe her attraction to him? Something she hadn't allowed herself to feel in over a decade?

That must be it. Wrapping plastic around the remains of her dinner, she thrust the box into the refrigerator and started a pot of coffee. For something to do. To keep her alert because this evening was far from over and that phone could ring at any time.

"Hey, Desi?" Kel said to her back as she stood at the coffeepot.

"Yeah?"

"You have trouble trusting, don't you?"

"Why the hell…" Then she broke off, everything inside her roiling uncomfortably, hearing her own words to him: *Just don't snow me.* Hardly the thing to say to a new acquaintance, and far more revealing than she should have allowed.

"Maybe," she finally said. "What does it matter?"

He didn't answer until she eventually turned around. He was still in the chair, feet propped on the battered coffee table. "I guess it doesn't."

But it did matter or he wouldn't have asked. While the coffeepot dribbled and steamed, she folded her arms and stared at him. "Are you worried you can't trust me?"

He shook his head. "In some ways I'm very trusting. You can't get through combat without trusting the guy beside you. You don't even have to know him, but you trust him with your life."

Again an uneasy flip of her stomach. This was getting to her and she didn't want it to. She hardly knew him and this wasn't a therapy session, but she felt as if he were picking at scabs inside her.

"Anyway," he said, "you're right, it doesn't matter. Not my business, casual question, forget it."

But no question was casual when it rattled her all the way to her bones. Without a word, she went to her bedroom and closed the door.

What the hell was going on with her? Usually she

was calmer than this, job oriented, letting little else disturb her.

So why was she suddenly shaking? Why did the betrayal and rape suddenly feel like yesterday? All this time she'd successfully buried it, but now it was rising up like some monster from the depths. Shaking from head to foot like an aspen leaf in the wind, she crawled onto her bed and curled into a tight ball, as if she could hold it all in.

But now that it had surfaced, it wouldn't go away. Memories flickered through her mind, limned brightly with terror and anger and disbelief. It had happened. But while it was happening, she'd been filled with disbelief. Only afterward did the horror hit her, the fear, the anger.

Joe, laughing at her protests, pulling at her clothes. Batting his hands away, trying to squirm away, only to find herself pinned by his much greater strength and weight. Begging. Oh, God, she had begged him to stop. She hated that craven begging, but it was all that was left to her when she couldn't get away.

Joe telling her she was enjoying it when every cell in her body was drenched with fear, desolation, violation. Feeling helpless. So helpless.

Then, when he'd left her on the bed, rising and dressing, saying he'd see her the next day... She had been frozen in a block of ice until that very moment.

Then the fury hit. Galvanized her. She jumped from the bed and the jackass had stood there smiling, enjoying her nakedness, apparently expecting a goodbye kiss. What he had gotten was a savage goodbye knee in the groin.

Then she had grabbed her clothes from the floor and fled naked into the night. Never, not once, had she told anyone about it. Shame smothered her voice.

After all, she must have done something to invite it, right?

Except years later she knew she hadn't asked for it. She'd been trying to stop it from the instant it started.

Now she understood. So why did the sense of shame remain? The distrust she could understand, but the shame?

She turned her head, biting the corner of her pillow, seeking some control. She didn't want to start crying. She hadn't cried about it since back then. She'd moved past it, built a good life, and Joe was consigned to hell in her mind.

Except…except maybe it wasn't as much in the past as she told herself.

The night remained quiet. The phone didn't ring. But it was a long time before she found sleep.

Chapter 5

Kel had never done this kind of job before. He got the basics, but he wasn't experienced in having to create a whole persona for a job.

Which was probably why he seemed to have made some serious mistake with Desi. Over the next few days, she barely talked to him, simply walked out every morning before dawn, and some nights didn't return until well after dark.

He considered moving back to the motel, since he was obviously making her uncomfortable, but he couldn't do that now, and it was all his own damn fault. Deciding to accept her invitation to use the bunkhouse had been a mistake. Of course, it would have been a mistake to stay at the motel once he was identified as an old friend of hers. Everybody must know about the bunkhouse and would probably wonder even more if he'd stayed at the motel.

This situation was far worse. This was where she lived, yet she was doing everything possible to avoid him.

When she came in at night, she nodded, grabbed some coffee and food and took it back to her room. From the sounds he guessed she had a radio or TV in there. So he sat out front, wondering what he could do to patch this up a bit.

And every day he went into town, wandering around, engaging in conversations. Just making himself visible. Soon two other investigators would arrive to play the role of his clients, but until then, he had to hope that word would get back to the illegal outfitting ring.

Maybe the word would move faster once he had some "clients."

He really needed to be thinking about what he was doing rather than fussing over a woman he hardly knew. But fact was, Desi had touched him at a deep level. He gave a damn, for some reason known only to the gods. He sure couldn't figure it out. Yeah, she was attractive, but the world was full of attractive women of every shape and size. So why was she occupying such a large portion of his thoughts?

Because, he realized suddenly, he felt guilty. Felt absolutely sure that he was responsible for whatever was troubling her. Seemed crazy, considering they were virtual strangers, but he had to have done something, and he felt guilty about it.

Maybe when he saw her tonight he'd tell her he'd stick to the bunkhouse room so she could have her apartment back. Small enough thing and wouldn't raise the eyebrows that moving back to the motel would.

Yeah, that was what he needed to do. Keep clear unless he needed her for something work related. Hell, that was the only reason he'd introduced himself to her to begin with.

Okay then. Feeling a little more settled, he went to the diner and fell into a surprisingly fruitful conversation. Excitement pinged him.

And he felt an urgent need to share the tidbit with Desi.

So much for avoiding her.

Desi finished some paperwork in her office. A guy had shot two deer instead of one, and she and Jos had had to work out bullet trajectories to be sure it had been accidental as he claimed.

Six hours later, they were sure it hadn't been accidental. From the blood on the ground, from the discovery of a second bullet casing, to the fact that this magic bullet had passed cleanly through two deer..., Nope. Even if it had passed through the first, it should have lodged in the second.

So now the carcasses waited in the freezer for necropsy and she had to record everything she and Jos had found in painstaking detail. If the forensic pathologist found something to uphold the man's claims, it would be over. If not…well, it would be far from over.

In the meantime, she'd relieved the man of his gun and had it in the evidence locker. If he was cleared, he'd get it back along with the meat of one deer, since he had a license. She didn't think he was going to get either one.

She also couldn't figure out why he'd reported it to Game and Fish. Had he regretted it once he'd done it? Did he fear someone would report it if he brought home two deer? Was he just trying to get ahead of the problem? Or had someone seen what he did?

She'd probably never know. He hadn't been very talkative. Once he declared it was an accident, his cooperation had stopped. Inexplicably. He had to have known he couldn't legally keep both deer, accident or not. So why shoot the second, unless he thought no one would ever know? Then his call to her office?

She rubbed her chin, thinking, and it occurred to her that he might not have been hunting alone. Maybe he was covering for someone else. Well, the bullets they'd managed to find with the metal detector would determine if both had been fired by his gun, or if another weapon had been involved.

Sighing, she turned off the computer, turned off the lights and went upstairs. Light gleamed from the window beside the door, so she guessed Kel was there.

Feeling uncomfortable, she kept climbing. Even she knew she had been rude to him, and without giving him a reason for her behavior. By now he must think she was weird.

Sadly, she didn't think he'd be wrong.

Her feet growing heavier with reluctance, she opened the door. Kel wasn't sitting on the couch, but instead standing, as if he were waiting for her. On the counter there were takeout containers.

"I've got news," he said. "If you're interested."

Her heart quickened as she closed the door behind her. "Good news?"

"I think so. I was at the diner today when a man asked me about my outfitting business. Said he had a friend who was interested."

She waited, then said, "It's possible."

"Yeah, but he didn't stop there. He said he knew some other outfitters, but his friend wanted someone cheaper."

"And you said?"

"That I could work something out, but first I had two clients coming in a couple of weeks I had to take care of first."

She nodded. "Then?"

"He said he'd get back with me. I asked for his friend's phone number, but he didn't give it up. Someone's nosing around, and after he left a nearby patron at the diner remarked the guy wasn't from around here."

"That *is* interesting," she admitted.

"Brought you dinner again," he said waving at the counter. "Something a little different. Anyway, it's not much, but it may indicate we're getting the action we wanted."

She nodded and tossed her insulated vest over the back of the couch. "Thanks for dinner. So you might have someone nibbling around your hook?"

"I hope so. So much investigation, thought and planning went into this over the last nine months that I'd hate for it to go bust. We've gotta catch these guys."

"Yeah, we do." With effort, she summoned a smile. He was trying to be nice, trying to include her, and she didn't have to be abrupt with him. He was keeping his distance and wasn't pushing himself on her in any way. Evidently her signals were clear.

The realization didn't really make her happy with herself. Kel was a nice man, as near as she could tell, and he really didn't deserve the cold shoulder she was giving him. They were colleagues, so maybe she ought to just get over herself.

She grabbed herself a coffee and one of the takeout containers and sat on the couch, using the coffee table.

The counter and the coffee table were her only choices for eating. No room for even a small table.

He had brought BLTs tonight, Maude's triple-layer sandwich that except for the lack of turkey would have made a great club sandwich. "I love these," she said. "Thanks."

"You already thanked me."

She glanced up, wondering why he'd felt the need to say that. "Something wrong?" she asked.

"You," he answered bluntly. "I don't know what I did to make you upset with me. Maybe it's none of my business. Or maybe you just do this to everyone. Maybe I'm crazy, but you seemed friendlier at first. Anyway, your business. I can live with the ice. What did you do today?"

Her appetite vanished instantly. She put her sandwich wedge back into the container and didn't know whether to look at the wall or at him. She was still feeling raw, still trying to bury her memories of Joe, and talking about it would only open it all up again. And all because he'd had to sketch a cover story about what he was doing here.

Was that really lying? she asked herself. It had been necessary; he had a role to play, bad guys to catch. Maybe she'd overreacted. But why? Because she found him attractive, attractive enough that she'd warned him not to snow her?

He must be really wondering by now how well screwed together she was, and an honest check of herself suggested he had every right to wonder. Odd behavior with no explanation.

He was probably even wondering if they'd be able to work together, the way she was treating him. He'd said he'd learned to trust the guy beside him, even if he was

a stranger. The situation right now couldn't be much different for him. He had trusted her, had told her what was
going on. Then she became distant.

Sheesh. But how to get past this? How much to reveal?

"I told you. A guy lied to me once," she heard herself
say through stiff lips. "Sweet lies. I believed him until
he raped me."

He swore quietly, as if it bothered him as much as the
first hearing. The room, small as it was, suddenly felt
very large and very empty, as if she were standing on
some cold mountaintop all by herself, removed from everything and everyone. She closed her eyes, feeling an
icy emotional wind blow through her, surrounding the
gaping hole Joe had left in her.

"I haven't lied to you…" His voice trailed off. "The
cover story I gave that deputy when she was here. Is
that it?"

Without opening her eyes, she managed a jerky, stiff
nod.

"Oh, man." He paused. "Desi, that was different. It
was my cover story. Have I lied to *you*?"

"How would I know?" The words came out muffled,
her lips remained stiff.

He swore again, this time not so quietly. "I guess you
can't know. But this is a working relationship. You don't
have anything to fear from me. We're going to catch a
gang of poachers. That's all. You don't have to trust me
beyond that."

Somehow that hurt, too, but she didn't know why. A
professional relationship was exactly what she wanted,
wasn't it? God, how had she turned into such a mess?
She'd buried the past, moved forward, become compe-
tent at her work, had a few friends both in and out of the

department. In short, she'd had a life she was content with until this man had shown up.

He was offering to keep things just where they'd been when he arrived. That shouldn't hurt at all. It should reassure her.

So why this crazed, mixed-up reaction? She was usually fairly good at separating herself from irrelevant matters. Focusing on the relevant. His cover story had been necessary and she knew it, so why couldn't she distinguish it from the real lies that had once wounded her?

Eventually she opened her eyes. He wasn't eating either. He held coffee in his hands and had his head tipped back looking up at the ceiling. Probably wondering what he could do about any of this.

He really didn't deserve this reaction from her. Not one bit. She'd been thrilled to know he was working on the poaching, had known that he was undercover, and had invited him to stay here as part of a frankly-stated cover story.

"I'm sorry," she said in a smothered voice. "I can't explain... My reaction was out of line..."

"Stop," he said, a clear command even though his voice remained low. "No apologies. I get it." He lifted his head and stared straight at her. "What I want to know is can we get around this enough to work together?"

She reached deep inside, searching for the woman she had been before this temporary breakdown. "Yes."

"Then we'll be fine. As for the rest...I understand post-traumatic stress. I told you what broke up my marriage. You're not responsible for the triggers. I'm just sorry you have to live with it."

"I haven't done this before. At least in a very, very long time."

"Maybe not. And maybe you haven't had some guy practically living with you before, a man you barely know. Whatever. My cover story apparently took the lid off the pressure cooker, and for that I'm truly sorry."

"If I'm not responsible for the triggers, then how could you be?"

At that, one corner of his mouth lifted. "Fair enough. I promise you I will never lie to you about anything except this damn cover, okay? If you think I'm lying tell me. I'm not a liar by nature. And when it comes to women, I usually give more truth than they really want."

For some reason that surprised a weak laugh from her.

He spread one arm. "I'm no Casanova. What you see is what you get. One great big rolling stone who never wanted to settle down after the first marriage went south because of my own PTSD. Safer to avoid entanglements when you can't trust yourself."

She hadn't thought of it that way before. But in part, wasn't that what she'd been doing since Joe? Not being able to trust men, that was what she'd always thought. But how about being able to trust herself? This wasn't looking good for her.

"Just go with the flow, Desi," he said after a while. "If I trigger you again, do me a favor and let me know right away, okay? Now I know how much lies bother you, but there may be other things."

She nodded slowly, facing the possibility. She might have chosen her career in part because she could avoid the kinds of relationships that might be a problem. Focus on the job, on catching miscreants, on dealing with men safely from behind a badge. Funny she'd never thought of that before.

But whyever she had chosen this career, she loved it.

Of that she had no doubt. Every morning when she put on that red shirt, she felt as if she were involved in a nearly sacred mission: protecting the wildlife and the ecology. Then her thoughts turned back to Kel.

"What triggers you?" she asked.

"Very crowded places. Narrow streets. Short sight lines. I've gotten over the loud noises problem, and for a while there I couldn't drive without feeling every other vehicle on the road was a potential bomb. That's gone, too. The triggers have lessened with time, which I guess makes me luckier than many. But you know…" He fell silent.

Eventually she prompted him. "Know what?"

"You have no idea just how nervous I can get in the mountains. Which means I picked a very strange career."

She began to feel some strong sympathy for him. "That's not getting easier?"

"Yeah, actually it is. Like I told you, I spent all summer hiking around up there. A little desensitization while I worked. It helped, but didn't entirely wash away the nerves."

He was trying to make her feel comfortable with her own craziness, she realized. Exceptional, considering how much he had to reveal about himself. He probably wasn't any more comfortable with talking about these things than she was.

"Thanks, Kel."

"For what?" He smiled again, a dim smile.

"For being so honest about something you'd probably rather not discuss."

At that he just shook his head. "No reason not to discuss it. The world is full of wounded souls, not just veterans. We all need to look out for each other. Now will you please eat? It's already eight, and I'm sure you haven't eaten in hours."

"Not since breakfast," she admitted and lifted the wedge of sandwich she had dropped. "And I do love BLTs."

"Then eat. I need to as well."

He went and got the other takeout box and dug into it as if it was the only thing he was interested in.

Somehow she doubted it. With Kel, she felt he was always thinking about something. But then, she did the same thing.

"A guy shot two deer this morning," she said.

He looked up and swallowed. "Seriously?"

"Yeah. Weird. He said it was an accident, but from the evidence Jos and I found, it doesn't look like it. What I don't get is why he reported it. He had nothing to gain. Doesn't even get the extra meat if it *was* an accident."

"Nope," he agreed. "That's strange all right. So you thinking someone else might have been there? That he's covering?"

"Maybe so. I just can't imagine why."

"Another mystery," he remarked as he resumed eating.

Desi glanced his way from time to time, feeling much better now. It was as if a boil inside her had been lanced, just by owning up to what was disturbing her. She needed to remember that for the future. Sometimes self-protective silence wasn't the answer.

Kel had begun working on his second sandwich, but suddenly looked up. "Did you ever get any help? After your rape, I mean? Or were you all alone?"

She stiffened. What right did he have to ask? Then she forced herself to be honest because he'd been so honest with her. "No. I spent two days crying and then I felt ashamed. I didn't want to tell anybody."

"So he got off?"

"I doubt he was able to walk for another week."

That drew a genuine laugh from Kel. The sound of it made Desi smile. Okay, they could handle this. It would all work somehow.

Several hundred miles away, a phone rang. The pony-tailed man closed his office door and answered. "Yeah."

"It's me," said a familiar voice. "One of my guys met the new outfitter working out of Conard City."

"Hell, that's good hunting." And no surprise to him.

"I know. Anyway, we need to do some more checking, but he says he's already got two clients and is looking for more. Price negotiable."

"Be careful and be sure. Got a call from Hugh yesterday. One of his men found another new outfitter operating around the Bighorn Mountains. I don't know if these two guys are together or not. And if they turn out to be legit, we've got to leave them alone."

"I get it," said the voice on the phone. "But negotiable prices doesn't sound legitimate to me."

The ponytailed man agreed. After he hung up, he spent a long time staring at the huge state map on his wall, marked up to show the best places to hunt this fall.

Negotiable prices meant trouble for all of them. If this guy kept it up too long, there'd be a price war.

Someone was going to have to move out, and it wasn't going to be the ponytailed man or his business associates. They were all certain of that, but the ponytail man was more certain because he had sources. He had some control over this mess.

Four years as a sniper had taught the ponytailed man that it was no harder to kill a man than it was to kill game. He could do it.

And he didn't especially care if he needed to.

After they finished eating, Kel helped Desi move the two deer into another freezer and tag them.

"Both bullet wounds are through and through," he remarked as they wrapped the remains in more plastic. "How likely is that?"

"Not. Jos and I checked the trajectory of both wounds and they don't add up to one bullet either. But straight through the second deer? I suppose weirder things have happened."

"Maybe with a cannon," he said. "No, you're right, it's possible. Unlikely, but possible. I'm long past thinking anything is impossible. Still."

She closed and locked the freezer putting a label on the outside of it. Every hunting season, what with one thing and another, they often filled these freezers before cases traveled through the courts and the meat could be donated.

She locked the shed behind them, then they climbed the stairs again. The night wind was getting stronger and colder. Whispers of winter carried on its breath. At the top landing, she stopped and looked back toward the mountains. They were barely visible against the night sky, just a darker presence against the stars. No lights. She'd been watching every evening, checking periodically for fires or bright lights. All quiet, evidently.

The moon would come up later, and it was fast approaching full. A hunter's moon. She just hoped no hunters were planning to take advantage of it.

She heard a yip and yowl, soon accompanied by others. "Coyotes," she remarked. "They don't usually come so close to town."

"Any reason they would tonight?"

She shook her head and turned to open the door. "Nothing I'm aware of. They seem to find enough food without human pets or garbage. I guess we'll find out if we're growing a problem."

"Anybody around here trap them?"

She lifted a brow at him as he closed the door behind them. "What do you think?"

One corner of his mouth lifted. "Of course."

She nodded and pulled her vest off. "There are some people who run trap lines as a business to augment their income. The pelts are worth a little. And if a rancher starts having a problem with them, he might put a bounty on them. But you know that."

She was rambling, telling him stuff he had to already know. Well, talking about coyote trappers had to be safer than anything else that came to mind. It helped her keep a distance, and she needed distance, something she was only beginning to realize.

As usual she went to close the curtains on the front window, open to anyone who drove by on the road out front. For the first time, she wondered why she did that. There wasn't that much traffic. No one would be able to see very far into the apartment from the road so far below, but she did it anyway. Her desire for distance?

Regardless, she closed them, telling herself that quirk or not, it might be best until they settled the whole issue of the illegal outfitters. As for the rest of it...well, she had most of her life left to deal with whether she was screwed up or just overly cautious.

Distance could be a good thing. Don't let anyone inside the gates until you really knew him or her. Sensible rule.

But why Kel's presence was bringing all this out... she squirmed inwardly. Was he somehow striking her as special? The sexual attraction she felt was a constant hum, but she was doing a fairly good job of keeping it in the background. She guessed she was still uncomfortable feeling that way about any man.

Big deal. He'd find his bad guys—or not—and move on again. All she had to do was survive a few days or weeks without doing something stupid.

She could do that, right?

Kel spoke and she realized she had been standing staring at the curtains she had just closed.

"Desi?"

"Sorry, lost in thought." She turned slowly. He was still sitting casually in the chair, legs loosely crossed, but nothing diminished his impact. It felt brand new and fresh all over again. Dang! Such a sweet ache, one she had almost forgotten.

One she usually quashed immediately, but this time she seemed unable to make it go away. She considered just going to her room, but it was a small room, designed only for sleeping, really. Not a small cave full of things she could do to occupy herself. Spartan, in fact, with one lamp, a tinny clock radio and small TV, a phone and a rocking chair squeezed into a corner. She'd tried to read in there, but the light was miserable.

So no, she wasn't ready for that confinement. Nor would it do any good. She had to work with Kel for a while, so she'd just better get used to it.

She returned to the sofa. "So you think you might have had a contact today?"

"Can't be sure," he admitted. "Still, it felt like I was being sounded out, and not as a guide. I mean, if you were going to hire me, wouldn't you want to know what I had to offer? If you were asking for a friend, you'd have at least some of those questions, right?"

"You'd think so. But it may have been so spur-of-the-moment he didn't have any questions."

"He seemed to want to know if my price was negotiable. Then he walked away when I said it was, and someone in the diner remarked he wasn't from around here."

He'd already told her that part and now eyed her curiously. She wondered if he guessed she was struggling to find safe ground. He probably did after their frank discussion about triggers and flashbacks. He didn't question the direction she took, however, and that was fine by her.

"I feel a little raw," she finally said. She owed him something after the way she had cold-shouldered him.

"I'm not surprised."

She believed him. "It's been more than ten years, Kel. I ought to be way past this."

"Sure. Right." He sighed. "If only the mind was that malleable. We'd all erase our bad memories and move on in eternal sunshine."

She curled her legs under her, leaning against the arm of the couch. "That would be nice, wouldn't it? Pie in the sky."

"We can dream, can't we?" He leaned forward, uncrossing his knees and resting his elbows on them. "The thing is, I keep reminding myself that we're the sum of our experiences, good and bad. I'm not sure I'd want to erase everything. Some of it, yes, but not all of it. If bad memories do nothing else, maybe they can make us more compassionate. I hope they can. Maybe they give us a little insight to what someone else is suffering."

She nodded slowly, uncertain what she thought. She hadn't exactly been moving mountains of compassion since Joe. No, she'd decided to expend her efforts by saving fish and animals, by protecting the entire ecology for future generations. Not exactly compassion.

"Like you," he said, surprising her. "How many civilians do you think I feel comfortable talking about my PTSD with? I stick with veterans' support groups when it comes to that. I don't expect to be understood by anyone else. But there you are, experiencing it in your own way, and I felt I could share with you. And you understood."

"Some of it," she said hesitantly. "I don't understand where you've been."

"And I won't talk about it for that very reason. But you understand some of what it did to me. I appreciate that."

She wrapped her arms around herself, considering his words. He'd made her feel special. He'd forged a link in a bridge they might be able to cross, at least about one thing, a very private thing as he said. Amazingly, that made her feel better. "Thanks, Kel."

"No thanks needed. All we did was give each other some room to breathe."

An interesting way to look at it, but accurate. Room to breathe. A tightness in her had begun to ease while they talked. Slowly she unfolded her arms, uncoiled and went to the kitchen to get more coffee as hers had grown cold. "Want some fresh?" she asked.

"Thanks." He rose and joined her in the small space, dumping the dregs in his cup down the sink. While she filled it for him he asked, "Think you'll get any calls tonight?"

"Probably not. Right now we don't have any reason to maintain a night patrol. No signs of illegal baiting or anything else that might cause us to stake out the woods. It's mostly quiet." Maybe too quiet, she thought. If there was one thing you could say with reasonable certainty about human nature, it was that there were a lot of people who seemed to want to get away with something.

Of course, that didn't mean she couldn't have a quiet night every now and then during hunting season.

Kel returned to the chair, and she followed a few seconds later with her own mug, this time sitting with her feet on the floor and her coffee on the table in reach.

"So dawn patrol in the morning?" he asked.

"Yeah, unless something happens tonight." She gave him an inquisitive look. "You have no idea how long you might have to wait before your plan works…if it works. Doesn't the waiting bother you?"

"I have a long experience of waiting. It doesn't bother me like it used to. But I have things to do. For example, I found a small storefront I may rent. I need a place that isn't here at your station to make me look like I really am setting up business."

She blinked, astonished. "You're going to put a sign up out front?"

He laughed. "Hell no. But I need an address, a place for people to reach me, to make it look like I'm settling in. I may appear to be buttering you up, but I can't run my illicit hunting business out of your place. Man, wouldn't that cause people to turn tail? So no, I need a business front, and I think I found the place. Small, cramped, just enough room to throw around some camping supplies, a few hunting rifles and shotguns…make it look like I'm set to be a guide."

Holding her cup, she leaned back and thought about it. It made sense, she supposed. He could appear to be pursuing her at night and working by day. "Do men really think women are that stupid?"

He stiffened. "What do you mean?"

"That you could sweet talk me into not doing my job to the best of my ability. Do men think it's really possible that a female warden would look the other way because some guy is romancing her?"

"Some would certainly," he answered straightly. "Not all of us think that way. I certainly don't, but some guys… well, I admit I suggested making it look like I was getting on your good side. It's the kind of thing some con would try. That's not me. I have greater respect for a woman's intelligence."

"So don't hold the idea against you?" she asked, sourly amused.

"Absolutely. I know how some guys think. Doesn't mean I'm the same."

Fair enough, she decided. Glancing at the clock she saw it was past nine. "Time for me to hit the sack. I need to be on the road before sunup. The TV works, by the way, but we have limited channels. No sports package."

He shook his head. "TV's not my thing. Mind if I read a book?" He indicated the bookshelves.

"Help yourself. It's an eclectic collection. I think every warden who ever lived here left some volumes behind."

When she rose, he rose with her, then surprised her by touching her arm lightly. He might as well have hooked her up to an electrical current. Her whole body started vibrating. She hardly dared look at him for fear of what he might see in her face.

"Desi? Any way I can help, just let me know."

"I think your plate is already full enough," she answered. "But thank you."

Then she strode off to her bed, eager to escape the ghosts from her past that he seemed to be resurrecting.

Or maybe he was waking something new. Either way, she didn't want it.

Chapter 6

Kel heard Desi wake while it was still dark outside. A glance at the battered digital alarm clock beside the bed advised him that dawn was still a couple of hours away. She hadn't gotten a lot of sleep.

He stood and stretched, listening to joints pop as they loosened up. A few more stretches and he felt ready. He flipped on the light in the bunk room and pulled on some casual Western clothes that looked as if they'd seen better days. They had.

He was glad he and Desi had talked last night. There was a bit of comfort between them now, and considering that they were nearly strangers, they'd managed to cover some difficult ground. For both of them.

Most people just didn't get how PTSD could make you react sometimes, how it could throw you back in time so that you were hardly aware of where you were, or could make you irritable and angry for no good reason. It was almost as if your own skin didn't feel quite right anymore.

He jammed his feet into hiking boots, tied them quickly, then stepped out into Desi's side of the upstairs. He found her in the kitchen scrambling some eggs, making some toast. The aroma of coffee drew him.

"Morning," he said.

She looked up from the stove. "Morning."

"Get enough sleep?"

"Enough," she answered. "Barely."

"I kinda thought so."

"What are you doing up? You could sleep a few more hours. There's not gonna be anyone around to rent you that storefront this early."

He leaned against the counter. He liked looking at her, he noted as he watched her finish making her breakfast. If he'd met her under other circumstances, he'd be trying like mad to get her attention in a different way. Instead he answered her question. "Do you have any idea how uncomfortable those cots are? And you're talking to a man who can sleep like a baby on rocky ground."

He watched everything about her change in the instant before she cracked a laugh. "That bad? Really?"

God, he wished she'd smile more. "I'm not sure why, but yes. Maybe I just don't move enough."

She lifted the pan from the stove, and turned to him with it. "You want these eggs? I can make more."

"Thanks but it's too early for me. I'll get something later. You pack a lunch?"

"Already done. Ham and Swiss on rye." She scraped the scrambled eggs onto a plate and he could see she'd added something green, probably peppers, and cheese. She'd also made herself four slices of rye toast. It looked good.

"So you get out there before the official hours start and patrol the roads?"

"Essentially, yes. We all do. Anyway I find a parked vehicle, I stop and listen. I'd better not hear a shot before the appointed time."

"And if you do?"

"Then I walk in. Or I wait by the vehicle. I mean they've got to bring their kill out soon."

"So they're not all falling over each other out there?"

She laughed, shaking her head. "You said you spent all summer hiking up there, Kel. You know how much land is out there. We'd need half of Wyoming hunting right here to have them stumbling over each other."

"Which makes your job challenging."

"You know, I realized a long time ago that I wasn't going to catch them all. Nobody could and some enforcement is better than none. Being random about who we catch keeps the guys who think about edging around the law a whole lot jumpier."

"I guess it would. You never know when a warden might swoop in."

"That's the idea." She paused to pass him a mug of coffee before coming around the counter and sitting on a stool to eat. "Help yourself to anything when you get hungry."

"I'm going to the diner when it opens. I'll have to eat there. You know that place is a great source of intelligence."

She gave a little snort. "Kinda like the churches. The community's beating heart. Or gossip central. I like it there, too. When I first started here, it was a great way to make connections. I went in wearing my red shirt, and right away I was sharing my table with five guys. They were checking me out, but that's the first step. I made a lot of friends over the next months. You hang out there enough and one of them will warn you if they think someone suspicious is looking for you."

"They will?" The idea surprised him, but he guessed she would know. He'd seen how small Afghani communities could be like that, but he hadn't expected it here. Maybe because he was used to being one of the guys no one really wanted around.

"Sure," she said, carrying her plate to the sink and setting it to soak in a small dishpan. "By now they all know where you're sleeping at night. That should speed things up for you."

Then she pulled on her belt, holstered her gun and donned her outerwear. Swiftly she left, leaving him feeling as if he had just seen a wraith, here and then gone.

Her words had struck him, though. *They all know where you're sleeping.*

Hell, he hadn't given one thought to what that might mean for her. Sure, she could say they were old friends, whatever, but it seemed a whole lot different when phrased the way she had.

They all know where you're sleeping.

Why had he been too stupid to think of that before? This wasn't some major city. He might be making things harder for her.

But she hadn't objected. She'd offered the bunkhouse, such as it was. Maybe it didn't matter any more here than it would have in a major city.

Or maybe it did, and neither of them had even considered it.

He didn't mind dangling himself as bait, but he didn't want her in that noose with him. He figured these guys had a motive to kill him. What if they thought Desi knew what he was doing?

Would they try to remove her, too?

Her daily job involved going out and talking to people, every one of whom was armed. And while game wardens and other conservation officers weren't exactly on the top of the list when it came to being shot in the line of duty, it happened, and such killings were on the rise nationally. A dangerous job, like law enforcement of any kind.

And he might have set her up for more.

Damn. Needing something to do, he rounded the counter and started washing her breakfast dishes. It sounded so casual, his suggestion that he make it look as if he were buttering her up so she wouldn't scrutinize his activities too closely. But what if the ring he was hunting read it differently? It didn't seem likely because she was a warden and that should protect her from their suspicion. She devoted her life to trying to stop the very thing he was pretending to do, the very thing that ring did.

No reason for them to think she was in on it. But *They all know where you're sleeping* sounded sinister to him now. God, he'd royally screwed up.

He grabbed some more coffee and sat at the counter, reviewing everything he'd done, what might or might not be known, and trying to figure out just how much danger he'd exposed Desi to.

It was too late now to move back to the motel. Everyone knew he'd moved in here. Maybe he needed to solidify the story over the next few days, making it clear he was sleeping in the bunkhouse. He could do that casually enough without making it seem like he was sending a message.

But would that be enough? He'd come here knowing he would need Desi's help. It wasn't a one-man job. But he'd been hoping to tap her network of friends, the people who called her when they saw something suspicious. The romancing her part had only been intended to create an impression that he was sweet-talking her. The instant she claimed him as an old friend had set this stone rolling. Who'd leave an old friend at the motel when she had a bunkhouse on the other side of the door? So he'd moved in, the natural thing.

Well, he supposed it was good that it looked natural, but even so he was beginning to wonder if he was cut out for this undercover stuff. He might have inadvertently put a woman in danger because he hadn't been quick enough on his feet, because he hadn't even really thought about what could happen.

He'd have to find a way to adapt. He was used to the best plans going awry, an inevitability in combat situations. He'd deal with it. But it made his heart skitter uncomfortably when he thought about how Desi might have been dragged into more danger.

Damn, the woman was growing on him, and it couldn't have been clearer that she didn't want to grow on anyone.

Maybe he needed his head examined. No time for that now, though. Soon two of his colleagues were scheduled to arrive for a "hunt" and he needed to get that storefront space up and running. Stake himself out like a Judas goat.

That had been the plan all along. He'd assumed he could do it because he'd been in much more dangerous

situations. But he hadn't often been in them with someone who hadn't volunteered.

Then he had a thought. There appeared to be empty
rooms above the storefront. Moving in there would also
seem like a natural step, and would draw attention away
from Desi. If it were possible, he needed to do that. It
wouldn't destroy the "old friend" designator like moving into the motel would. It would appear as if Desi had
simply offered him a cot until he had a better place to
rest his head.

Satisfied that he needed to take care of that ASAP, he
decided to make a light breakfast because he was going
to eat at Maude's diner again in a couple of hours. Put
his finger to the wind. See if anyone had noticed anything unusual.

Desi liked patrolling before dawn. She loved the dark
peace of the woods, pierced only by her headlights. It was
a dangerous time, too. If anyone out there didn't wait for
first light, she could be mistaken for game. Of course,
that could happen at any time, orange vest and cap or no.
Some hunters were just too quick on the trigger, like the
guy who'd mistaken his hunting partner for a game bird.
Yeah, the partner had been wearing orange, but it wasn't
visible through the brush. So the brush had rustled, and
the hunter had made a bad choice.

At least no one had died, but she'd given quite a stern
lecture to the offending hunter about not shooting when
he couldn't clearly see his target. Not that he seemed
to need the lecture at that point. He'd been distraught
enough to see the error in his ways, but the lecture was
required anyway. The other hunter went to the hospital

but was all right and refused to press charges. Both of them were lucky men.

And the first hunter lost his right to hunt for a while.

The sad thing was, she'd seen that more than once, heard of it too many times. It kept her cautious when she got out of her vehicle. Everyone sitting in a stand right now, or who had tracked a game animal and was just waiting, was eager. Too eager. Intentional or not, that made them dangerous.

While she prowled the roads looking for vehicles pulled to the side, her thoughts wandered back to Kel. Boy, had she hightailed it out of there this morning. Earlier than she had really needed to, but she could excuse it because it allowed her to patrol some of the more distant parts of her area.

But seeing him this morning, freshly wakened, a little rumpled...well, he was only more attractive. Dang, she needed to keep her mind in the game, not her urges. The guy would probably be gone in a few weeks; he was here only for business. She couldn't have picked a worse guy to suddenly get attracted to.

It made her so uneasy to feel that tug toward him, that pleasant ache for him. She'd managed to quash all that for years. But here she was doing it again.

Then it struck her that maybe she was responding to him because it was safe. He *was* going away. No complications. Nothing messy. And a good reason to park her yearning and not act on it.

Anyway, after last night and their intimate conversation, she felt better about everything. She'd shared something she had never shared before and her confidence had been accepted with caring. He'd shared something he probably didn't share outside a group of vets, and she appreciated the importance of that. A special guy.

Part of her was sorry to realize that he'd be moving on as soon as they solved this, or a soon as the WIU decided this wasn't working.

Every time she thought about it, the idea that a whole ring of illegal outfitters was operating in this state, she got a real burn going. Occasional poaching happened because people were people, but to take large sums of money from out-of-state hunters who couldn't or wouldn't wait to get a permit for the game they wanted? Who wouldn't pay for even the most basic license and take their chance in a drawing like everyone else?

She knew those out-of-state licenses were expensive, but there was a reason for that: to protect hunting for residents. It would be awful to have locals shunted aside as wealthy trophy hunters snapped up licenses in huge numbers. Plus, it helped support Game and Fish, who were looking after a whole lot of things for people who paid other fees all year round. Call it a makeup fee. Paying for year-round services that out-of-staters planned to use for only a few days. Services that made it possible for them to find game here.

But then her thoughts started drifting back to Kel again. She could have laughed at herself if she weren't troubled about her own state of mind. Stuck in a rut, she decided. But it wasn't the first rut she'd met in her head.

As the road made a hairpin turn, she saw a pickup pulled over to the side, lights off. This was far out from anywhere, so it wasn't surprising that someone had gotten here well before first light.

Still, she probably needed a little chat with them, unless they were camped somewhere in the woods. Under those circumstances, trying to find them would be a waste of time. She switched on her roof bar and red-and-blue flashers. The swirl of colors made the darkened forest around look eerie.

She put the pickup in Park and set the emergency brake. Just as she was about to climb out, the driver's side door of the truck ahead opened and a man climbed out.

People often did that, but she wished they wouldn't until she was out of her vehicle with complete mobility. At least he didn't try to approach

She unlatched her seatbelt, felt for her sidearm, making sure she had clear access, then climbed out, keeping the open door between herself and the man.

"How's it going?" she called.

"Dawn could hurry up," the man answered. "Seems like I've been sitting here forever."

"Not much longer. You have any loaded weapons in your truck?"

"Not loaded, but yeah, me and my buddy got a couple of rifles."

"Take them out slowly please and leave them in the bed of the truck."

The man seemed to have no troubled with that. He reached inside the cab and pulled out two hunting rifles in padded carrying cases, and laid them in the bed.

"You need my buddy to get out, too?" The guy asked.

"Not really. Just checking licenses. Sorry about the guns but caution requires it."

"I get it."

"Any other weapons?"

"Hunting knives. You want them in the back, too?"

"Please."

Once the weapons were taken care of, she approached.

"Just the standard check. You get anything good in the drawing this year?"

"Elk," the man said proudly as he handed over his license, permit and ID. "My buddy already got elk and moose a few years ago. Some people get all the luck, don't they?"

She heard the guy inside laugh. "I shared the meat with you, Bob."

Bob grinned. "He did. Invited me and the family over for dinner a few times."

Desi smiled. "I hope you'll be doing the cooking this year."

"Count on it. Doby's wife has the best recipe. I'm planning to beg for it."

By the time she finished checking them out, she decided that she really liked both of the men. As she got ready to return to her vehicle, she paused and turned back. "We've got a poaching problem," she said.

Bob shook his head. "Don't we always? I hate it when they take the big game. Say, Warden, can you tell me something?"

"If I know."

"Does the poaching affect the available permits for the next year?"

She hitched her gun belt to a more comfortable position. "That depends. We do our best to count the herds and then decide how many we can afford to harvest. If there's been a lot of poaching, then yeah, the population might decrease and we might offer fewer permits."

"I figured," said the guy in the passenger seat. "You getting on top of it, Warden?"

"We're trying. It seems to be on the increase, though. Say, if you gentlemen see anything suspicious while you're out here, will you let me know? I'd like for both of you to be able to win big game permits next year. Likelier if we can offer more."

"I know," said Bob. "Believe me, if I see something I'll be in touch."

"Just don't try to police anyone. Wouldn't want you getting hurt." She passed him her card. "You can call night or day. This time of year I sleep on the phone."

That caused both of them to laugh. She waved and climbed into her vehicle again, switching off the light bar and flashers.

She thoroughly enjoyed encounters like that. After both men were safely back in their truck, she drove on.

Then her mind, as if it were attached by a rubber band, snapped back to Kel. All she could do was shake her head at herself. Most of the people she met on this job were like the men she had just talked to. Regardless, for her own safety she had to keep her head in the game. Completely in the game.

Sexy, fuzzy thoughts about a man weren't going to help her. Nope, pure distraction. But then she laughed. It had been so very long since she'd allowed herself that distraction. It was kind of fun.

Kel rented that storefront he'd been looking at, paying the guy for six months. He and his headquarters team had debated that, whether a very short-term lease would make him look more suspicious, or whether it would lessen his threat to the ring they were after. Finally they decided on six months as a good compromise. It meant Kel wasn't planning on quitting, that he wasn't just a one-time threat to their income stream.

In the meantime, he now had a place to put all the

camping gear from his pickup. Yeah, he'd just have to load it all up again when his "clients" arrived, but he could make a show of checking it all out, like he was getting ready. The rifles and pistols he kept in the truck. By the time he was done with that, it was lunch hour and he headed back to Maude's diner to get something to eat and listen for anything that might perk his attention.

And for the first time he felt as if he were being watched.

There were a lot of people in the diner; any one of them could be staring a bit. But it had started, the first prickles, as he was unloading his truck. Just prickles, easily dismissed. Now it was stronger, and he looked casually around the diner. He forced himself to eat, then return to his storefront to lay out all the camping gear for inspection. None of it really needed it, but it made him look serious if anyone was interested.

Dang, he thought finally as the afternoon began to wane. He had to get out of here. He was having crazy feelings, and he honestly didn't know if he could trust them.

Back at the warden station he saw four more official vehicles parked out front. Desi must be having a pow-wow with her colleagues. His curiosity piqued but he couldn't just walk in on them. Instead he headed upstairs and let himself in.

He could hear voices and laughter from down below, but couldn't make out any words. He hoped he hadn't caused her any problem by showing up while everyone could see him, then brushed the thought away. Probably they all knew he was staying here by this point.

He went to the sink, washed the coffee carafe and started a fresh pot. Out the window over the sink, he caught sight of two wardens carrying a plastic-wrapped carcass out to the evidence freezers. More poaching?

His interest quickened again and he wished he could just go down and ask. Well, he could wait for Desi. He doubted she'd refuse to tell him. It wasn't like it was a state secret.

At least the feeling of being watched had stopped. He hated that skin-crawling, hair-raising sensation. Most people could sense it and dismiss it, but after where he'd been, he was unable to ignore it. He was also unable to trust it. With time he'd begun to understand that not all his reactions were justified by what was happening in the present.

Parsing them was the tough part. Real? Not real? Twinges from the past or something going on now?

He was on his second cup of coffee, thinking about finding a grocery to buy some food for Desi's cupboards and fridge, when he heard the trucks out front rev up and pull away from the station. The confab appeared to be over.

He thought about going downstairs, then decided to wait. He didn't want to force his company on the woman. But soon enough he heard her climbing the wooden steps outside.

She entered the apartment with a smile, still wearing her red shirt and jeans, vest hanging open. Her nimbus of curly dark hair looked windblown and her cheeks were rosy. "How's it going?"

"Got my storefront," he said as she closed the door. Then a thought popped into his head. "You never did say what happened with that eagle."

"The one the kid shot with an arrow? Wonder of wonders, Mike Windwalker says the bird can be released in just a couple more days. Mrs. Eagle is going to be thrilled."

"That's great news." Best news he'd had in a while, he realized. Did that make him pathetic or not? "I made coffee and I was thinking about going to the grocery. I should replace the food I've used and add some more."

She reached the coffeepot, still wearing her jacket, and paused to pour. "No need. I think most of what you've eaten has been at the diner."

Not exactly true, but he wasn't going to argue. He felt strangely awkward, as if their heart-to-heart last night had left him uneasy somehow.

She turned, leaning back against the counter, mug in both hands. "Calvin Lake, one of my wardens, found another trophy kill. This time a bull moose."

"God! Where?"

"Close to the edge of this section. Might have been an accidental crossover from a neighboring area, but that's still illegal, as is wasting the meat."

"At this point it hardly matters if the hunter had a permit."

"Exactly. So we were talking about what we might be able to do. Five of us. Hardly an army. But I did talk to some hunters in the backwoods who promised to keep an eye out and let me know if anything made them suspicious." She sipped her coffee. "I hope you can catch these guys, Kel, because I'm pretty sure we won't be able to without more resources."

He sighed. "This is a flyer, you know. We can't trace them. The money…well, it's either all in cash or being handled out of state. No phone numbers to be traced. We've gone back five years trying to get a handle on just one person but we haven't gotten it. They're good.

Too good. We need someone with loose lips, or we need to catch someone in the act. We need evidence and we need names."

"I know," she answered. "It's just so hard to believe that an operation like this could fly under the radar."

He snorted. "Look at the Mafia. How many years did that take? It'd be easier to collect the evidence if we had one subject. But even then it could take a long time."

She nodded. "So you want to go to the market?"

"I was thinking about it. Only fair I should buy my share of the food."

She surprised him with a crooked smile. "And I don't have much around here. I don't usually buy for more than a couple of days at a time. Who knows what I might want three days from now?"

That made him laugh, but as she grabbed her keys and suggested they go together, he realized it wasn't the market he wanted, so much as he wanted to test himself. To see if he still felt watched. If he was on the edge of another slide into temporary instability. Because if he was, he needed to warn her and the guys who were coming to hunt with him, if it lasted.

Because he might not be entirely trustworthy.

The grocery wasn't exactly modern, but it was spotlessly clean and well lit. Definitely not a chain, though. It wasn't crowded, making it more comfortable for him, but occasionally they passed people, all of whom greeted Desi in a friendly fashion before moving on. No time for introductions and he was glad to leave it at that.

He threw items that appealed to him in the basket without asking if they were okay because he intended to pick up the entire tab. He suspected she might argue, but although she minimized it, he *had* been eating her food and drinking her coffee.

Then they came on a couple with a small child, maybe three.

This time he got introduced because the man wanted to chat. Turned out he was the chief of police, Jake Madison, a strong-looking man with dark hair and a friendly smile. He introduced his pretty, very pregnant blonde wife, Nora, and their towheaded son James. "So have you learned anything about the poacher?"

Desi shook her head. "I wish. I sent some tissue samples to the lab to see if the sheep was sick, but we're not going to get very far without something more. Were you able to fix your fence and keep the wolves away?"

Madison nodded. "It didn't bring down much fence. Larry and I fixed it in a few hours. I'm thinking that barbed wire probably damaged the sheepskin if the big-horn broke through itself. So maybe I had some fencing down before it came through. No way to tell. As for the wolves, once the carcass was gone and we'd deodorized the place, Larry and I took turns keeping watch. As best I can tell, the wolves disappeared back into the mountains."

"Well, that's good news at least."

"Yeah." Jake smiled, then his gaze traveled over Kel. "I've heard about you. Starting an outfitter's business?"

"That's the plan. I've got two clients coming in a couple of weeks."

"I suppose since you're with Desi you've got an outfitter's license. I couldn't find it online but I did find you have an application in."

Kel almost stiffened, but caught himself in time. "Yeah, they say it won't take much longer on the app.

As for the guys coming, the law says I can act as their guide as long as I don't charge them, so if my license isn't approved they may get lucky."

Jake nodded. "It can take some time to get things squared away on the website. I didn't mean to offend you."

"It's okay," Kel answered. "But you can call the department if you want." He knew that would be safe because all official channels would back him up.

Jake smiled. "No need. I know how Desi feels about poaching. If she finds an unlicensed outfitter, she's apt to treat him worse than a charging bear. I hope your business goes well."

Kel stopped him as he started to move on. "Do you have a lot of trouble with hunters on your property? Are you posted?"

"I'm posted all right. And four or five times a season somebody decides to ignore that. It's enough to make a man think about electrifying his fence, at least parts of it."

Kel laughed. "Unfortunately, I bet all those parts are inconveniently far away."

Jake's smile widened. "True. Which is not to say I haven't caught hunters entirely too close to the house. But Desi can tell you all those stories. Nora and I need to get going before the tot gets hungry."

Nora spoke for the first time since saying hello. "Desi? If you find time, we're having a little get-together at the ranch on Sunday afternoon. Bring your friend and an appetite."

"Thanks, Nora. I will if I can find time."

Nora laughed. "I know you won't. Maybe in the springtime."

"Nice people," Kel remarked as they moved on. "Did I just get a warning?"

"Maybe." Desi looked up at him from the corner of her eye, a smile tugging at the edge of her mouth. "See what I mean about a network?"

Kel laughed again, fighting down an urge to hug her because she looked positively cute right now. "I'll mind my p's and q's. So I've already had a background check? Pretty fast."

"I'm surprised you wanted it to hold up. Jake's a smart man, and so is our sheriff, Gage Dalton. They smell anything funny and you may have to explain yourself to more people than you want to."

Kel thought about that as he made an extravagant purchase of T-bone steaks. "You got a grill?"

"Out back if you want to stand in the cold. Propane, not charcoal."

"I can stand it. I've stood worse conditions."

He watched her expression grow thoughtful and was sorry he'd destroyed the light mood. He hadn't meant to; the truth had just popped out. "Tonight then, if you're going to be around."

"Yeah, I get tonight off unless something really big happens. It's a busy time of year so we spent the meeting figuring how to cover for each other. Trying to take into account who has kids they want to see, a doctor's appointment, whatever."

They used the cart to get the groceries to her truck. He'd gone a little overboard and she hadn't objected when he paid, probably because of the way he had splurged. No reason she should pay for his expensive tastes.

As they were driving back to the station, however, he began to consider if he'd done the right thing by hanging so tight with her. Not just because she might be in danger, but because would anybody, including the ring he was after, actually believe he was operating without an outfitter's license? The immediate assumption was that she would do exactly what the chief of police had done: check him out, friend or no friend.

He pulled out his cell phone and called home base while they drove. "We got a problem I hadn't thought of. I may need to take a few more people into my confidence, and make sure nobody gets the idea I'm licensed if they call." He listened to Farley. "Yeah, I know, but we're putting the senior warden out here in a difficult position. Police are checking up on me. I can talk my way through it, but it's not going to point the bad guys to me."

Farley was listening but still concerned. "Look," he said, "I get why you put in my app, but make it look like it's been yanked because I was bad once. Okay? And I'm going to talk to the local law about what's really going on. We've asked the senior warden to keep it under her hat. I'm sure the sheriff and police chief can, too. They all deserve to know what I'm up to."

When he hung up, he realized they'd pulled into the station parking lot, and Desi was looking at him, smiling faintly.

"What?" he asked.

"You're an honest man," she said simply.

"I try to be. I'm not cut out for undercover work, as I'm discovering. I keep making mistakes. I should never have listened when my bosses told me to hook up with you as if I'm edging my way around you. Well, your chief of police made it clear today that it's not working. He cares enough about you that he wanted to make sure I wasn't lying to you. So...I screwed that one up, and now that I have, some of those who might be worried about you need to know what's coming down the pike. Because I need to lose that application soon. The sooner the better. And what if your sheriff decides to check after it's gone? No, I need to cover your butt and mine by telling the truth."

"I hear you."

He felt himself returning her smile. "You're not a fool, Desi. But you've got friends around here who care enough about you to find out if you're being misled. That's pretty special. It's also a situation someone didn't count on. Good job, Warden."

"Me? Why?"

"Because you've got the most effective network in the world. People who give a damn." With that he slid out of the truck and took a deep breath of the fresh air. Evening was just beginning to move in. Maybe too late to cook steaks tonight. But when would he have the chance again? The way this woman worked, there wasn't a whole lot of leftover time.

Probably good, because if he hung around her too much, he'd be trying to get her into bed. The need was growing in him, a constant humming when she was around. It was getting harder to behave himself.

But he was playing a dangerous game, apparently not very well, and that concerned him even more.

Not for himself, but for her.

Chapter 7

The ponytailed man was sitting with his friend, the bearded man, the two of them sharing some beer and nuts while watching a recorded football game they'd missed on Sunday.

"The client list is getting full," the bearded man said. "Usually I don't like latecomers, but it looks like we're going to have a banner year."

"I saw. You checked everyone out?"

"Like always. You know we have to worry less about phonies now that everything is word-of-mouth. I check older clients about new clients in addition to everything else. We're safe. Except from competition."

"Yeah, competition. Another one has turned up near Yellowstone. Anyway, I've been running checks. Two haven't applied for licenses. One has an application in the system, but I heard just before close of business that it's going to be denied."

"Which one?"

"The one in Conard County. My source says the guy's hanging out with the warden there. Her old friend it seems."

"Hmm." The bearded man fell silent. "Hanging with the warden? Either he's good at lying or she's that blinded."

"If he's an old friend of hers, she might well be blinded."

"Could be. Or they could be working together."

The ponytailed man put his beer bottle down. His heart accelerated. His buddy was edging too close to the truth, and he didn't want that. It might reveal too much about his contacts. "In what way? She's willing to turn a blind eye?"

"Or maybe he's helping her."

Slowly the ponytailed man turned toward him, wondering how to redirect this. "What exactly are you saying?"

"That maybe she wants to get one of us. The bighorn Rod did last week…big mistake. On a rancher's land, for God's sake? Might as well post a sign. No way the carrion feeders could clear out a carcass that big fast enough on private property."

Ponytail man nodded. "Point taken."

"Hell, he might as well stamped it with a sign. We know the wardens are hot on poaching. They have no idea how many animals we take down because we don't leave a trail very often. Now she knows she's got a trophy hunter for sure, and she managed to find some other carcasses over the last two years. They could be random poachings, but one on the chief of police's property? Posted property? We've got too much skin hanging in the breeze.

"They can't prove anything. Not yet. But you do a background on this Kel Westin. Former army Ranger. I ask you, who is he a bigger threat to? Us or the animals?"

Ponytail man took a couple of swigs from his long-neck before replying. "Us," he said finally. "So you think she's got an old friend helping her?"

"That's my read. The license app? Cover. They're working together."

"Then I guess we need to stay away."

"Oh, don't give me that crap," bearded man said. "There's a lot of trophy animals in that area. We can't meet our demand if we pull out, not without making it obvious what's going on by having so many more game animals poached in other areas. No, we can't just shut down our operations there."

"Then what?"

"We may have to take them both out, the warden and her friend. But we'll have to wait a bit and see."

Ponytail man wasn't opposed, but he hoped his friend kept his yap shut. "Don't tell the others what you're thinking. The fewer who know, the better."

The other man nodded. "Amazing how fast someone can disappear for good out there."

As cold as it was, the baking potatoes took longer than usual on the grill behind the station, then when it came time to cook the steaks, Kel turned the heat way up to sear them. He used the finger test to determine when they were medium rare, then carried the bowl of potatoes and covered platter of steaks upstairs, hoping they wouldn't be cold by the time they reached the plate.

Over the years he'd gotten used to eating a lot of cold food, but that seemed like a rotten thing to do to a steak.

When he entered the apartment, he smelled broccoli, probably from the casserole on the counter. "Desi?"

"I'll be right out," she called from what sounded like her bedroom.

He started setting two places at the counter then froze as a thought struck him. Something wasn't adding up. He was a man used to following orders, then thinking on the fly as situations developed. He never *made* the plans.

He certainly hadn't made this one, and for the first time he wondered why the hell they had wanted him to apply for a license. The idea was to convince the bad guys that he was running an illicit operation like them. So why should it be possible for someone to check up on him and find out he was being considered for a license?

What the hell would that accomplish, except to possibly remove him from suspicion by the ring? And that wasn't the point of this operation at all.

Unless they thought they might learn something from who called to verify that he was getting a license? Same with the other guys in their various parts of the state?

It might be. Damn. He started moving again, finishing the place settings as he heard Desi emerge from her bedroom.

Something stank, but he'd spent an entire career feeling that something stank then just followed his orders and pursued his assigned objective. Usually the stink had been more imagined than real, and he seldom trusted his own instinct when it came to laying a plan anymore. Above his pay grade, as they used to say in the army.

For the first time he wondered about the plan. About the people who had made it. Having him embed with Desi had been their plan. It put her at risk. Had they just assumed she'd check on his licensing? But why, when he was supposed to tell her exactly what he was doing here?

"That smells wonderful," Desi said as she slid onto a stool. "A feast. Do you eat this way all the time?"

"Hell no," he answered. "Just once in a while. A treat."

He pushed a foil-wrapped potato onto her plate, added one of the steaks, and left it to her to get a serving of the broccoli.

The questions wouldn't lie down, though. He had to force them aside for further consideration later. Right now he needed to focus on great food and great company. On Desi. He didn't want her to guess that he was beginning to feel as if all of this would blow up in both their faces.

Because something was wrong, and he was no longer just a soldier. No, now he was supposed to be something more, which meant he needed to figure a few things out.

Quickly.

Desi thought Kel was tense as he sat beside her eating, but she didn't know whether to say anything. They ate silently for a while, she remarked on how good the steak was, then waited for more than a monosyllabic response. It didn't come.

Finally she couldn't stand it anymore. "What's going on, Kel?"

"Sorry, I'm thinking. I don't mean to be rude."

She hesitated, wondering if she should just let it go. The guy had a right to think, after all. But something was troubling her as well. "Why did you say you have an application on file? Why'd you tell them to pull it?"

She saw him stiffen a bit, then he put down his fork and turned to look at her. "I'd really like to save this discussion for after the meal. It's too good not to enjoy. Promise I'll tell you later."

"Okay. But are you even tasting your food now?"

At that one corner of his mouth lifted. "I'm concentrating on it. Sorry I'm so quiet."

"It *is* really good," she agreed. "I hardly ever let myself splurge like this."

"Well, I have an advantage. I'm getting disability checks for my knees."

"Really? They must be bad."

"Pretty torn up," he admitted. "The checks aren't that big, but enough that I can buy a steak now and then."

"Cool." She thought it was, too. The guy had apparently been injured while serving his country and deserved at least some compensation for it when the effects were lingering. "You said you have a lot of pain."

"Anybody with torn-up knees has a lot of pain. When I can't take it anymore, they'll give me new knees. I'm not in a rush."

"I wouldn't be either," she admitted. "I've heard it hurts like hell and the pain doesn't always go away."

"How could it not hurt like hell when you consider what they're doing to your leg? But that's not what's holding me back. I'd be laid up for a while, I'd need physical therapy, but they told me I only get one replacement per knee and it has to last the rest of my life. So…" He shrugged. "No rush here."

"You seem to get around pretty well."

"I do. It's harder on rough ground, and I have a barometer in my knees. You know, the joke about the old guy who claims his rheumatism says it's going to rain? Well, my knees prove it's no joke. But a lot of pain management, for me anyway, is simply accepting it. And never running out of ibuprofen."

The way he said the last sentence made her laugh quietly. "But how can you hike the mountains, then?"

"I ignore it. You get so it's more like background noise until something happens to jam it to the foreground. Everybody has pain sometimes, and a lot of people have it all the time. I'm not special."

She kind of thought he was but suspected he wouldn't appreciate hearing it. Sitting almost shoulder to shoulder with him like this made her acutely aware of him. She didn't know what smelled better, the food on her plate or him.

She had to make herself focus on her dinner rather than him, but that seemed the wisest course, all things considered. "So you're going to talk to the sheriff and the police chief about your mission?"

"I think that would be smart. Is there any reason I shouldn't? You think they're both trustworthy?"

"I'm sure of it. I'd trust either of them with my life."

"Okay then."

"Frankly, I'd be happier if they knew. You think my network is good? Theirs are far better. Between them, they probably know damn near everything about everybody in this county."

"That's useful." He snared the last bite of his steak, then turned his attention to the remains of his potato.

The steaks were large, and Desi looked at him. "If you're not fussy, I hate to waste this steak and I'm stuffed."

"I never pass up good food. Far too often my diet consisted of freeze-dried everything. Maybe it's not supposed to be possible, but I could swear the freeze-drying sucked all the flavor out."

"Lots of hikers and campers around here use that stuff."

"Then maybe they don't have taste buds."

She laughed again, delighted by the way he could find humor in odd places. "I hadn't thought about that."

"No reason you should. But I'm sure I have a good set because I can taste this dinner."

She was glad to see him tuck into her steak. Sure, she could have put it into the fridge to eat later, but it wouldn't be the same. Besides, he was evidently still hungry enough to want it.

She slid off the stood and carried her plate to the sink then hesitated before returning to her accustomed position on the couch. He'd said that he would explain to her what had happened this afternoon when he made that phone call.

And for the first time things weren't looking as simple as she'd initially thought. It struck her that she knew very little about what was supposed to be happening here except that he was hoping to be approached by the bad guys. Not much of a plan. Maybe his military experience had made him a good improviser, but counting on that didn't seem like planning.

He carried his dishes to the sink and rinsed them before bringing a fresh coffee with him to sit on the chair facing her. "Time to talk," he said.

She felt her heartbeat accelerate. "Something wrong?" she tried to ask casually.

"I don't know, but I'm not feeling good about any of this. You want to hear why? Maybe a second perspective will clear the fog."

"Sure." Tucking her legs beneath her and leaning on

the arm of the couch, she waited, all ears. Since looking at him was distracting, she stared down at her legs.

"They sent me out here to start an outfitting operation, bare-bones and cheaper than the guys we're after. On the face of it, that would get their attention if I'm cutting into their revenue stream. But I was supposed to be operating in their area, under the table, not above it. And I was supposed to let you know what I was doing here and see if we could cozy up a bit to make it look like you'd have no interest in checking me out."

She bristled a little. "Is that what they think of me?"

He spread a hand. "I don't know, Desi. Honestly, I don't know, but I don't know what's going on here either. I mean, you're a senior warden and everyone knows you rose fast. Why would they disrespect you?"

"Because maybe some of them think this was an affirmative action type of promotion."

She realized he had frozen, his hands going perfectly still. After a minute he said, "Has anyone said that to you? Hinted that?"

"Of course. It gets back to me. Some think I slept my way into this job. Every woman faces stuff like this, Kel. Surely you know."

"I've heard," he said, then rose from the chair and started pacing. "Never knew anyone who'd faced it. Maybe I can be blind."

She hesitated. "Kel? It was never a problem that I was aware of when I was just a warden. The guys were pretty good about treating me as just another colleague except for occasional locker room lapses, which I ignored. This promotion though... I'm way young. And there are guys with a lot more experience who probably thought it should be theirs. I can understand."

"You shouldn't have to understand," he said, pivoting to face her, his eyes at once hard and fiery. "You shouldn't have to make any excuses. All *I* heard about you was that you were exceptional and that the guys who work with you really like you."

She shrugged. "Well, I don't work with all the wardens. I don't even know a lot of them very well. Sure we meet, work together sometimes, but it's pure work. Some I might not even recognize on the street out of uniform."

She paused. "You know, this job is often very solitary. You remember that famous Texas Ranger saying? *One riot, one Ranger.* I'm not going to claim we're anything like those guys, but most of our work is just as solitary. Endless hours of patrolling, sniffing around for anything that doesn't look right. Given how solitary we are most of the time, it's not surprising that some might have an unflattering opinion of me. I meet with my fellow wardens here, we have summer barbecues, families included, we work together when necessary, and we bond. I can't say that about most of the rest of the wardens, at least with regard to me."

He still looked angry. "So you just brush that talk off?"

"What else am I going to do? My part of the world seems to be okay. They can have the rest."

He swore, paced the room a bit more then finally dropped onto his chair again, clasping his hands. "I realize I'm trying to swim upstream here, but I am so damn offended by that I'm practically spluttering."

She smiled, touched by his reaction. "Thanks, Kel, but let it go."

"I can't. I worked with some of the first female Rangers. I was glad to have them on my six. They were as good as the best. I don't get the problem, and I don't get why you should have to put up with this."

"I'm not putting up with much," she reminded him. "The guys I work with are all fine."

He continued to scowl for a while longer, ceding the discussion to her, but when she took another peek at him, she noticed his expression was changing. "Kel? Something wrong?"

"Something's very wrong and I wanted to talk to you about it since you're now in it up to your neck. To begin with, I'm just a soldier. I don't make the plans. I carry them out. So maybe I didn't think hard enough about this."

"How so?" He was beginning to make her uneasy, very uneasy. Something was wrong with the plan? She had her own job to worry about and plenty to keep her busy, so she hadn't thought about his end of all this. Something was bugging him? That didn't make her feel very comfortable.

"It doesn't add up. They wanted me to look like I was running an illicit operation yet they put in a license application for me. They said it was because if anyone called to check up on me they'd be able to record whoever called. But does that make sense, Desi? Does it really? I assumed they knew what they were doing, and now that feels like a mistake."

Her heart quickened and she unfolded her legs so she could lean forward. "What are you saying?"

"I don't know what I'm saying. I'm thinking out loud. Something isn't adding up. I want to figure out what's wrong. So start with the insanity of me having an outfitter's license app on file. Why? Does that make it look like I'm doing something illegal?"

"Not really," she admitted. "In fact, I never expected to hear Jake say he'd checked on you and you say you had an application in. If I expected to hear anything it was that you needed to get going on an application."

"Exactly. Then the part about cozying up to you ostensibly so you wouldn't check on me. Cripes, Desi, I walked in your door and told you exactly what I was doing. Did I really need to do any more than that? Why would anyone think that getting close to you would make me look like trouble to the ring we're after? All it does is put you closer to the problem. Was that necessary?"

"No." She could see why he was troubled, and now she was troubled, too. She hadn't given much thought to any of this except that she hoped the plan worked because at least some of the poaching would be stopped. For a while anyway.

"If I spend much time hanging with you, no poacher is going to try to have a talk with me or warn me off either. We're too close. And that's what they wanted at HQ. Us close."

Desi felt cold ripple through her and goose bumps rise on her skin. It was an internal ice in a warm room. She hadn't experienced that often, but she knew what it meant. She sensed something terrible on the way that would change her forever.

"Us close," she repeated. "But Kel...whose neck is in this noose? Yours? Mine? Ours? And if it's me or both of us, what the hell is really going on?"

"I'm beginning to wonder," he answered grimly. "I agreed to be staked out like a goat, but I didn't agree to anyone else being staked out with me. Now you might be. That's plain wrong."

"But there's no reason..." She shook her head trying

to clear it, feeling her insides clench with emotions she couldn't even parse. "Why would anyone want me involved like that? Because I've been raising the roof over all the poaching out this way? Because I've been requesting more wardens to deal with it? That's not a reason to want to hurt anyone is it?"

"God knows. I guess it depends on which bar got rattled. But it still doesn't add up. Why make it look like I'm legit at all? Like I could get away with anything if we're hanging together?"

A thought so disturbing occurred to her that she had to squeeze it out. "What if I'm a suspect in the poaching?"

He practically gaped at her. "Oh, come off it, Desi. You've got a stellar rep with the department, and if you were poaching why would you be raising the roof about it?"

She raised her gaze to meet his. "Then maybe I'm in someone's way."

That did it, Kel thought. When he'd arrived in this place, he'd met a calm, pleasant woman who was very much in control of herself and her job. She felt seamless, as if she'd gotten it all together and liked it just the way it was.

But now... Her face was pinched and she seemed to have shrunk just a little. The thoughts running through her head were clearly unpleasant. He wondered how many relationships she was rifling through trying to figure out who might want to harm her in some way.

Pointless exercise. But something pulled at him until he stood up and crossed the room. Sitting beside her on the couch, he wrapped his arm around her shoulders casually. "I'm just speculating, Desi," he reminded her.

"Asking questions I probably should have asked before I came out here."

But she gave a quick, negative shake of her head. "No. You're absolutely correct that something's wrong. I've had my head in my day-to-day work, and I really haven't thought much about what you're doing and how it all would work. How pieces might fit. It was your job, not mine. I was just glad the trophy hunting was getting the attention it deserves."

He was relieved when she softened a bit, leaning into his side, but he could tell she was still asking the hard questions. "You know," she said, "maybe I really have been a pain in the butt to someone. Someone important enough to want me out of the way. Not necessarily dead, but maybe diverted. Maybe that's why you were supposed to get close to me, so I'd be distracted by you, or leave it all up to you. But who and why?"

"That would have to be someone who's profiting from the ring."

"I know." Her voice was quiet. "It also means someone important enough to get their fingers into your assignment."

Everything inside him stilled, the way it did in the moments before a fight, when every sense was on high alert but the mind quieted, open to every impression. "I knew these guys were making loads of money, but I never thought of them as having pull like that."

"Then maybe it's time we started to." Turning her head, she rested it in the hollow of his shoulder. He could feel her warm breath on his neck, an enticement almost impossible to resist as electricity began to dance its way to his groin.

Ah, hell, he thought. This was something neither of

them wanted. He was going to be dead or out of here fairly soon. She'd been raped and he suspected she hadn't been with a man since. This could only muddy their thinking, muddy everything. More important, he didn't want to leave her with any more wounds.

But she felt so good pressed to his side, and her cheek resting in the hollow of his shoulder...well, that felt like trust. Real trust. He wasn't sure he deserved it considering the trouble he might have brought to her door.

Holding her like this, a gesture meant to show caring, was making it hard for him to think straight. Well, to think about anything but her, that was.

But he knew he needed to. Since the moment the police chief, Jake Madison, had mentioned that he'd checked up on Kel, the entire picture had changed. As if looking through broken glass, for the first time he noticed that these pieces really weren't fitting.

How to put them together? He knew what his assigned task was: to draw the illicit outfitters out somehow. At least one of them. He should get a threat, an offer, some contact that would give him a person and maybe even a real name. A wedge. They certainly needed one, and every other way they'd tried to track this group down had failed.

They were like ghosts, invisible except for the chill of their passing. The signs, the trophy kills, the large campsites that left nothing useful behind. But none of those trophies had ever found in state. That meant they were going to other places, and it was like a hole in a picture that said something was wrong.

He was equally sure they hadn't found most of the carnage or even the locations of where these hunting parties had gone. Those mountains up there and around the state could hide a lot of things easily and quickly.

They'd gotten whispers, hints, that something illegal was happening on a larger scale than usual. Desi had certainly raised a lot of attention about the increased trophy hunting over the last few years. And had the hunting been legitimate, they wouldn't have left the meat behind. That big no-no had given them away as much as anything.

He closed his eyes, still thinking, and felt Desi lean into him even more. He tightened his arm around her instinctively. "Desi?"

"Hmm?"

"You know it's wasting the meat that's giving them away."

"I thought so. They want something much smaller coming out with them, something they could hide. Hiding an entire large game animal...well that's whole lot harder. We do spot checks all the time to make sure the harvested animal was taken with a permit. But something you could hide in a big box or under a tarp with machinery? Like a head? Yeah, that's why they don't take the meat."

"That's what I was thinking."

"And that gets us nowhere," she sighed. "Kel, I've been over this again and again for the last couple of years. Every time I stumble on one of these. Well, stumbling is the right word. There's so much wilderness out there, so many places we can't really keep an eye on. We have to look for things we can't see."

"I was just thinking that. Looking for holes."

"Exactly. It's almost as if we have to see what's not there. I thought it would be so great if they approached you. Then we'd have an idea where to start…as long as their approach wasn't to kill you."

He felt her shudder a little. He was touched that it bothered her that much. "I knew what to expect when I agreed to do this. But I don't know the relationships among the players."

"Which players?"

"Let's start with Game and Fish. I've only been at this for a couple of years. I don't know what the network is, who owes whom what, if you know what I mean. Could someone up the chain in Game and Fish be in someone's pocket? I never even thought about it until your police chief mentioned that he'd checked me out and found out I'd applied for a license. At first I thought of it as good cover with the local authorities, then it jarred me seriously. That's why I called and told them to yank the app."

He turned a little and felt her breast press against him. Uh-oh. But despite the sizzle that ran through him, he didn't want to make her aware of the contact. Didn't want to make her uncomfortable by pulling back. He drew a steadying breath and tried to continue his thoughts.

"That made me wonder, too," she said. Did she sound a little breathless? He wasn't sure, but he was headed that way himself. "You applying for a license could be a big *stay away* flag to the illegal outfitters. But why?"

"My question exactly."

She sighed again and moved a little closer. He thought it was unconscious on her part, but he stiffened a bit as he resisted the urge to respond in a sexual way. His whole body was coming alive to her.

"Am I making you uncomfortable?" she asked quietly.

"I wouldn't say uncomfortable."

"Then what?"

He felt her head move and he twisted so he could look down at his shoulder. She stared up at him with a steady questioning gaze. In an instant, he was undone.

"Hot as hell," he said bluntly. As soon as the words slipped past his lips, he waited for her retreat. He was no expert on the kind of suffering she'd endured, but he knew something about post-traumatic stress and he was certain she would fly away. He felt her tense, but she didn't move.

"Me, too," she whispered. "But I'm afraid."

This was so very dangerous, he thought. Dangerous because of what had happened to her. Dangerous because he might cause more wounds without intending to. But she needed something right now, and it wasn't rejection.

He raised his hand, running his fingers through her dark nimbus of curls. "I like your hair."

"It's convenient."

"Also cute. Desi, there's no need to jump into anything. I understand your fears. You *do* make me hot. I feel like a volcano ready to erupt right now. But I think we should take this slowly."

She bit her lip, looking disappointed and almost relieved at the same time. Ah, hell, maybe she was feeling rejected. Not knowing how else to clear that particular notion, he twisted some more and found her mouth with his.

Nothing demanding, just a light brush of lips over and over, designed to help her relax if she could. Designed to nurture the fire just a bit but not douse it or turn it into a conflagration. Although he wasn't far from one himself. But he judged she needed gentleness as much as anything. Care, patience, wooing. She had to be ready and he somehow didn't think she really was. What she was feeling might be an awakening, or it might vanish to be buried again.

She laid her hand on his chest and gripped the dark flannel of his shirt. The sensation caused a shower of sparks behind his eyes. Ah, sweet, sweet woman. His groin, which had been aching, began to throb. Danger. He was too close to following his natural urges.

Slowly he lifted his head, brushing a last kiss on her lips. "So sweet," he whispered.

Her eyelids fluttered. "I didn't know," she murmured, her voice breathy.

"Didn't know what?"

"That a kiss could be so nice."

At once he found his self-control. It snapped into place like the jaws of a crocodile. She didn't know a kiss could be so nice? Her words speared him until his chest ached for her. My God, what had this woman been through? Had her rapist been her first and only?

Forget his attraction to her, he had a strong urge to rend something, smash something, hunt down the SOB...

"Did I do it right?"

He closed his eyes, battling fury, battling pain for her. "You did it right," he said. "Very right." That she should have to wonder about the smallest touching of lips? That guy must have assaulted her in ways that weren't physical. She might say he wasn't able to walk for a week, but that wouldn't remove the experience or stinging words. Only fresh experience would, and she apparently hadn't allowed herself any.

Opening his eyes, hanging on to his temper, he gave her another soft kiss. "I want to do it again. But like I said, let's take it slow."

"Because of me?"

Double damn. Was he messing this up? "Because I want it to be perfect and right for both of us. Okay?"

She nodded, then let her head fall against his shoulder. Relieved, he snuggled her in, astonished that this self-assured woman had exposed so much vulnerability to him. Vulnerability he had never imagined could be part of a woman who presented such a confident face to the world.

He felt a little shiver run through her, then she softened completely. Staring at nothing, he held her and wondered what he was walking into. What he might be dragging her into. Because something was rotten, and it was easier to think about that than to think about the ache in his groin and how much he wanted Desi.

Chapter 8

Desi spent a restless night. She kept waking, remembering their kiss and feeling scalded with embarrassment that she had asked him if she had done it right. What was the matter with her? The only good thing about it was that she already had Kel pegged as a trustworthy man who wouldn't use her vulnerability and uncertainty against her.

But that didn't leave her any less embarrassed by that damn question.

Worse, she didn't like being weak, and she'd been weak enough last night to ask that awkward, revealing question. Weakness was something she'd determinedly expunged after Joe, swearing she would never again let anyone use her that way. Well, that had blown up last night. She supposed she ought to be grateful that Kel didn't seem inclined to push, and she didn't much care whether it was because he was a gentleman or because he didn't want her. She had to raise her barriers again, fast.

Then there was the other stuff. When her cheeks stopped burning, she couldn't help but feel a burst of adrenaline and anxiety about what was going on here. She'd never dealt with anything like this before. She knew her job, knew her rules and the law, and never before had she wondered about the possibility of politics and lies creeping into the department. The wardens she knew and had actually worked with didn't strike her as the sorts who would get involved in anything illicit. A bunch of good, honest people. Like Kel.

But the questions he had raised...she stared into the darkness and wondered. He was definitely right: something was very, very wrong.

But what?

He'd been frank from the outset that they wanted him to cozy up with her. That bothered her more now than ever. Did someone suspect *her* of breaking the law? Had they never imagined that Kel would be so forthright in his approach? Or was someone afraid of her and trying to shut her down? Or shut them both down?

It sure wouldn't stop the poaching if both of them were hamstrung in some way and didn't even know it. Maybe her whole involvement was to make sure that no one poached here for a while. Not this group, anyway.

Ah, it wasn't making any sense. She was glad when her digital clock sounded its alarm at three o'clock. A quick breakfast and she'd hit the road to be on patrol before dawn. The time she was likeliest to catch someone stretching the rules.

She dressed swiftly in her red flannel shirt, jeans and hiking boots. Just as she started the coffeepot, Kel emerged from the bunkhouse. He didn't look as if he had slept well either.

"Morning," he said.

"Morning," she replied, smothering a yawn. "Sleep well?"

"Not likely. You?"

"Me neither."

They shared a look of understanding that somehow eased her embarrassment. Although she doubted he'd spent any time thinking about that tentative kiss, and certainly not as much time as she had.

On impulse she asked, "Want to ride shotgun today?"

"Sure. I'm not getting much done around town yet."

"When do your hunters arrive? A couple of weeks you said?"

"That's the plan, although at this point I wouldn't be surprised if that changed. Nothing's going according to what I *thought* was the plan."

"No kidding."

He came around the counter. "Move over and make toast. I'll do the eggs."

Oddly, she didn't mind being nudged aside in her own kitchen. What she *did* notice, however, was just how small it was. Finally she moved the toaster and sat on the far side of the counter, making a stack of buttered toast.

Not that she minded bumping into him. At this point she was feeling crazy enough to want to keep bumping into him.

But business first. Part of her was surprised she'd offered to let him ride shotgun, and part of her was surprised he'd agreed. She guessed they had more talking to do, although without information it was all probably pointless.

A kind of sour mirth filled her as she buttered yet another piece of toast. Should she be making an enemies list? In all her years with the department, she'd never even remotely felt the need for that. Sure, some guys resented her, but she suspected they weren't a majority, and even if they were, so what?

No, if someone were trying to mess her up in some way, it had to do with the poaching. Heaven knew she'd been making enough noise about it. Her area had an awful lot of poaching, more than most. It was bad for the game animals. Maybe it was bad for her, too. Maybe they were wondering what the hell was going on out here. Maybe Kel was watching *her*.

She stiffened, her hands stilling, toast and butter forgotten.

"Desi? Something wrong?"

"No. No." Quickly she spread butter on the last piece of toast as Kel reached for two plates and placed fried eggs on them. She loved dipping toast in egg yolk but she suspected she wasn't going to taste a thing this morning.

Once he'd filled the mugs, he slid onto the stool beside her and began eating.

She bit into a slice of toast, absently dipped in yolk, and wondered if she should just come out and ask him. But he wouldn't tell her if it were true, and if he were as good a liar as he'd had to have been to get this far with her, then how would she know if he was telling her the truth? Cripes, hadn't she just decided he was a truthful man? What was going on inside her head?

Maybe she was just feeling paranoid, not a usual state of mind for her, not since the year after her rape, but if she was, she certainly didn't want to advertise it.

Of course, all the questions he'd raised last night about

what was going on had definitely created a paranoid atmosphere. Now she was wondering about everything. Great.

She stared down at her plate until Kel said, "What's wrong? Didn't I make the eggs right?"

"They're fine," she answered, her mouth feeling dry. She quickly sipped coffee. "Just thinking."

"There's a lot to think about," he agreed and resumed eating.

Oh, yeah, she thought, cutting up egg and wiping the whites around her plate to coat them with yolk. Using another piece of toast, she began mopping it all, shoving bits with her fork onto the bread.

Well, if he'd been sent to watch her, he wasn't exactly doing a great job of it. How many days had he spent wandering around town, finally renting a storefront, and leaving her to do her job unhindered? If he were watching her, wouldn't he want to spend more time doing it while she was on the job?

He could have come up with a lot of reasonable excuses, like getting the lay of the land, learning the roads… But he hadn't. He'd said he did that last summer.

So maybe it *was* paranoia. And maybe not surprising on her part. She maintained enough self-awareness to know how little she trusted men, and last night had busted right through one of her strongest barriers. Nobody had touched her since Joe. Not sexually. But last night she'd let it happen. So maybe she was throwing up a fresh set of barriers, among them suspecting Kel of lies when as far as she could tell he hadn't lied once to her.

Because she hated lies. Loathed them. Her contact with Kel last night had shaken a lot of things loose, things that frightened her.

"Kel," she said quietly.

"Yeah?"

"I think I got triggered last night." Hard to say, but clearly true. If nothing else it might cover for any odd behavior on her part today.

He didn't answer immediately. "I'm sorry," he said. "Won't do that again."

Astonishingly, that hurt. She'd practically asked for it, but it hurt when she got what she wanted. Man, she was turning into a mess, and she didn't like it. Whether he wanted to or not, Kel was throwing her off-balance.

She took over the chore of washing the dishes just to have something to do. Kel apparently sensed he wasn't wanted because he disappeared into the bunkhouse for about twenty minutes, then returned ready for the outdoors.

She quickly pulled on her own insulated vest, her heavier jacket and made sure her gloves were in her pocket. Ready for the day, physically if not emotionally.

Everything she needed was in her truck, but Kel paused to get his pistol as well as an orange vest and cap out of his. Safety first.

Then they were speeding toward the mountains, a starry sky overhead, a heavy moon sagging into the jagged peaks.

"Hunter's moon next week," he remarked. "I like that name even though it doesn't mean a thing anymore. I wonder where it came from?"

"Native Americans," she answered. Here she was on firm ground. "It was a traditional time to hunt deer that had fattened over the summer, or smaller prey that only came out at night, like foxes or coyotes. The last big hunt before winter."

"Thanks for explaining. I'd always wondered but never thought to look it up," he remarked. "And I bet some people still try to use it that way."

"Count on it. If it's bright enough, they won't need to reveal themselves with artificial lights."

"So how do you handle it?"

She gave a short laugh. "Patrol. Listen for gunshots. Hope for a tip from somewhere."

He fell silent, leaving her chained in the misery of her own thoughts while they finally bumped off pavement and started up the access roads into the mountains.

A couple of miles passed before he spoke again. "Do you get a lot of tips?"

"Sure. People who've entered the drawings every year and never gotten a big game permit can become awfully talkative when someone they know took game without one. Or when they hear about it. No one likes people who wantonly kill the game, or wantonly waste the meat. What's been bugging me is that I haven't gotten a single ping on these trophy hunters. Not one."

"Which means they're not local?"

"That would be my guess."

She heard him drum his fingers. Right now the trees crowded in, making it feel like they were driving through a dark tunnel, blocking out the sky and moon.

"You've been asking for help," he said.

She was sure he knew the answer but she gave it anyway. "You bet. I probably annoyed the hell out of a few people."

"Is it unusual not to get it?"

Suddenly she understood where he was coming from. "Maybe," she said cautiously. "Usually a few wardens can be freed up to come help, but while the poachings have been on the increase, the numbers were hardly big enough to cause a major flap. Besides, it's not like it isn't happening elsewhere, too."

"How much would a few more wardens have helped?"

"Truthfully? In a case like this I don't know. More ears to the wind, more boots on the ground. This is a large area we're patrolling here. Ordinarily I'd say five wardens were enough to be a deterrent and to take care of the cases we actually could track down. But this has been so…" She shrugged a shoulder and steered them around a bumpy curve. "I don't know," she said finally. "It's been egregious but it hardly amounts to an epidemic. Whoever these guys are, they're apparently careful not to take so much that wardens are crawling all over these mountains."

"Or any other public grounds either," he noted. "Same kind of thing around the state. Hence, you get me. With a half-baked plan, I'm beginning to think. Yeah, we need a wedge, a way to get a look at this ring. Just one person, one phone number, one talkative trophy hunter. Just one. It's kind of amazing, though. We have a pact with thirty states to report this kind of business, and not one whisper from out there about trophies inexplicably showing up. They must have a taxidermist in their pocket. Out of state."

"So maybe we'll never get them until I fall face first into their camp stove."

That drew a laugh from him, and the tension began to leave Desi. No need to be paranoid. Nothing about Kel seemed evasive. Last night…well, best to leave that alone. Especially if all it was going to do was make her paranoid.

Around a bend and there was a truck parked alongside

the road. Desi immediately pulled up behind it, glanced at the time, then put her truck in Park and set the emergency brake. Then she turned on her rear and front flashers, leaving the roof rack dark. The truck chimed repeatedly as she climbed out, leaving the keys in the ignition. She was glad that Kel stayed put. This was *her* job.

She could see the backs of two heads as she approached. They swiveled around, then as her boots crunched on gravel, she heard the driver's window slide down.

"How's it going?" she asked as she approached.

"Waiting," came the answer. An elbow lifted, perching on the door frame. She stepped closer and saw a face that she thought she recognized. "Bill Grayling?"

He smiled. "I wish I could say I'm glad you remember me. Howdy, Warden. This here's my son, Tom. Warden Jenks, Tom."

The younger man nodded.

"So you got your privileges back, Mr. Grayling?"

"I sure did." He reached into the front pocket of his hunting vest and pulled out papers. "See for yourself."

She pulled a penlight out of her pocket and scanned the papers. They appeared to be in order. "Good job, Mr. Grayling," she said as she handed them back. "Tom, are you going to hunt, too?"

"Give her your papers, boy," Bill said gruffly. "You don't want trouble like I got."

Desi smiled. "All about the rules now, are we?"

"Believe it," Bill said as he passed his son's papers to her. "Weren't no fun losing my gun and having to stay home when I shoulda been hunting for my family. 'Twasn't a fun winter. My wife weren't happy with me, I can tell you. Lean pickin's."

"I'm sorry. But I see you're waiting."

"Damn straight," Bill said. He took his son's papers back from her and turned them over to Tom. "Clock says twenty-five minutes. That right?"

Desi looked at her watch. "Exactly. You seen good game out here?"

"Lotsa deer. It'd be nice if we could both bag one, huh, Tommy? Lots of hungry mouths at home now with the grandkids."

Tommy smiled. "There sure are."

"Good luck to you both. Say, Bill, you seen anything around while you were scouting, anything that didn't look right to you somehow?"

Bill started to shake his head. "Not really. Lots of people have been scouting since late summer. Plenty not from around here, but that's not unusual. Folks want to know where the hunting is good."

"True. Well, thanks, Bill." Desi started to turn away.

"You know," Bill said slowly, "there was a guy…"

Desi faced him again. "Yes?"

"He was on horseback, headed into the back country."

"Did you talk to him?"

"Just a bit. I remarked how hard it would be to get any big game out of the back of beyond, and he said he had pack horses he'd bring. And maybe some friends."

"But that struck you as odd. Why?"

"Because I was at the drawing for the big game permits. Always wanted to get me a moose tag. Anyway, this guy mentioned looking for bighorn, and you know what? I'm pretty certain I didn't see him at the drawing. And they wasn't no leftover permits afterward."

Desi felt something prickle along her back. "You sure?"

Bill looked at Tom. Tom hesitated, then said, "Maybe we're wrong, but I don't remember him at the drawing neither."

"Did you get a good look at him?"

Bill shrugged. "Can't tell you how tall. He was on a horse. Seemed in a hurry, too. Just asked me if any bighorn were moving down yet. Well, yeah, they're coming lower now, but at the time, not so much. Course, they weren't in season yet."

"See any dogs?"

That arrested Bill. "Yeah," he said. "Didn't like it. I mean, what kind of scouting can you do with a pack of dogs? Any game that wasn't sick would run far and fast."

Desi pulled out her pad and pen. "Tell me everything you can, Bill. About the man, the horse, the dogs, who was with him."

Bill's eyes widened a shade. "Poacher?"

"I don't know, Bill, but I'd sure like to talk to the guy." She wrote down the vague description Bill and Tom provided her and thanked them.

"I'll tell you," Bill said. "I see 'em again I'll call you. Maybe take more notice. Since I paid for my crime, seems like everyone else should, too."

The way he said it made her laugh. She wished them luck again and headed back to her truck.

Desi climbed in, turned off the flashers and eased around the pickup. As soon as they were back on empty road, Kel spoke. "That looked like an interesting conversation."

"It was. Bill and I go back aways. I always had a feeling he might be skirting the law, but never found any proof until two years ago. I caught him hunting after sunset. A good hour outside regulation time. So he lost his gun and his license for a while. Anyway, he's legal again."

"I gathered that or you wouldn't have left him there."

She supposed she was explaining too much. She sometimes had a tendency to do that. "Sorry. I asked him if he'd seen anything that bugged him. He remembered a guy on horseback with a pack of dogs, which he thought was ridiculous if you're looking for big game. Anyway, the guy asked him about the bighorn and whether they'd started to come to a lower elevation. The thing that bothered Bill most, however, was that he was sure the guy wasn't at the drawing for the big game permits. And his son agreed."

"So they're out here," Kel remarked. "Description?"

"Not much. They couldn't guess height because he was on a horse. Head covered by a cowboy hat that shadowed his face. So it's a vague description. They seem to think he had dark hair, along with six billion other people."

"A pack of dogs, though. I wonder if we should check with vets in the area?"

"There's only one here, but he could check others, I suppose." She didn't hold high hopes though. Lots of people with the room had multiple dogs, and some dogs *were* used for hunting within very strict limits.

For example, if dogs hounded that bighorn down the mountain until it died at the Madison place, that was strictly illegal. Dogs could be used to chase wildcats, but little else. But why use the dogs to bring the animal down so close to civilization? Unless it had been wounded and had taken off, so the dogs were used to keep it from running into impassable country. Or maybe the dogs had just gotten out of hand.

She chewed her lip thinking about it. A pack of dogs. Given that it was illegal to let dogs harass, chase or harm most game, what use would a pack of them be except for something illegal, because if you had that many of them, how likely was it you could prevent them from going after something they shouldn't? Bill was right, but more than he knew.

"Given the law," Kel remarked, "it doesn't make sense unless he was after mountain lions. But he asked about bighorn."

"Believe me, I'm adding two and two."

Up and down narrow back roads for the next several hours, finding campsites set up in a few places. Twice they stopped to check deer being loaded into trucks, but nothing was amiss. Being a weekday, it also wasn't very busy. Come the weekend…

But the relative peace of the morning was shattered just before noon by a radio call from Jos. His voice crackled over the air. "We've got a hunter down." He gave coordinates, Desi responded and turned her truck around, heading out to help. She didn't spare the gas.

"Will we have to carry him out?" Kel asked.

"Probably."

"I'll help."

It was a good thing they both had their seat belts on. The road was bumpy and they'd probably both have gotten concussions if they'd been free of restraint. Desi slowed only when she knew the bumps might be bad enough to damage an axle, and then only when she couldn't find a way around.

"When he said hunter down," Kel asked, "did that tell you anything?"

"Gunshot. Otherwise it would have been *hunter injured*."

"That explains a lot," he remarked as they jolted again.

She guessed he was referring to the way she was pushing the envelope with her driving. If she hadn't been so familiar with these roads, she wouldn't be doing this, but she didn't bother to tell him. She needed all her attention for driving.

She used her siren to get past two pickups carrying game, gave one wish that she could check it out, and kept going. Someone's life was in the balance. That mattered more than anything.

At last she got as close to the coordinates Jos had given as she could. No other official vehicles had arrived yet, but she wasn't surprised. She had been closest. She pulled up behind Jos's truck and scrambled out. From the back she pulled her folding stretcher and a first aid kit. Kel took the stretcher from her.

Then they hurried into the woods. Desi keyed her radio. "We're in the woods approaching you, Jos."

"Good. I'm gonna need some help with the other guy, too. He's half-crazed."

"He did it?"

"No, and that's not calming him down any. But wait till you get here."

They trotted through the woods, avoiding obstacles. It shouldn't be too far, Desi thought. Maybe a mile from where Jos was parked. Had the wounded man's companion somehow managed to make a cell connection from the woods? It was getting easier to do that, but it still wasn't exactly reliable.

So the guy's hunting buddy hadn't shot him. The information sharpened Desi's senses, and she saw that

Kel was scanning the woods as they hurried. He hadn't missed it either. He was also limping a bit and ignoring it.

Someone else was out here. Probably an incautious hunter now on the run. Probably nothing deliberate. Probably.

The light coming through the evergreens was greenish, but every so often they broke into a patch of deciduous trees that had shed their autumn leaves and into bright sunshine. The contrast could be almost blinding, but there wasn't enough of it to cause Desi to pull out her sunglasses.

The radio burst with static. "I hear you," Jos said. "Two of you?"

"Yeah, Kel is with me."

"Good," said Jos.

He'd asked and she wondered why, then understood. He was worried about who else might be out here. A shooter. Maybe it hadn't been accidental, but she doubted Jos could know that.

Then they burst into another clearing where bright light shown through the skeletal fingers of the trees. Jos was kneeling beside the wounded hunter, both of their orange vests nearly glowing, except where the one was bloodstained. Another man huddled at the edge of the clearing, looking terrified. "Why?" he kept saying. "Why?"

Good question, Desi thought. There wasn't enough cover in this clearing for anyone to mistake the fallen man for an animal.

She dropped to her knees beside Jos. The wounded man's eyes were open. He looked a bit dazed, but he was breathing.

Kel dropped the stretcher beside them, then went over to the huddled man and squatted down.

"It'll be okay, buddy. We're here. Wanna tell me what happened?"

"I don't know," the man groaned. "Never saw anyone. Just standing here looking at the GPS cuz Don had seen some moose near here."

"That's Don over there?"

"Yeah, is he gonna die?"

"No," Jos answered firmly. "We're going to get him out of here." He looked at Desi. "Bad wound in the shoulder. We gotta get him to the road."

She nodded and turned to open the stretcher. "You called for help?"

"I tried but couldn't raise anyone but you, and the guy was bleeding so badly..."

"You come help us carry your buddy out," Kel said to the other man. He took him by his arm and helped him to his feet. "You can do that, right?"

"Yeah." He didn't sound very convincing but at least he was willing to try. Then he said something that explained a whole lot to Desi.

"Jeez, man, just like Iraq. Sniper bullets coming out of nowhere!"

"I know what you mean," Kel said. "But this isn't Iraq, is it? Look at all the trees. Never saw anything like that, did you?"

"No...no..."

"And what's the first thing we need to do?"

"Get Don out of the line of fire."

"Then let's go do it."

Line of fire? Desi's scalp prickled and she looked around quickly. Sniper? Maybe something more than a gunshot out of nowhere had set this guy off. But now was not the time.

The three of them managed to get Don on the stretcher. Jos and Kel took the head end while she and the friend took the foot. She used her free hand to try to call for air evac. For a while, all she got was static, but then she connected. She described the situation tersely and recited the coordinates as they hurried through the woods as fast as they could. "We'll meet you on Hessler Road."

"You guys got here just in time," Jos remarked. "I was so busy staunching the bleeding that I gave up trying to get through. Maybe they could have put a Stokes basket down there."

"Too tight," Desi said. "You were right. Bleeding first or the rescue would be pointless. Anyway, the road'll be better."

"Yeah." Jos shook his head. "At least I didn't lose *my* head. I don't get it. The guy was putting pressure on the wound, but as soon as I arrived he just freaked…"

Desi quickly glanced at the other man, across from her at the foot end of the stretcher. He didn't even seem to pick up on that, but a quick glance back told her that Kel had and he wasn't pleased.

But Jos was young and this wasn't the time to educate him. Later maybe.

One thing for certain, the mile back to the road seemed to take longer this time. They paused once to switch sides of the stretcher, and she was glad to see Don's friend was calming down.

"What's your name?" she asked as they resumed the hike.

"Thor Edvaldson, and I hate the jokes."

"I would, too," she answered pleasantly. "So you didn't see anything at all?"

"Not until Don was hit. The woods seemed quiet, almost empty, which was frustrating Don because he blamed it on the dogs."

"Dogs?" Her ears pricked.

"Yeah. Maybe a half hour before the shot we passed four guys on horseback. Don took exception to their dogs and told them to leash them. I guess I don't have to tell you why. Anyway, they laughed and just kept going."

"Don didn't try to follow them, did he?"

"Naw. He was ticked though. Figured they'd ruined our hunting for the day. So maybe they were as careless as they were stupid. I don't like people who break the rules."

"Neither do I." Now the skin on the back of her neck felt like it was crawling. "Did the men say anything else?"

"I don't..." Thor paused. "Well, Don told 'em to get the dogs out of here or it was going to waste his moose permit. That seemed to interest them, but they just kept moving."

"Interest them how?"

"Not sure. Like they might be looking for moose, too? But who the hell takes a bunch of dogs on a moose hunt? Guarantees you won't see a single animal."

Unless, Desi thought, you wanted to drive them, herd them, cluster some up and pick the best. She saw what dogs could do on the ranches around here. She couldn't imagine any reason why hunting dogs couldn't be used the same way...which was why it was forbidden.

When they reached the road, Jos radioed to find out how long before the helo arrived. "Five minutes," came the clipped response.

"Jos?" Desi asked. "Was the wound through and through?"

Jos nodded.

She looked at Thor again. "Mr. Edvaldson, what did you do when Don was shot?"

"Hit the ground."

"Training," remarked Kel. "He was probably flat before Don finished falling."

Desi nodded. "So…given the way Don was hit, any idea what direction the bullet must have come from?"

Thor lowered his head, thinking. "Upslope to the north of us. Northwest, I'd guess. When it came through his shoulder it just missed me. He was pointing that way, to where he'd seen some moose a couple weeks ago. Seems like there were some elk, too. Anyway, I was standing mostly behind him, just a bit to the side so I could see where he was pointing. He'd bent some twigs to mark his path last time. GPS isn't always reliable up in these mountains." Then he fell silent.

Kel clapped his arm. "You gonna be okay, man?"

"Always okay sooner or later." He stiffened as the sound of rotors became audible.

Kel spoke again, clearly demanding his attention, probably for good reason, Desi thought. "Want to wait and go back with us, or take the flight?"

"I ain't sick."

"I know, but we could be here for a while."

Yes they could, Desi thought, turning back to look at the woods. Metal detectors and a search for a needle in a haystack. With some police assistance.

"Jos, call the sheriff. We have a crime scene."

The helicopter hovered overhead and the side door opened. A refurbished Huey, it was a workhorse. Pretty soon a metal arm stuck out the side, and a helmeted medic began lowering a basket for Don.

"We can put you in a harness," Kel said to Edvaldson. "Don might be grateful not to be alone."

So that's what happened. Don went up in the basket, and a few minutes later Thor followed him in a harness. He left his hunting rifle beside the road. In the background Jos's radio crackled, almost inaudible with the rotor noise. Jos must have turned the volume all the way up.

"I hope you don't mind," Kel said to Desi. "But he needed to get out of here."

"I could tell. For a while he wasn't here at all."

"Being shot at can do that."

"Good job drawing him back," she said sincerely.

He half smiled. "I think you did most of that."

Desi doubted it. First pulling on gloves, she picked up Thor's rifle and checked it out. "Hasn't been fired," she said, before putting it into the back of her truck.

"Sheriff's on the way with forensics," Jos said. "If you guys want to go, I can lead 'em back in."

Desi waited a moment then asked, "Did those guys with the dogs sound legit to you?"

Jos shook his head. "Not if they were really there."

"You think Thor is lying?"

"How would I know? But either he's making up something or the guys they ran into really were there. But even if they were, why the hell shoot someone just because he saw you? And why only one of them?"

"Good question."

"Maybe," said Kel slowly, "whoever it was thought he got both hunters with one bullet. You heard what Edvaldson said. Maybe he hit dirt so fast it looked like they'd both bought it."

Jos nodded, stretching and compressing his lips as he thought.

Desi turned to Kel, wishing she could get rid of the skin-crawling feeling. "So why shoot and assume they're dead? Why not finish it?"

"Because one shot can look like an accident, but two can't? Because if they were both shot, how likely was it they'd get help before they died?"

"Ugly calculus." Desi shook her shoulders, trying to ease the deepening tension.

"Murder always is," Kel replied. "So they managed to get a cell connection up here?"

Jos nodded. "Amazing. It was all broken up and I'm sorry to say that some good, long minutes were wasted while I tried to understand what had happened and get their GPS. *That* apparently was working, and Edvaldson managed to give me coordinates, thank God. Without that…" He just shook his head and closed his eyes.

"Jos?" Desi asked. "You want to leave this to me?"

His eyes snapped open and she could see fire in them. "Hell no. I want to find whoever did this."

"Not likely," she pointed out. "All that can be done at this point is collecting evidence."

"I don't care," he said succinctly. "Bad enough we can't catch all the poachers. This is worse. I gotta do something, Desi."

"I understand." And she did, but he was so new to this, relatively speaking. It was a shocking incident, but she'd seen other hunters shot, usually by a careless companion. This was Jos's first time. "Be proud of yourself. You didn't lose your head."

"Unlike his friend."

At that Kel strode up the road, away from him.

"What's with him?" Jos asked.

"Thor is a vet, Jos," she said, keeping her tone as pleasant as she could. "That gunshot snapped him back to Iraq. Thank goodness he didn't start shooting up the woods."

Jos fell silent, finally saying, "Oh. Yeah. He said..." He trailed off and looked after Kel. "Him, too? He's a vet?"

"Yes."

Jos swore. "I'm sorry, Desi. Should I apologize to him? I was shook up and being stupid."

"Maybe not just yet. Later. I think he needs a moment to himself." Maybe more than a moment, she thought. He'd handled Thor Edvaldson beautifully, but she couldn't imagine he hadn't been reminded of ugly things in his own life.

With effort she forced her attention back to immediate matters. "You get any blood on you?"

"I don't think so. The Edvaldson guy was using a T-shirt wrapped around the shoulder to apply pressure. He got covered with blood, but I pulled on my gloves before I took over."

"Check and make sure. I've got bleach in my truck if you need to wash any off."

"Sure." Jos looked down and started to peel off his bloody blue rubber gloves. Just as long as none had gotten through them or his clothing... She scanned his face and saw no blood there either.

Jos looked up, and he appeared haunted. "I'm not sure how much good I did. Maybe the bleeding slowed because he'd almost bled out."

There was always that ugly possibility. But she reminded herself that Don had managed to open his eyes a bit. And he'd still been breathing when they airlifted him.

"You did everything you could," she said firmly. "Everything. Me, I'm going back to the scene, keep an eye on it. You bring the lawmen back when they arrive?"

"Sure thing."

She glanced to where Kel stood, hands in pockets, staring at the woods. She gave him a little wave, then turned to hike back to the scene. It shouldn't have been left unattended, not that they'd had any choice.

Anyway, needle in a haystack barely covered it when it came to finding the bullet or a casing. That shot could have been fired from some distance, and it was anybody's guess where the bullet had wound up. She hoped the sheriff brought his new K9 Unit. The dog would probably be better than the metal detectors, given how many bullets had likely been fired by hunters in this area over the years. And that wouldn't even include other metallic trash.

Hell. If she'd been unhappy about the poaching before, now she was almost blind with fury. Bad enough killing animals without a permit, bad enough wantonly wasting the meat, but to shoot a human being? For what? Because he'd seen them, seen the dogs? Really?

She wondered if something else had happened, something that Thor hadn't noticed or had forgotten. He'd sure been hanging on to reality by a slender thread for a while there.

She heard feet crunching pine needles and leaves behind her, and she didn't really need to glance back to know who it was. "Are you sure you want to do this?"

she asked before he reached her. "This has got to be a lot more like Afghanistan."

She thought of the way he'd stood there alone up the road, hands in his pockets, staring at the woods. An ache for him pushed aside some of her anger.

"Yes," he answered just as he reached her side. "Whatever lunatic shot Don might still be around."

"I doubt it."

"So do I, but why take the chance?"

She couldn't argue with that. "This whole thing stinks. If it was an accidental shot, the guy obviously ran. If it was deliberate, why hang around?"

"Because bullets carry identifying marks."

"True. But useless until we find the weapon." She plowed on, scanning the woods. "I'd like to try to figure out where the shot came from, if we can. Thor said Don had broken some branches to guide them. Maybe that'll help."

"It'll at least have us looking in the right direction. But if the bullet deflected any when it emerged from Don, that's not going to help a lot."

"No." Which brought up a chilling idea she hadn't wanted to consider. "Thor was standing almost behind Don. Maybe the shooter *meant* to get them both."

"I was pondering that."

"God, Kel! This isn't supposed to be a war zone."

"I know." His voice lowered a bit. "But it sure as hell feels like one now."

Chapter 9

Fifteen minutes later they stood at the edge of the clearing. Efforts to save Don's life had really stirred up the ground, not that she thought footprints would be any help in this case.

In the bright sunlight, one thing sure stood out: blood on the dead leaves, probably more in the dead pine needles and soaked into the ground. "A lot of blood," she said. She wasn't squeamish by nature, but somehow this was different.

"A lot," he agreed. "But it always looks like more than it is. It takes about six minutes for a grown man to bleed out from an artery. This went on a lot longer. Thor had time to apply pressure. Clearly from what Jos said, Don was still bleeding when he arrived and he had to work at stopping it. So it's more than we can see, but not enough to kill him."

"Which says what exactly?" She hated the note of impatience in her tone.

"I'm just thinking, trying to envision. I don't want to walk all over that blood. It's evidence. I'm trying to figure out how to get a sight line without doing that."

"Sight line?"

"I know how snipers work. He'd have to find a clear sight line through all these woods. That limits his range. Let me think about it."

He knew how snipers worked? That made her heart lurch. She hadn't really given much thought to all he might know, all he might have seen, all he might have done. Or the size of the burdens and scars he must carry. God, he seemed so well-balanced, but here he was talking coolly about *snipers*?

She couldn't stop the words from emerging. "Were you a sniper?"

"Not in the way you're thinking."

"What am I thinking?"

"That I was trained to do that job. I wasn't. But I learned some things from those who were. And, I *was* a soldier, remember? If I can't figure out a sight line for a shot, who can?"

He had a point. "Stupid question," she said.

"Natural one," he replied. "Relax, Desi. I'm not going off the rails here."

Was that the impression she had given him? She felt awfully small just then. Following on Jos's ill-conceived comment, he must be feeling really good right now.

But he'd fallen silent, scanning the clearing intently. Then he took a couple of steps to the side. A minute later he pointed. "Come here and look. You can see the bent branch."

She stepped to his side, but he moved her in front of him and pointed again. "See it?"

"Yeah." It wasn't a bent branch, but a broken one. A trail marker. She looked past it. "So they were probably standing much like we are, looking in that direction."

"Probably," he agreed.

"But the forest is thick with undergrowth and saplings there."

"It's not a good sight line," he agreed. "I have only the vaguest idea of what direction he was struck from, so let me work my way around and see what I can find."

She was busy listening and looking at everything else. The forest had absorbed the shooting and subsequent ruckus, and had moved back into its normal patterns. She listened to the breeze in the tops of the firs, a faint sigh. Other sounds of small animals scampering across the floor reached her. Birds were rare above eight thousand feet, but she heard the distant call of an eagle. The turkey vultures had probably already begun their southward migration. A few crows might be hanging around in piney areas, but they weren't as common as they once were. Some did prefer the heights, however, at least until late autumn. Regardless, birdsong wasn't a chorus this time of year up here.

But the important thing was that she could not detect any sign of disturbance from wildlife. The shooter must have moved on, and peace had returned.

Despite this, the hunting for bighorns, at this altitude, would soon become excellent if it wasn't already. They moved down from the high crags as the autumn deepened, looking for lower valleys for mating.

A good reason for hunters to be about, especially on

horseback because carrying large game out of here required help. But dogs?

Bothered, she shook her head as if she could shake loose a useful thought of some kind.

"Desi?"

She looked over and saw Kel a few feet away. He gestured for her to come over. She took two steps and he put her in front of him again.

"See?" He pointed.

It took her a moment, but she *did* see. A straight line between the trees, though it didn't go that far. A few hundred feet?

She followed the invisible line across the clearing. It led directly to the bloodstain. "Okay then," she said on a long breath.

"No accident," Kel said. "The shooter could see."

"And I don't believe in magic bullets."

"Me neither."

Bright sunlight on Don and Thor, both of them in orange vests and caps...definitely not an accident.

"I'll move a little farther, keep looking for other possibilities, but between the bent branch and what Thor said..."

"Yeah." Desi's tone was clipped. Her stomach rolled over just once. She'd dealt with a lot in her career, but murder was a first. Forcing herself to calm, she looked at her watch. "The first of the sheriff's team should be arriving within a half hour. Maybe sooner if they push it."

"Okay." He walked a little farther around the clearing, apparently checking for other sight lines, but as she stared at the one across from where she was positioned, she felt certain that this was it. If so, the sheriff wouldn't have to search that far for expended casings.

Maybe they'd find one, if it hadn't been picked up. Then she turned around and glanced at the woods behind her. She doubted that a bullet would have had enough force to embed itself in a tree after passing all the way through Don, but she had no idea which type of rifle or load had been used. Some could travel quite a distance, but they weren't usually the kinds of guns used for hunting. You needed power, yes, but you didn't want bullets flying for a thousand yards or more if they should happen not to hit a tree. Nor did you want a bullet so strong it would rip open the far side of your quarry. Best case, the bullet entered the game and didn't go beyond. Not that that could be guaranteed.

God, her head was racing in circles with this. She'd seen accidental shootings as a warden, but never a deliberate one. Nobody in their right mind would do such a thing.

Kel returned to her side. "That's it. That's the only remotely decent sight line I can find."

She pivoted and faced it again. "This must be hard for you."

He surprised her by slipping his arm loosely around her back. "It's got to be harder for you. I've seen worse."

"I imagine. But this…a trigger?"

"Not so much for me as it was for Thor, but don't ask me why."

"It was like he was in two places at once."

He sighed. "I'm sure he was. And it had to be all the harder because his memory of Iraq wasn't squaring with what his eyes were seeing even if his mind tried to shift to the past."

She leaned a little closer, surprisingly grateful not to be alone right now. For a person who naturally enjoyed the solitude of the woods, the feeling crept through her like a warning. Something inside her was changing. For the good? She didn't know. "So he was aware he was here?"

"As far as I can tell. I'm not saying it's not possible to slip so far into a memory that for all intents and purposes you're living it again and everything else vanishes. He just didn't strike me as having fully severed the connection with here and now."

"Have you ever?"

"Slipped my moorings in time? Once in a while. Not recently, though. Yeah, I still have triggers, but I know where I am."

She nodded. That was usually what happened to her. She'd know perfectly well where she was and who she was talking to, yet her brain spilled things that should have been said to Joe. She sometimes only realized it when someone would begin to look at her oddly, as if she were overreacting to something. Thank goodness it didn't happen often. She seemed to have a very narrow set of triggers.

"Thanks for the hug," she said presently. "I guess I need it. This is really getting to me. It's so senseless and brutal."

"Yeah, it is." He tightened his arm briefly. "Just let me know if I'm trespassing too far. This is bad enough without me upsetting you."

"It's a hug, Kel," she said, failing to achieve the humor she wished she could. It *was* a friendly hug, nothing to set off her memories of the rape, but it sure felt good. She made up her mind to accept the comfort and stop analyzing it.

Because right now, as the horror really began to come

home, she needed the comfort. It surpassed her understanding that someone could attempt murder for no real reason except the possibility that...the possibility of what? It just didn't add up. "Do you think the shooter might be one of the poachers? That he feared he might be remembered coming through here with a string of horses?"

"Don't a lot of people do that?"

"Not with a pack of dogs."

"True. Maybe. But murder ratchets things up an awful lot. Greed can make men do terrible things, but this seems excessive."

"That's what I'd say, but it happened." Sickened, she stood staring into the pool of sunlight that revealed the day's ugliness, and wondered how even a hundred illegal hunts could be worth this.

By the time the sheriff's deputies and forensic team arrived, Desi had returned to her normal, calm demeanor. The tension had left her face. Kel rather admired her for that. It wasn't as if she saw a murder scene every single day.

He watched her talking to the sheriff, Gage Dalton, and that deputy he'd met, Sarah Ironheart, and some other older man who with long dark hair streaked with gray. Other deputies set up a ring of yellow tape, and once he'd pointed out the probable sight line, they blocked that off as well.

The light was beginning to change as the afternoon deepened, and it wasn't long before generator-powered spotlights arrived. And just after them a K9 Unit appeared, a caramel-colored Belgian Malinois with straight-up ears and an eager, intelligent face. The deputy who held his leash looked almost as eager as his dog.

Kel half smiled. He somehow suspected this man and his dog didn't see a whole lot of official activity locally. Hours spent training couldn't make up for that.

Then the sheriff approached him. One look at Gage Dalton said the man had been to hell and back, confirmed both by his limp and the burn that scarred the side of his face.

"So you're the new outfitter I've been hearing about," Dalton said without preamble.

"Must be," Kel answered amiably. "Say, can you step away from here for a moment?"

Dalton tilted his head a bit. "Sure." He jerked his head back toward the road, and kept walking until the stream of arriving deputies and forensics people trailed off. Then he stopped and faced Kel. "Well?"

"I'm not going to flash my credentials in case somebody happens by, but I'm actually with the Wildlife Investigative Unit. I'm posing as an outfitter hoping to get some leads on a ring of unlicensed outfitters."

Gage studied him for a minute. "Desi knows."

"Of course she knows. Until you, she's the only one I told."

Gage looked past him into the woods. "There's been an increase in poaching. I know it's been bothering the hell out of Desi. Then that sheep on Jake Madison's land. Jake was hopping mad, thinks somebody used dogs to chase it down."

"Yeah, she told me."

Gage's dark gaze returned to him. "And this guy who got shot saw men riding with a pack of dogs."

"Yeah."

Gage nodded slowly. "On a personal level, I've never

been interested in hunting. I get that other people need the food or whatever. But I have to say, somehow I've always had the impression that hunting should be sporting. The animal should at least have a chance."

"That's what most of the regulations are designed to do."

"Two years ago," Gage went on, "there were some dogs menacing antelope. There are a lot of ranch dogs around here. Most do what they're supposed to, but sometimes some of them get a notion to chase game."

"I've heard of it."

"Desi and her wardens, with a little help from us, managed to round up the dogs. The ones we traced, the owners got fined. But all of the dogs...put down."

"That's the law."

"I know. What I was getting to was how much that bothered Desi. Law or no law, I think she felt like we ought to be putting down the owners rather than their dogs."

That drew a short laugh from Kel.

"Yeah," said Gage, smiling crookedly. "She cares deeply about animals. I'm not so sure she feels that way about some people. Good quality in a warden, I guess. She's great at what she does." He veered the topic sharply. "What do you need from me and my deputies?"

"Eyes and ears. Desi's too busy doing her job, I can't be everywhere and I'm damn sure I'm not hearing everything because I'm an outsider."

"I can guarantee that. No problem. My deputies are excellent eyes and ears when they know what they should be listening for. A ring of illegal outfitters, huh? I heard of one guy a couple of years back who didn't get caught until someone actually checked on his license. Amazing. He apparently made a tidy sum, though."

"They do. There are a lot of people willing to pay small fortunes to bring home a trophy. People who make assumptions they don't question, don't bother to find out whether the outfit is licensed...well, I don't need to tell you."

Again that crooked smile from Gage. "Trust me, you don't. I got a pretty good idea of what people are capable of from the years I was an undercover agent with the DEA. Which sometimes makes me a bit like Desi."

Kel arched a brow.

Gage laughed. "I'm sometimes more inclined to like animals. But most people around here are good folks. Not perfect, but good. That's why I stayed. Well, that and my wife. Anyway, I'll let you know if we pick up on anything."

He turned to go back to the crime scene then paused. "A pack of dogs, huh?"

"That's what he said."

"I don't like that at all. We don't need you here anymore unless you want to stay. I'll try to shoo Desi along, too. I realize she's law enforcement, too, but what we need to be doing now...no reason she should hang around. Honestly, I don't like the way she looks."

Neither did Kel. Honestly. That calm, professional exterior had returned, yet right now he felt as if it were a facade. She got furious about an animal being poached, but she got sickened by attempted murder. Her moral compass was just fine.

His? Maybe.

* * *

To Kel's relief, Desi was finally persuaded to leave Jos on the scene and depart with Kel.

"It's *my* scene," Jos argued.

Desi studied him. He was, after all, a young man who couldn't have many years of experience. Kel awaited her judgment, hoping she'd give Jos the approval he seemed to want. That she'd tell him she trusted him to take over for her.

"Sure, Jos," she said. "I appreciate it. You've done great today. But if you have any…repercussions from what you had to deal with earlier, don't be afraid to tell me. Some things really affect us."

Jos nodded. "I can handle it. I *need* to handle it."

Probably so, Kel thought as he and Desi climbed into her truck. Jos had done well dealing with the wounded man, and now he needed to do something, anything, to help catch the shooter. Some imperatives couldn't be ignored for the sake of the soul.

Desi remained silent throughout the trip back to the station. He left her undisturbed, wondering if she'd be able to find out if Don had survived his wounding. He supposed she would, as an investigating officer.

He'd also had plenty of time to think about the event, so he wasn't exactly surprised when Desi parked her truck in front of the station and said, "The shooter thought Don might have recognized him."

"I've been thinking about that."

"No other reason for it. This is going to heighten the scrutiny around here, which doesn't serve these guys at all. So…"

She pulled her keys from the ignition, threw open the door and climbed out. "Let's go upstairs. I'm starving."

"Want me to run into town and grab something?"

"Only if you want to. I'm sure I can do something with eggs and some bacon."

He could cheerfully eat breakfast at any hour of the day or night, so he slid out, waited for her to lock up, then followed her up the stairs.

While she paused to dump her gear and get more comfortable, he started a pot of coffee. Only then did he remove his vest, jacket and weapon. Desi stood in the middle of the living room, clearly lost in thought, so he let her be. He pulled out the eggs, hunted up the bacon in the lower drawer.

She spoke, clearly with half her attention. "If you want, there are some thin sandwich steaks in the freezer. They'd probably thaw quickly."

"Okay." He pulled those out, too, then went out to stand near her. "Desi? Are you okay?"

"I don't know," she replied. Her voice sounded taut, stretched. She was holding it all in. All of it. His hands clenched and unclenched as he wondered what boundaries he dared to cross with her. This was taking a toll on her and he urgently wanted to find some way to comfort her.

What had started as a straightforward assignment seemed to be growing into a huge mess, and part of his concern now was Desi. She was no longer just the warden he was supposed to hook up with. With each passing hour he cared more about what all this might be doing to *her*. Yeah, he hated the poaching, but he'd never guessed that it might upset Desi even more. Or that murder would stalk the forest and mountains. Now she mattered as much as what he'd been sent here to do. Maybe more. And he was worried for her.

Feeling like a lug who might be doing everything wrong, he slipped one arm around her shoulders as he had earlier in the woods. She'd appreciated it then. Maybe she wouldn't despise it now.

Almost the instant he touched her, she turned into him and wrapped her arms around his waist. A little astonished, but relieved, he hugged her with both arms and simply waited.

She felt so good leaning into him, warm and soft in all the right places. His body responded even as his mind rebelled. Wrong time. Absolutely the wrong time.

Closing his eyes, he held her and tried to step down on natural desires that sometimes had no place. Right now was one of those times.

He knew little enough about Desi, but he suspected this was the first time she'd seen a man maliciously shot. He didn't have to try very hard to remember the emotional and psychological transition he'd had to make when it all became real for him in the Rangers. An internal earthquake.

While it wasn't battle today, it had been bad enough in its own right. Peaceful woods had been shattered by horror that shouldn't happen here in this safe place. What you expected on a battlefield wasn't what you expected to happen in your own backyard to people who were simply hunting.

Now Desi wasn't just worried about the hapless game animals, she was probably worried about other hunters and her own wardens. How could she not be?

"What's happening, Kel?" she asked quietly. "What the hell is going on? How much money is a man's life worth?"

He cleared his throat. "Never having put a price tag on one myself, I couldn't tell you."

"I can see it in self-defense, but this wasn't. Not even if he thought Don could recognize him. He could have come up with some excuse for what they were doing with the dogs. Anyway, he had no reason to think Don or Thor would tell anyone about it. So why try to kill them?"

She rubbed her face against his shoulder as if to wipe it clean of memory. The gesture tightened his chest. "Hell," he whispered.

"What?"

"Some people are truly twisted, Desi. Maybe we don't run into them often, or when we do we don't recognize them. Psychopaths or whatever they're called now. Charming, smart, seemingly nice, and utterly without conscience."

"Like Joe," she whispered.

Joe? Then he made the connection. "Maybe, I don't know. Did he ever express regret or apologize?"

"Never. What he did was brag about his conquest."

He swore silently. People like Joe didn't deserve to breathe free air. "Well, there are people out there who don't care about anyone or anything except themselves and what they want. So yeah, a guy like that wouldn't have any compunction about shooting someone. But these types are usually smarter than that. Did they think these hunters' bones would never be found? I don't know. Surely an alarm would have been raised. Someone would miss them. Their truck was on the road, right? How long would it take for the forest to scatter their remains beyond hope?"

"Probably not long," she answered. "Not long at all. Wolves, bears, coyotes… Three days? Maybe four?"

"So whoever did this must have figured these guys were on a long hunting trip. It's a weekday. Maybe nobody would expect them back before Sunday. Or maybe later. Anyway, I'm sure the sheriff will look into that. Regardless, it wouldn't take long for enough to disappear that nobody could be sure what happened to them."

"Maybe not," she admitted. Her voice had grown softer, quieter.

"That's why we bury our dead, Desi." He closed his eyes, remembering Afghanistan, how quickly the carrion-eaters would start to circle in the air above. How quickly scavengers would arrive to grab what they could. Nature cleaned up the dead.

All of a sudden, he felt Desi stir against him, moving back. Immediately he let go of her, feeling an emptiness in his arms.

"Today had to be hard on you, too," she remarked. "I'm sure you've seen worse, but I saw how you helped Thor find himself. Here I am trying to take it in, and you're probably dealing with some pretty bad memories."

"I'm okay," he assured her. For now anyway. He'd felt a couple of tugs out there in the woods, a couple of times when he felt he could have slipped his moorings, but he was getting better at controlling it. Helping Thor Edvaldson had probably helped him has much as it had helped Thor.

"Yeah," she said, then went to the kitchen.

Withdrawn, he thought, worry tightening his chest all over again. She was pulling somewhere inside. He knew all about that. He also knew it could work only for so long. Had she learned how to do it after her rape? Maybe.

Cussing silently, he watched her start cracking eggs into a bowl, watched her turn on the big pan on the stove and lay bacon strips in it. He ought to help, but he could sense the bubble she had put around herself. A line of protection from everything, a place where she could remain cool and nothing could touch her.

Except she'd already been touched. As mad as she'd been about the bighorn, this reaction didn't seem right. Something in her was on overload but he wasn't sure what, if anything, he could do, or even if he should.

"I'm gonna cook those steaks and eggs in the bacon grease, if that's all right," she said without looking at him.

"Can't imagine what bacon grease could ruin."

Her head nodded, but didn't turn toward him.

"First thing I wanted every time I came home," he continued, "was a mess of bacon. A hamburger was second, but first I wanted my fill of bacon. You should have seen the look on a waiter's face when I'd sit down in some diner and tell them to just keep the bacon and coffee coming."

"They probably don't hear that every day."

"When I was still married," he said, dredging the words from some place deep inside, "my wife wouldn't cook that much of it and wouldn't let me. Unhealthy. Well, I didn't give a damn. I'd just walked through war and come out the other side. Like I was going to worry about a heart attack twenty years down the road."

That caused her head to turn a bit. "Fatalistic?"

"Yeah," he admitted.

"Scrambled or fried?"

"However you want." He waited, hoping she hadn't dived right back into her bubble. "I stopped being afraid of dying. I was more worried about the dog."

"Dog?" She half turned then, giving him a sidelong glance.

"Yeah. Lots of stray mutts out there. They are generally despised and roundly mistreated. It's a hard life for almost everyone there. People living close to starvation, just barely eking out a life…well, it's a brutal way to live for too many. So I guess rescuing a stray dog must have seemed…well, maybe thoughtless. Why feed a useless animal when people were hungry? Especially one that's considered unclean. Anyway, I worried about the animal. I was afraid someone would torture it or beat it while we were out on patrol."

"You had to leave it behind?"

"Let me put it this way. When you're creeping over terrain maintaining complete silence, camouflaged… do you really want a dog giving you away by prancing around or barking?"

"I guess not." She moved the bacon a bit in the pan.

"Anyway, we must have seemed mad to the locals, but we couldn't resist. Cammi did as much for our welfare as we did for his. Interestingly, after a few months, the locals started to change their attitudes. So maybe we did something for the general welfare of Afghanistan's mutts. At least in that locale."

"I thought people everywhere found dogs useful. I thought that's why they got domesticated in the first place."

"They're also scavengers," he answered quietly. "It's kind of a vicious circle. If they're not fed, they'll find something to eat. What they find is sometimes repulsive."

He watched her grow very still, then she nodded. "I can see that."

"We were talking about what would happen to human remains up there in the woods today. Well, that can become a religious problem for some people."

"I get it," she said, almost sharply.

He bet she did.

"What happened to Cammi?"

"One of the guys has been trying to find a way to get him back here. Latest word is that he might be brought here in a couple of months. There are organizations that will help now. It wasn't always that way."

"No, I heard about that. Violation of general orders or something to keep a pet. Shoot on sight."

"Pretty much."

She turned then, looking at him from haunted eyes. "And we think humans are so superior."

"I wonder often," he admitted. "What can I do to help with dinner?" Time to shift to safer ground. He shouldn't have brought up the dog, but she'd asked if he was afraid of dying. Not anymore. He'd left that in the dust a long time ago. But that damn dog? Yeah, that was different. He could close his eyes and remember it curling up beside him on his pallet, or licking his hand or face until he pulled out of some dark well he'd sunk into after a buddy was wounded or killed.

His need to protect his buddies had extended to Cammi before long. He had become part of their unit.

"Kel?"

He started and saw Desi looking inquisitive. He guessed he'd dropped out. "Yeah?"

"You...okay?"

"I sometimes wonder what okay is," he said, then walked over to the bar. "Need help?"

"It's almost done. I was just wondering why you got so quiet."

"It's been a day." A day that had him thinking about a dog he hadn't seen in years. The last thing he needed right now was to have memories stalking him, knocking him off-kilter. Wandering the byways of Afghanistan wouldn't help anything.

He closed his eyes, took a few relaxing breaths and firmly centered himself in the here and now. He'd lived the past. He didn't need to relive it.

Far across the state, the man with the ponytail threw a paperweight across the room, denting the wallboard. He didn't care. He was furious. He gripped the phone so tightly that his knuckles ached.

"What the hell was Randy thinking?" he demanded again.

"I told you, he thought the guys could identify him."

"And report what? That he was on horseback and had dogs? That still isn't a crime, or doesn't Randy realize it?"

"I don't know what the hell Randy realizes," came the answer. "You talk to him. Right now we got bigger fish to worry about. I got word that new outfitter is undercharging us by a fair amount. There are too many of them in this state right now trying to horn in, but we got three hunts planned for Conard County in the next two weeks and we can't have our customers hearing they could have gotten the service cheaper."

"Wouldn't be as good as what we provide," the ponytailed man snapped. "And now because of Randy, we're going to have wardens on the lookout for anything and everything. Hell, he didn't even kill the guys, did he?"

"No."

"So what good did he do? The guys might not have recognized him before, but they're sure going to be trying now with the help of law enforcement. You ever see one of them Identi-Kits? Do me a favor and tell Randy to find a bolt-hole and stay in it for a good long time. We can't have him running around out there. Hell, now everyone's on guard over that way, including that new outfitter I bet."

"We'll take care of him."

"He was the *only* one you were supposed to take care of, him and that big-mouth bitch of a warden. Now we got a bigger headache. Damn it."

He slammed the phone down. What poaching hadn't been able to do, one of his own men had just done. They were on the radar now, and quiet and careful as they might be, it was going to take time for things to cool down.

He punched the wall. Two plus two. He bet the law could add those numbers just as well. Now they'd be wondering more than ever about the poachers. Now they'd be keeping an extremely sharp eye out.

Damn Randy to hell.

Chapter 10

After dinner and cleanup, Kel and Desi sat in the living room. The lengthy silence seemed pregnant somehow, but Kel didn't want to disturb it. At least he didn't feel as if he should vanish. He'd had enough of that with his ex-wife, and felt surprisingly content to be accepted in someone's space.

Because it was a fact, once civilians got past *Thank you for your service*, they usually didn't know what else to say or do. Hurried on as if escaping. He didn't blame them necessarily, but it had made him even more reluctant to hang around in crowded places. He'd kind of gone undercover for himself when he chose to make his home here in this underpopulated state, and had left his military service behind. Except in the Game and Fish Department, there were quite a few other vets. They got it.

Desi had no reason to get it, yet she seemed to. If he did something to concern her, she merely asked if he was okay. When he said he was, she accepted it whether she believed it or not. No badgering, no demand to share the most intimate parts of himself.

But as they sat there, little by little he felt the air becoming charged. He was certain it wasn't him. Glancing at Desi, he saw her looking down at her lap, her hands tightly clenched.

"Desi?" he finally asked.

"You know," she said slowly, "you're the first man I've let hug me since Joe."

That shook him, but he wasn't sure if she wanted him to say anything. She'd even let him kiss her ever so briefly. Where was she headed?

"I'm glad you let me."

"I...want to tell you. I don't know why. This day has been just awful. Why should I dredge up more ugliness? But it's pushing at me, Kel. Pushing hard."

"Then let it out." He was prepared to listen, and was sure she couldn't possibly tell him anything more horrible than the things he'd already experienced.

"But it's not right. You came here to do a job, not to listen to me dump. You don't even know me very well. I should talk to someone else."

"Like who?" he asked mildly. He suspected she had a very short list of real friends or she would have talked to one of them already. Mostly her relationships appeared to be built around her job. "Sometimes," he said, "it's easier to talk to a stranger who gets where you're coming from than to talk to someone who really knows you."

"You might be right," she said slowly. "I don't know. I just know it happened a very long time ago, I buried it and moved on, yet here it is pushing its way up again like a backed-up sewer."

Man, did he know that feeling. "Then let 'er rip." So she thought she'd buried it and left it behind. Not really, not when he was the first man to kiss or hug her in all this time. Burying the dead didn't always work when they left souvenirs behind.

"It's a stupid story," she said.

"You can stop right there."

Her head jerked up, her eyes sparking. "What?"

"I'm not going to listen to you say being raped was stupid no matter how it came about. You can leave out that commentary, because it's not true. The guy was evidently a slime. No reason to think any part of it was stupid."

She looked down, unleashing a long breath. "Okay. I *felt* stupid. I felt like I should have known, should have picked up on something, but I didn't."

"Still not true," he said flatly. "You were the victim. Don't give him any excuses, and don't blame yourself."

She jumped up. "If you're going to edit everything I say, then what's the point?"

Oh, she was mad now. He almost smiled. "The point is to make it clear to you that you should stop beating yourself up. This is all on him. Every bit of it. Are you going to condemn yourself for being trusting? I hope not. But you're certainly not stupid. I know that for a fact."

She almost gaped at him. He patted the couch beside him invitingly but she didn't move. Okay, not ready for that level of trust yet.

He waited, his insides knotting with concern for her, a feeling that surprised him. He hardly knew the woman; how was he getting so involved so fast? Because he'd learned to avoid involvement. Anger was a safe place to live if you couldn't be numb. Yet almost from the moment of meeting Desi, not only had he desired her, but he'd felt other emotions for her. She called to him in ways that troubled him more than simple passion.

"Okay," she said finally. "Screw the gory details. I'd dated Joe three times. He seemed okay, he was charming and I was st—" She cut herself off sharply. "I was nineteen. Inexperienced. I had a few casual dates in high school, but nothing like Joe. He made me feel so... special. Anyway, I hadn't heard anything bad about him around the college, he seemed nice enough, so when he asked me to come to his off-campus apartment to listen to music, I didn't even hesitate. I was excited that he was so interested. I think I was falling in love."

She broke off again, and now she was pacing. "He overpowered me. No alcohol, nothing. Just him overpowering me and telling me I really wanted it, over and over..."

"Bastard," Kel said quietly.

"Yeah." At least she didn't argue with that. "Wooed with sweet lies until I was cornered and then..." She trailed off. "Why am I telling you this?"

"Because you need to."

"Do I?" She faced him. "I was a virgin, Kel. That was my one time ever."

He swore and this time he let some of his pain and anger show. Her anguish deserved an echo from him.

"So now you know." She wrapped her arms around herself, and for the first time the strong, confident Desi completely vanished, leaving a small, stricken women behind. He wanted to go to her, but was afraid of the chain reaction he might set off.

He absolutely had to let her lead. He dared ask one question. "Did you tell anyone?"

She gave a little gasp as if she'd been punched.

"What?"

"I can't believe I completely forgot it. I've been telling myself for years that I never told anyone. But I did. My roommates."

"And?"

"It was like they didn't hear me. I don't know if they thought I was overreacting, or lying or what. But I never spoke of it again."

He closed his eyes at the image of her being laughed at when she had been viciously violated. God, no wonder she'd sought the woods and kept a safe distance. No wonder she'd completely forgotten it all this time. Her roommates had given her a second wound, almost as bad as the first. He was willing to bet that after that she had trouble becoming close to women, too.

Hell. He wondered how she'd pasted over her scars and what was tearing them open now.

Idiotic question, he realized suddenly. The answer was as plain as the nose on his face. He'd kissed her. He'd touched her, even if only for a comforting hug. He'd gone places she hadn't let another man go in all this time.

He stood up. "I guess I should go stay at the motel."

She froze, then gaped at him. "Am I that repulsive?"

Where had that come from? "No," he said. "Absolutely not. But you wondered why you suddenly felt the need to dump all this when it's clear this is not something you talk to anyone about."

"So?"

"So I'm triggering you by my very presence. Hugging you, kissing you, that must feel like the very edge of your worst nightmare. So I should clear out. We'll find a way to work this crazy assignment without me crowding you. Damn, I'm even beginning to wonder if I was sent here just so I'd be out of somebody's way. The longer I'm here, the more I wonder what I'm doing. Regardless, I'm clearly upsetting *you*."

He'd taken just one step toward the bunkhouse when another bit of understanding practically punched him in the gut. If he walked out now, after what she had just shared with him, he'd be no better than those friends who had ignored her all those years ago. He'd leave a rejection in his wake. "Aw, hell," he said under his breath.

"Kel?"

He faced her again. God, he wished he could wipe that tension from her face, the ghosts from her gaze.

"Don't leave," she said.

"If I'm making you uncomfortable, dredging up the past, maybe I should."

She shook her head. "Maybe some things need dredging. Anyway, even if you're triggering me, I still liked it when you hugged me, and I still liked it when you kissed me. Maybe I'm just taking a painful step on a path I should have followed a long time ago."

He took a moment, choosing his words carefully. "What path would that be?"

"Healing. There's burying and then there's healing. But I'm sure you know that."

Yeah, he did. He also knew that healing could be far more painful than burying, and could take a lot more effort.

After a moment he went to sit on the couch. "Okay. You want to take a break from this? Talk about something else? It's up to you, Desi."

She averted her face, remaining still and silent for a few minutes. He let her be. She must be feeling very exposed and vulnerable right now, so he had to follow her lead. Besides, intentionally or not, he guessed he had pushed her in some way when he had said he would leave. Maybe all that time in therapy after he'd come home for good had taught him something, he thought sourly.

Finally, she looked at him. Then haltingly she crossed the floor and lowered herself onto the couch beside him. Not enough to touch, a good six inches between them, but a remarkable sign of trust.

"How did you become so understanding?" she asked quietly.

"Well…I've lived it, dealt with some trauma, went to therapy…which helps a little but somehow doesn't get rid of the nightmares… And if that's made me more understanding then good."

"Good? You can say that? I can't even imagine the horrible experiences you've had."

"No, you probably can't, and I'm glad of that. But it remains, the psychologist I worked with at the VA once told me something. I'm not sure if it was pointed at me, just a general statement or an off-the-cuff remark."

She turned her head a little, looking at him from the corner of her eye. "Yes?"

"She said the usual stuff about what doesn't kill us makes us stronger. It may be true, but I wasn't buying it back then. Anyway, then she came at it from a different direction. She said all the bad things that happen to us? If we let them, they can make us better people, more understanding and more empathetic." He passed a hand over his face, feeling suddenly very weary. Life, he sometimes thought, was a burden that never quit. "I didn't really hear it at the time, I was too self-absorbed, too angry, but it kind of stuck. And maybe she was right."

"That sounds like making lemonade out of lemons."

He nodded. "Maybe so. But what else are we going to do?"

She grew silent again and he let her be. Nothing helped the nightmares that clung. Nothing but time. Seeing her peer into her own abyss had caused him to look into his own a bit. He tried to do that as rarely as possible, but in the dead of night, sleeping, there were no defenses, and waking from a nightmare confused about where he was…well, nothing prevented that. Time had helped, but it hadn't cured. All he could say with any truth was that he'd learned to better control himself and his mind.

"The past can't be changed," she said eventually.

"Nope." He wished it could, but he was sure that billions of other people often wished it could be and with the same lack of success.

Time passed. Seldom had Kel felt as aware of minutes slipping beyond reach. He'd been in situations where minutes dragged endlessly and he wished them gone, but never before had he felt them eluding him, and worse, that no one could know how many of them were left.

Desi suddenly rose, and there was something determined in the way she moved. "I'm going to call the hospital and check up on Don, and the sheriff to find out if they've learned anything. Then you and I are going to have a talk about this plan of yours."

The call with the hospital was brief. Despite Desi's position with Game and Fish, they were reluctant to release information. All she learned was that Don was stable.

So next she dialed the sheriff's office and was immediately told to call Gage Dalton at home. He answered after a couple of rings. "Just got in from the scene, Desi.

I'm eating a reheated dinner that Emma sweetly saved for me. How about I drop by when I'm done?"

"I'd appreciate it. I'm troubled and I want to compare notes."

"You're not the only one."

When she hung up, she faced Kel. "The sheriff's coming over."

"Good," he answered and rose, stretching until joints popped.

God, he looked good, she thought. She wished she knew how to reach for what he seemed to offer. Then she reminded herself it was the wrong time. Maybe the wrong everything. More important matters needed her attention.

"You think he discovered anything?" he asked, shaking his arms and shoulders a bit. Clearly he wasn't good at sitting for long.

"I don't know, but he's had an opportunity to question Thor in depth. Maybe even to speak to Don. Anyway, I've got wardens I need to tell something before they go out in those woods. Their instinct, once they hear about this, is going to be looking for those guys and their dogs. I don't know if I want them all converging. We need to put our heads together."

Then, feeling her level of tension ratchet until her skin tightened, she asked, "What kind of cockamamie plan did the WIU have? How was this supposed to *really* work? You're one man. Why would anybody be nervous about what you're doing? I don't like this."

"Neither do I," he answered. "Not now." He shook his head a bit, then started pacing. "I don't know how much of this I've shared with you and how much I simply thought about, but I've been growing more and more troubled by this whole thing."

"Why?" She folded her arms and waited, feeling her heart accelerate a bit, her stomach flutter uneasily. If he was questioning it...

"Look, I was a grunt. I didn't make overall plans, strategies, any of it. I was the guy they'd tell *take this hill*, *this group of caves*, *this town*. Just that simple. One objective, me and my men, and it was my job to know how to do those things. I never had the big picture. I had my piece of it. They said do it and I did it. So when WIU said do it, I came without question to do exactly that. Impersonate an illegal outfitter, and wait for one of the bad guys to apply pressure. Get us a name."

He looked at her, but she had nothing to say. The only new information was what he had told her about himself.

"Anyway," he went on, "it was never my job to evaluate what I'd been told to do. It was my job to do it. I took this the same way. Go there, do this, wait for that. It seemed pretty straightforward, and my skill is adapting to the unexpected. Seemed okay."

"But now it doesn't?"

"Not since I found out I had an outfitter's application on file." He stopped pacing and put his hands on his narrow hips. "Something's wrong with that, Desi."

"I gathered." She sighed, folding her arms and leaning back against the counter. "It doesn't make sense, you're right. Those are public records. If anything was guaranteed to keep these illegal outfitters away, it would be your application license."

"That's how it struck me. Now the question is why in the hell would they want to do that?"

Her stomach began to sink. "You think somebody at WIU is taking you out of the picture."

"Or somebody with the pull. I've started to wonder if I wasn't sent here to be sidelined. But that couldn't be, not if they're shooting hunters they happen across."

She shook her head sharply. "We don't know that yet. And what purpose could it serve them to do that anyway?"

"You wouldn't think it would, would you. But...what if I'd been out there hunting today?"

"Then they made a bad mistake, because you were with me." Then his words hit her. She drew a sharp breath, felt her heart slam and her knees weaken a bit. "You think they might have been trying to frame you?"

"I don't know!" His voice rose slightly in frustration, and she watched as he reined himself in. "The point is, I'm beginning to feel as if I were sent here with blinders on. Either that or this is the lousiest operation ever."

"Might be both," she said slowly. Then she managed a small mirthless laugh. "You haven't been with the department long, Kel, but I can promise you, investigations like this can take years. I wouldn't be surprised if you had to hang out here for a couple of years if they don't get a break some other way. I remember one investigation like this that went on for three years and involved a dozen states. But right now, we don't even have one name, one lead to pursue."

"That's what I heard, anyway." He ran his fingers through his short hair. "Okay, maybe I'm making a mountain out of a molehill. But something stinks like three-day-old fish."

Desi eased onto a stool, feeling all her hard-won and well-practiced cool beginning to slip out of her grasp.

Emotions could be weakening. Anger was good, but she wasn't angry right now. Now she was worried sick and she didn't like it.

Looking at Kel, she wondered how she had come to care so much about what happened to him. Regardless of how she'd gotten here, she cared. The idea that he was being used like some puppet, or worse being set up...

She stopped her thoughts sharply. Now was not the time. "When Gage gets here, let's talk about this. He's done enough undercover work in his life to know if this is reasonable or unreasonable."

Having encountered Gage's capacity for coffee any time of day or night, she busied herself making a fresh pot.

She liked it here in Conard County. It had been a long time since she hadn't felt a bit rootless, but it struck her now that she was beginning to feel rooted here. Stupid thing to let herself feel when she could be reassigned at any time. Not that that was common. Many of her fellow wardens were working areas where they'd grown up and had friends and family.

She sighed as she started the pot brewing and realized Kel had joined her in the kitchenette. She turned a little and was startled when he placed his hand on her shoulder.

"I refuse to drag you into whatever this is."

His touch was welcome but his words were not. "I can take care of myself. Besides, I got into it, whatever it is, when I started raising the roof over increased trophy hunting. I was the one setting off flares. I know other wardens were concerned, but I made the most noise. Mainly because we have some of the largest herds of big game in the state. Plenty of trophies up there in the mountains. We're right on a major migratory route."

"True," he agreed.

"Which makes this a great place to hunt if you don't care about permits and all you want is a big trophy for your wall. I need more wardens." She snorted quietly. "And good luck with that. We're already spread pretty thin everywhere."

Her moment of weakness had passed. It was okay to be concerned about Kel, but not okay to feel it that deeply. In fact, given his background, he was probably the last man on earth who needed someone to worry about him.

Gage arrived a short time later. He'd ditched his uniform in favor of black jeans and a black long-sleeved shirt, although his jacket clearly bore the sheriff's emblem.

"So what's up, girls and boys," he asked as Desi brought him coffee. He took the easy chair, grimacing as he folded into it, and Desi and Kel sat on either end of the couch.

"I want to know what you learned today," Desi said bluntly. "You know what Kel's doing here, right?"

"Basically."

"Well, something stinks. Were you able to talk to Don? The guy who was shot?"

"Not yet. But we spent a lot of time with Thor Edvaldson." He shook his head a little. "Poor guy seems touchy about his name. I'd like to look inside the heads of his parents. Anyway, he did his best to give us a description of what he saw, but I don't think he was especially focused on the riders. More on the dogs. Seems he has a mild fear of them."

Then he turned his attention to Kel. "So they sent you out here undercover, your butt essentially hanging in the breeze, thinking maybe someone would tell you stop horning in?"

"Or something," Kel agreed. "Right now that's feeling like not much of a plan."

"It certainly isn't. When I went undercover I at least had targets. People we wanted to know more about or catch red-handed. This is…" Gage just shook his head. "So nobody has the least idea who these guys are? *Nothing?* From where I'm sitting that seems strange. How can they be so invisible? How is it that nobody in Game and Fish has a clue? They must have some ideas."

"None that were shared with me," Kel said. "I was told that they couldn't get a handle on anyone. That whoever was part of this ring had managed to get to the point where they didn't have to advertise but relied solely on word-of-mouth."

"Like drug pushers," Gage mused. "Okay, so somebody either needs to be invited to join the group, or to be pushed out by the group. Well, that's possible. Tricky situation, but possible. I assume you're pretty much ready to handle anything that might arise."

"It used to be my job, although the situation this time didn't seem as deadly."

"Didn't," Gage repeated. "Yeah. Today…" He trailed off. "I talked with Edvaldson quite a bit. Even after he let go of the shock, he didn't have much to say. Two men, six horses, four of which seemed to be pack horses carrying a lot, and a whole lot of dogs. He couldn't even tell me how many dogs. They scared him. So a whole lot could be three or four, or a dozen. I haven't been able to talk to Don, yet, but with any luck I might be able to ask him a bit tomorrow."

"Did you find anything?" Desi asked, even though her hopes weren't high.

"Actually yes. Kel was right about the shooter's line of sight. We found a bullet casing, thanks to the K9. Just one. Thor told me how he was positioned behind Don, and we sketched it out. Either the shooter thought he could take them both at the same time, or he didn't care as long as he got Don. Regardless, a .338 magnum shell is a pretty big round for hunting."

Kel stiffened. Desi whipped her head around to look at him. ".338 cal?" she repeated. "Definitely for big game."

"Yeah," agreed Kel. "And overkill for Don. He's lucky he survived."

Desi rose from the couch and went to get the coffeepot. She desperately needed to move. "So the .338 magnum suggests big game. But why in the hell shoot Don? Chances are, he'd have never mentioned those guys once he got his own moose."

"Maybe they didn't want him in the area?" Kel suggested.

"Or maybe they didn't plan on hell descending," Desi replied. "Like we talked about, in three or four days there wouldn't have been enough left out there to really know what happened. If he'd gotten both men."

Gage spoke again. "From what we know of where the two men were standing, that was probably his intent."

Desi nodded. "And Thor said he dropped instantly. Training. So maybe the shooter thought he got both of them. Regardless, he wasn't going to go back to be sure. His targets were armed, too."

"Maybe he didn't care if he got both of them," Kel said slowly. "Maybe it was misdirection."

Gage said nothing. Desi stared at Kel. "How so?"

"I'm not sure. But we're all talking about a shooter in the woods, not about trophy hunters. We're concerned about an attempted murder, not whether a big game animal gets taken. Or maybe it was a warning. Anyway, you were talking earlier about needing to make sure your wardens didn't all converge and possibly walk into something. That you're going to talk to them in the morning."

"That's a wise idea," said Gage. "This is a police job now, this shooting part of it. Yes we need the help of the wardens. Who knows the woods best? But Kel has a point. We're going to act differently now. All of us. And if the shooter had any point at all in attacking those guys, maybe that was it. Desi, how about I bring some of my people out here in the morning to meet with your people? Maybe we can work something out. It's always better to have more minds to look at something. Is that okay with you?"

"Of course it's okay," she said. "I want all the help I can get." But then she looked at Kel again. "What are we going to do with you? You're supposed to be undercover. If you're at this meeting tomorrow..." She hesitated. "I don't like this whole damn affair. Bad enough having dead animals."

"You two work Kel's part out together. I just want to catch me a bad guy." Rising, Gage said good-night and headed for the door, looking back just long enough to say, "Eight in the morning?"

"Make it nine. I've got to gather my people and some of them will have a bit of a drive."

"Nine it is."

He closed the door behind him and the silence suddenly seemed thick. Without a word, Desi picked up her radio and called her wardens, telling them there was a meeting at nine at the station. Everyone promised to be there.

Then she was alone with Kel, looking at a man who'd frankly said at one point that he'd been sent out here to be a goat. Problem was, that could be a fatal role.

The other problem was, neither of them was sure exactly how he was being used.

She felt sickened.

Chapter 11

While no inclement weather was in the forecast, the wind started blowing fiercely around ten that night. Desi listened to the forlorn keening, and for the first time in her life truly noticed how lonely it sounded.

She briefly gave some thought to going to Mahoney's Bar in town and eating some kind of appetizer just to listen to the sound of voices in the background and the music of the jukebox that Mahoney somehow miraculously kept working and serving up old tunes.

But there was Kel, too. Shadows seemed to be passing across his face, as if he were trying to avoid some unpleasant place inside himself, a place that might have been resurrected by the day's events.

Maybe he needed a break, too. "Let's go to town," she said.

He tilted his head. He was still sitting on the couch and looked up at her. "What do you want to do?"

"Hit Mahoney's Bar. Listen to the gossip or not. I just want to be in a crowd. I guess you wouldn't like that from what you've said."

He stood. "Let's go. Sitting around here thinking about something we know almost nothing about isn't doing me any favors. As long as you understand I might get an overwhelming urge to walk out, depending."

"Then we'll walk. I don't necessarily want to stay until closing. I just need to get out of here for a while and stop listening to the wind. God, it sounds mournful, like a funeral for all the world."

One corner of his mouth managed a small tick upward. "Good description. It isn't taking me any place I want to go."

Outside the wind felt even stronger. Tumbleweeds blew down the middle of the road and in the fields beyond. The moon had grown brighter, well on its way to full, occasionally occluded by a scudding cloud. Leafless fingers of some nearby trees did a skeletal dance, silvered by the moon, occasionally cracking under the stress.

"This feels like a good setting for a horror movie," Kel remarked.

Desi laughed. "It's beautiful, though. It reminds me of that line from 'The Highwayman.' 'The moon was a ghostly galleon tossed upon cloudy seas...' It does feel as if Halloween is near."

"I thought it was."

She laughed again as they climbed into her truck and drove the mile to town. They had to park a way down the street, though. Even on a weeknight Mahoney's was evidently hopping.

Inside warmth and the buzz of voices, along with raucous laughter, greeted them. Every booth and table was full, but a man at the bar, spying them, slid over one stool making room for both of them.

"Hey, Desi," said Matt Jackson as she slid onto the stool he'd just vacated. "How's it going? And who's your new friend?" Matt was a man of about Desi's age who spent his summers working construction and remodeling jobs wherever he could find them. Most of the summer he was out of town, but come winter he was always back and seemed to need only odd jobs. A smiling face, dark hair and eyes that were an unusual aquamarine.

"Hey, Matt," she answered. "This is Kel Westin. He's in town to set up an outfitter's business."

Matt leaned forward to see past Desi to Kel. "Howdy. It's odd now that I think of it, but I don't believe we've had an outfitter around here before. You going to be guiding?"

"That's the idea," Kel answered easily. "I spent most of the summer scouting in the mountains."

Matt nodded. "A lot of people do that. But you won't be guiding people from around here."

Kel chuckled. "No, the local hunters don't need me."

Matt laughed. Jim Mahoney, tending bar, came over for their orders. Kel looked at Desi. "You want me to be the designated driver?"

She shook her head. "I don't even have a beer this time of year. Never know when the phone will ring."

So Kel ordered himself an ale and she asked for a mocha coffee.

"Terrible thing today," Matt continued. "I can't believe Don Greaves was shot. Is he going to be okay?"

"I guess we'll all know more in the morning."

"When I was a kid, he and his father used to bring

over some venison steaks for us to enjoy. My dad never cottoned to hunting, but he never turned down a steak either."

It was Desi's turn to laugh. "I don't know many who would."

"You ever go hunting, Desi?" Matt asked.

"Never have the time."

"But if you did?"

She tilted her head, thinking about it. "You know, most of the wardens I know go hunting. But somehow..." She shrugged. "I spend so much time protecting those animals, I don't think I could bring myself to eat one."

That caused Matt a thigh-slapping laugh, and moments later some other men gathered around, beer mugs in hand. They all wanted to talk about the shooting that day, and all had very strong opinions about careless hunters. Kel twisted a little on his stool and just listened, nodding occasionally.

But soon talk turned to poaching. Desi knew she'd been making a lot of noise about it, but that was within the wardens' service. She hadn't realized how aware of it the locals were. Sure, they came to her when they suspected wrongdoing, but that didn't mean they had any idea of how big the problem was growing. Apparently, she was wrong.

Lefty Anderson, one of the men gathered round, leaned in. "We was talking before you got here, Desi. You know anything about a camp on the north side of Thunder Mountain?"

Her heart quickened. She glanced at Kel and saw his gaze had sharpened. "A camp?" she repeated.

"I ain't talking about a pup tent," Lefty said, keeping his voice low. Several of the other men nodded. "Showed up about a week ago, figured it'd be gone after a few days, but it's still there, just below the tree line. Bighorn territory. Now, I grant you, it ain't the kind of camp you see in them shows about safaris in Africa, but it ain't three men and a gun, if you get me."

Desi nodded slowly. "I get you. Think I should check it out?"

"Maybe so." Lefty changed the topic, turning his attention on Kel. "So you going to help them out-of-staters catch our game?"

Kel smiled faintly. "That's usually who will hire me, yes."

"Thought so." Then he swerved the subject again. "My granddaddy use to tell me 'bout the old days, when we didn't need no licenses to hunt."

Desi pursed her mouth. "What else did he tell you?"

Lefty laughed. "How we about lost all the fish and game. *His* granddaddy told stories about no fish in the rivers. And when my granddaddy was a boy, finding deer wasn't near so easy. So I get the point of licenses. Just wish we didn't have to share some of the ones for big game with outsiders."

"They're a comparatively small number and they pay higher fees," Desi explained. "Much higher. All that money is used to support our efforts to increase the herds and for the fish farms."

"I know."

Then another man spoke, one Desi didn't recognize. She was still learning the people in this area.

"Thing is," the new voice said, "those high fees are the reason we got illegal outfitters."

"I wouldn't be so sure of that," Matt argued. "These guys who want these fancy outfitters? They'd still want them even if we charged the same fees. They don't want to do the hard work we all do around here, scoping out the best places to hunt, finding buddies to help us carry our kill. They want to come in here, take a comfortable horse ride, sit in a comfortable camp, and have plenty of help for all the rest of it."

"Lazy hunters," said someone else.

Then a bunch of them looked at Kel. "You doing the five-star thing?"

Kel shook his head. "I'm just getting started. Anybody I guide is going to hunt pretty much the way you do."

Well, thought Desi as the crowd dissipated, that had seemed to satisfy at least some of them.

Except for the guy who had said the high licenses fees were the reason for illegal outfitters. Looking over Kel's shoulder as she started drinking a second coffee, she saw the guy looking at him. She couldn't imagine why he was interested but he was the one who'd brought up the illicit operations. Most people didn't think about them unless they made the news being arrested.

Odd. But then she shrugged it off. She'd heard a lot of opinions in her life, and a lot of people had said odd things. Matt announced he was headed for the restroom and departed.

As Desi faced the bar and stared down at her cup, she kept her voice low and said, "I'm going to need Lefty to tell me where that camp is. The north side of Thunder Mountain is a huge area, but it *does* sound like something I need to check out."

"I agree. It's not impossible, but it seems like a bad time of year to be camping for fun and pleasure. Something about hunting season."

She laughed, and glanced at him. He was smiling, and

strangely enough that made her feel happy. "I'm going to try to have a word with Lefty, see if he can give me a better location."

He surprised her by reaching over to cover her hand with his. "Be careful how you do it. Not every vibe in this bar is friendly."

Her eyes widened. "You feel that?"

"I never ignore it when I do."

She looked down at her cup and saucer. "Then maybe I should just ask for a flyover, checking for heat signatures. A camp ought to stand out easily, compared to the animals and small groups of hunters."

"Maybe."

She eased her hand from beneath his. "We need to go."

He nodded but before she could start to slide off her stool, Lefty slipped in beside her, between her and Matt's stools. "Hey," he said, and ordered a longneck. As he waited he pushed a small paper coaster to her with an almost invisible flicking movement of one finger. She covered it casually with her hand.

"Lefty?" she said.

"I've grown up with most of these people," he said quietly smiling like they were having a casual conversation. "Doesn't mean I trust them all. My number's on there if you want to call me."

"Thanks."

He grabbed his beer, saluted her with the bottle and returned to his corner of the bar.

"Ready?" Kel asked.

Desi closed her hand around the small piece of paper, crumpling it in her palm. "As ever. Early meeting."

She and Kel were just walking out when Matt returned. "Already?" he said.

Desi smiled. "I got work in the morning, Matt."

"So do I. I'll stumble through it." Then he laughed and mounted his stool again as they walked out.

Chapter 12

"I guess Lefty was getting some bad vibes, too," Desi remarked as they drove back to the station.

"So it would seem. What did he give you?"

"I'll look when we get back. I wouldn't think he'd have been so covert about giving me his phone number."

Kel surprised her with a laugh. "Covert. That's the last thing I expected to see in that bar."

She had to laugh, too. "I'm not used to a lot of cloak-and-dagger."

"How soon do you think we can get a plane up there to look?"

"I don't know. Considering that the camp was mentioned in front of a lot of people, it might move quickly... if your vibes were any indication."

"Like you said, Lefty seemed to have them, too. I'd like to know why."

She wheeled into the parking lot and brought the vehicle to a halt. She sat for a minute, drumming her fingers on the steering wheel before she finally switched off the ignition and released her seat belt. "Let's go inside, Kel."

The wind hadn't died any and was batting the truck hard enough to make it rock just a little. Hard enough that when she climbed out she had to lean to keep her footing. The night was no less beautiful, but she decided that mostly clear sky or not, it'd be wise to check the weather forecast tonight rather than wait for morning.

Upstairs she pulled the coaster out of her pocket and unfolded it on the bar. Kel leaned in to look over her shoulder. "Just a phone number," he said after a moment. "That's odd. I expected something else."

"Me, too," she agreed. Man, he was close, and he was making her thoughts scatter like leaves in the wind out there. She turned the paper over and saw what looked like coordinates. "Now, that could be useful."

"GPS," he remarked. "It can either make life easier or make it a hell of a lot harder."

"Yeah." At least he moved away to toss his jacket over the back of a chair, giving her room to breathe. His closeness had made her chest tighten with a miserable combination of fear and hope. She wanted him, but she was terrified of it.

Leaning over, she picked up the landline phone and punched in Lefty's number. To her relief, he was out of the bar.

"Lefty, it's Desi Jenks. Thanks for the coordinates. They're for this camp you saw, right?"

"Close to it," he answered. "You know the GPS isn't perfect up there. And they could have already moved. Anyway, as soon as I saw them I didn't feel right about it. Me and my buddies just avoided it. But it was right below the tree line, fairly good concealment from above. Camouflaged tents, maybe three horses and two dogs. We moved the other way and ran into a couple of tree stands."

"Tree stands?"

"I don't know many guys who'd haul them up there," Lefty said. "Especially since game is moving downslope right now."

Desi hesitated. "So what were you doing up there?" she asked.

Lefty laughed. "I go up there and hunt walking downhill. Works for me and besides I like the hiking part of hunting. Always have. But tree stands up there? You'd need someone to drive game toward you. Ballard and I thought they must be city slickers. Then I remembered that bighorn over at Madison's place. Now, what the hell was one of them doing down so low?"

Lefty let the question hang and Desi didn't discuss her speculations with him. "Thanks, Lefty. I'll get someone to look into it."

Before she hung up though, Lefty added something else.

"Desi? There was a stranger in the bar tonight. We get 'em from time to time, but this one…he kept watching your friend. Thought you should know."

"Thanks, Lefty." She bade him good-night. She looked at Kel. "Lefty says a stranger was watching you."

To her surprise, Kel smiled. "Then maybe this plan isn't a complete bust."

She wished she felt as sanguine about it. Of course, Lefty could be wrong.

Then, opening her laptop, she called up the weather. "Oh, heck," she said.

"What?"

"Snow in the higher elevations overnight. That's not gonna help an infrared scan from a plane. If the camp has moved, we might not find it without one, even with Lefty's coordinates. Anyway, the storm's no help."

"Not likely," he agreed. "One thing for sure, if they haven't moved yet, they're not moving tonight or tomorrow, so we can relax."

And then he astonished her by moving in and taking her hand. "Sit with me, Desi? Because for some reason this feels like an awfully lonely night."

She felt startled, but not unpleasantly so. Part of her wanted to run before anything bad could happen, but an even stronger urge overwhelmed fear. She wanted to know if sex could be good. All her friends thought so, and more times than she could count, she'd judged herself to be permanently damaged goods because of Joe.

"I run," she whispered. "I always run away."

"I'm not surprised." His tone had grown amazingly gentle. "I'm not asking for anything you don't feel comfortable with. I just want to feel close to someone right now."

She struggled to meet his gaze, afraid of what she might see there. Something critical? A heat she wasn't ready for? "You feel lonely?"

"Yeah." He let the word drop into the room. "I rarely felt lonely before. Always surrounded by the people I worked with. Always busy, never a moment… But I feel lonesome tonight."

That reached her in ways no sexy words ever could have. She understood loneliness. She surrounded herself with walls of it on purpose. Nobody got too close, not even people she called friends. Always a distance, always feeling like an actor in her own life...except when it came to her job. She'd given her heart completely to her work, and she told herself that was all she needed.

But sometimes... She let Kel take her hand and lead her to the couch.

"Just sit with me," he said. "We can talk. I'd like to hug you, but that's not required. It's up to you."

She felt a flutter of nervousness, but it struck her suddenly that this man had somehow pierced her defenses. Yes, she might still run, she might go crazy on him and act like he was Joe, but he made her want to take that risk.

She hesitated a bit, glancing back at the phone, knowing it was just an excuse. It was late and there wasn't another blessed thing she could do tonight.

Except test her own boundaries.

When Desi sat beside him on the couch, Kel could feel the tension in her. She was practically humming with it. He *was* lonely, not a usual state of affairs for him. He wondered if the wind was getting to him, although he'd sat out many stiff winds in his life, and listened to the banshee wails of it. Or maybe going to the bar and feeling like a total outsider. Not that folks had been unfriendly, but it was clear they cared about Desi, they knew her, they felt obliged to keep her informed. Good job as a warden. Good job as a human being.

He'd known that once. His unit had all been his best friends. His brothers and sisters. He supposed it wasn't strange that sooner or later he would start missing that camaraderie. But it made him feel even more of an outsider now that he was unsure why his bosses had put him out here.

Go there, do this was no longer sufficient. He was learning to need reasons, to want the bigger picture.

There was Desi, too. She had become a constant ache somewhere inside him. He wanted her, but it was more than that. He wanted to be friends, real friends, the kind of friendship welded in fire. Well, that might happen soon enough if that camp on Thunder Mountain turned out to be important.

Then she spoke, and he was disappointed that she was still thinking about the job.

"I don't know how soon I can get an overflight of that side of the mountain. And with the snow…"

"So we go up there, you and me. We get eyes on it if we can and watch to see what they're doing."

"Tomorrow?"

"Tomorrow," he agreed.

"Thanks. I'd rather not ask one of my wardens at the meeting in the morning."

He turned his head. "Why?"

"Because I don't want them in danger unless I can't avoid it. They all have people who care about them."

It was true, and reminded him yet again of the gulf between him and the rest of the world. "I think you have lots of people who care about you."

"Maybe." Then she shocked the breath out of him. "Do you want me? Sexually, I mean?"

He'd been propositioned before, but never quite so baldly. Desi apparently didn't know how to flirt, and there was nothing wrong with that, but he was touched by sorrow over how much she had missed because of one criminal man. "Of course I do. Can't you tell?" Stupid question, one which he wished he could yank back out of the air.

"I'm not sure. How can I be sure? I thought, maybe... but I read a guy wrong once."

Ah. He raised his arm, wrapping it around her shoulders and drawing her close to his side. She didn't resist, for which he was grateful. "I've been trying not to let it show. I didn't want to frighten you. Funny thing is, I learned that no means no when I was two years old."

"I've got a lot of *no* signs, don't I?" She almost sighed the words, then let her head fall against his shoulder.

"Perfectly understandable."

"Is it? Maybe I need to get over the past. I usually keep people at a safe emotional distance. Nobody gets really close. But you did, and I don't even know how. You affect my feelings. I care. So..."

"So? What *so*? Caring doesn't have to lead to sex. Would I like to make love to you? Most certainly. Do I need to in order to remain your friend? Most certainly not. I like you, Desi. I really do. I want to get to know you better. I admire the way you do your job. You have a great many good qualities. I've known you a short time, yet I have no doubt you'd have my back if I needed it. Or the back of anyone you know. I prize that. What more do I need from you? Not one damn thing."

"Oh, Kel," she said quietly. "You're so nice."

"No, I'm just honest. I'm not shining you on. I believe in honesty. Which is part of what is killing me about this assignment. But at least I could be honest with you and the sheriff. Still..."

"That's different."

"Is it?" He gave a short laugh. "I once read that the difference between a dope dealer and a DEA agent is that the agent lies. Now I'm wearing those shoes. I think the purpose is a good one. But I don't like lying."

"I'm sure you don't. I know I wouldn't."

But he knew he needed to turn this conversation around. She'd made herself so vulnerable by asking him if he wanted her. He'd answered, but he suspected not in a way that would really convince her. If she wanted to be convinced, and he wasn't sure about that either.

He tightened his arm around her shoulders until she raised her face, then cupped her cheek with his hand. Her eyes drifted closed. Saying not a word, he ran his thumb over her sweet soft skin, tracing her cheekbone, the shell of her ear...oh, that made a shiver run through her. He felt himself swell a bit in response.

"Kel?" she whispered.

"Yeah?"

"I want to get over this hang-up. Desperately. But what if I freak on you?"

"Then we'll deal with it. But somehow, I don't think you will."

Her eyes opened to half-mast. "How can you know?"

"Because we'll go slow and you can stop me at any point where you get uneasy. I promise."

The words were sweet to Desi's ears. She could stop him if she got frightened. He promised. Even from their short acquaintance, she believed this man did not make promises lightly. But she didn't know what to say, where to begin. She waited, poised on the cusp of trepidation and longing. Expectation and anxiety. Her whole body seemed to be quivering in anticipation, begging him to touch her, begging herself to let this continue.

He leaned in and kissed her. A butterfly kiss, the merest brush of lips on hers. Soft and exquisite and it might as well have been a match. Yearning speared hotly along her nerve endings. Hardly aware of it, she twisted toward him, raising her hands to his powerful shoulders.

But he just kept on kissing her lightly, as if he were in no rush, as if this gentle touch were all he wanted. It was certainly stoking the heat inside her.

His tongue ran over her lips. She gasped as a new trickle of heat ran through her, and when she gasped his tongue took the invitation and found hers.

Nothing forceful, nothing demanding, an almost playful caress of his tongue against hers. Astonished with delight, she tried to reciprocate, doing as he did, and felt a surge of triumph when he moaned quietly. But the triumph quickly gave way to confidence as she realized she could do this. She wasn't afraid, he wasn't scaring her and this was nothing like Joe.

Eagerness built in her like a growing storm. He forced nothing on her. Even his embrace was so gentle she knew she could escape if she wanted to. He made her feel safe.

And in feeling safe, she could let herself soar. Joy and passion, so long forgotten, lifted her on its incredible wings.

Kel sensed the change in her, felt her relax into his embrace, loved it when she started returning his kiss. Life had taught him a great deal of self-control, and he exerted it now even though this woman threatened to topple it completely with her tentative responses, with her welcome. Her need, he realized, was at least as large as his own, but she needed more than great lovemaking. She needed balm for her soul.

Few moments in his life had been imbued with such

importance as this one. Matters of life and death, yes, but this was different, a chance to help someone heal. Hushed awe filled him, even as desire's fire tried to take over.

"You're sweet," he murmured, trying to stay centered on her and her needs. To hell with his own. He knew what a gift she was giving him. How much trust she was offering. Continuing to caress her cheek with his thumb, he kissed her again, a gentle exploration of the warm cavern of her mouth. Then he trailed his lips to the side, finding the shell of her ear with his tongue. With each touch, with each breath he exhaled, she shivered again.

Her hands slipped from his shoulders to his back, as if she were trying to draw him closer. He refused to let her. Too soon. He wanted her to be so far into the experience that she forgot every last smidgeon of fear. He wanted her welcome to be unequivocal.

His traced a path to her neck with his tongue and her fingers gripped his back almost painfully. Murmurs escaped her, soft ones. Delighted ones. No protest.

He knew that for all intents and purposes he was making love to a virgin. Her rape didn't count as a sexual experience, but rather one of violence and abuse. This time had to be different. All he wanted was for her to move forward without fearing all men's sexuality. If he could manage that...

But she distracted him from the thoughts he was trying to hang on to in order to keep himself under control. His brain didn't want to think logically about anything, not when she pulled at his sweatshirt as if she wanted it gone.

He was happy to oblige, to become her plaything if it helped her or even just because that was what she wanted right now.

He helped her pull the shirt over his head, then drew her in for another kiss as her hands began to wander over his bare flesh. Need began to consume him. His loins ached. Desire pounded in his blood, nearly deafening him.

Control, he reminded himself, fearing he was losing the battle.

Her hands, at first tentative, grew bolder when she realized he wasn't pulling away, that he clearly enjoyed her touches. He hated the moment when she started to move back, sure he had somehow put her off, or that her fears were taking charge, but then her hands began to caress his chest. They wandered over him curiously, eagerly, and discovered how sensitive his nipples were.

"Like mine," she breathed.

If he hadn't been so gripped by pounding need, he might have laughed as she turned into an imp, teasing him until he could have lost his mind. When he gave in and shuddered with pleasure, she sighed and teased him more.

She liked having power over him, and he was only too willing to grant it. In conquering her past, she was quickly turning into an active lover and he adored it.

But soon having his shirt off wasn't enough. She started to tug at her own and he caught her hands. With huge effort, pushing back his hunger, he asked huskily, "Are you sure?"

Her eyes looked sleepy and her mouth, the mouth he had so gently plundered, curved into a faint smile. "Absolutely," she murmured. "Absolutely."

Desi wondered if ever in her life had she been as certain of what she wanted as now. The thought barely ruffled the surface of her excitement and longing for more. A gentle man, one who was giving her control, demanding not a thing from her. She wouldn't have believed a man like Kel could have existed. He looked so powerful, so in charge, yet had never tried to control her in the least way, not even at the outset. A man so comfortable in himself that he seemed to have nothing to prove.

A man who made her feel safe enough to take a risk. As he helped her pull off her sweater and the turtleneck beneath it, she shivered in anticipation. She hovered on the cusp of discovery, at a place far beyond any she had ever visited before. Joe had terrified her and hurt her. This man was helping her make the climb in her own way, in her own time.

A sense of amazing freedom filled her even as passion carried her ever deeper into its grip. Her whole body seemed alight with need, the throbbing at her center at once delightful and consuming. She felt an emptiness there, a need for something to answer that ache.

But Kel didn't give it to her. Not just then. He reached for the clasp of her bra, asking, "Okay?"

"Yes." The word came out tight as excitement hammered her even more strongly. When she felt the clasp release and her breasts spill free, she gasped, acutely aware of the air touching her skin, of a man's gaze, then his hands, then his mouth.

He leaned in and kissed her again, but as he did so he cupped her breasts, squeezing just a little, running his thumbs over her hardening nipples, a sensation so powerful that a moan escaped her. As if wires reached from her nipples to her core, everything inside her tightened then began to throb hungrily in time with the light brushes of his thumb. Instinctively, her tongue reacted with the same rhythm, echoing her need.

Her entire body demanded satisfaction, her thoughts flew away and she became mindless with hunger. Then, he startled her. He leaned back on the couch and drew her over him, so that she looked down at him.

"Your way," he said, a raspy murmur.

Her way? She didn't have a way. She'd never...but the instant of fear flew away as he lifted one of her breasts until he could pull her nipple into his mouth. The strong sucking ignited her. Every concern or hesitation vanished.

He was hers, for tonight anyway. Here and now, he had given himself to her.

Power filled her. Doubts fled. She might not know much, but she grasped what she needed.

Rearing up, she reached for his belt. A sound escaped him and soon he was helping her. With his thumbs and a wiggle he pushed his clothes below his hips. Letting her see him, revealing how much he wanted her.

No secrets. Curious, driven by feelings she barely understood, she closed her hand around his erection and felt his entire body jerk. When she started to withdraw her hand, afraid she had hurt him, he closed his own around it, holding her to himself. Then, carefully, he showed her how to stroke him.

The moans that escaped him then delighted her, but deepened her need to feel the same way. He felt so smooth, so strong...

Unable to stand another minute, she wiggled off him and stripped away the last of her clothes. As she did so, he pulled a condom from the pants that still tangled his legs and rolled it on. She was past noticing, past feeling the chilliness of the air, and she had only a vague understanding of what she needed but when he tugged her hand and drew her over him, he showed her.

He guided her until she straddled him, then drew her down until his erection pierced her. The feeling was so exquisite she lost her breath. The emptiness was gone, in its place came instincts as old as time.

"Ride me," he said gruffly. Gripping her hips, he showed her, and soon her body took over, driving her toward the answer she wanted beyond everything now.

She rode him. Higher and higher she rose, the pounding ache in her loins driving her like a whip, harder and harder and...

She shattered into a million flaming pieces, the world disappearing in a supernova of suns, only dimly aware that Kel thrust one last time. Her cry joined his moan, then she seemed to faint.

When she returned, once again aware of something besides her own pleasure, her insides still warm, clenching in a slower rhythm, she was aware of Kel beneath her. He moved her a little, withdrawing himself from her, and as she felt him slip out she wanted to stop him.

But she didn't have the energy to protest, and when his powerful arms surrounded her, holding her close, she never wanted to move again. The aftermath was almost as beautiful as the event itself.

Eons later, or perhaps only a few minutes, Kel stirred again. "I need to take care of business. Want a robe?"

She hated the idea of him letting go of her, leaving her for even a short time, but reality was returning and couldn't be denied. The sweat drying on her skin was chilling her. "Thanks," she said thickly. "Back of my bedroom door."

"I'll be right back," he promised, giving her a quick kiss as he sat up. With evident reluctance, he placed her on the couch beside him.

Now she was getting really cold, but he returned swiftly, giving her her robe before heading back to the bathroom. Standing, she pulled it on and for the first time realized he had left her with a pleasant ache between her legs.

She had made love with a man. All of a sudden it hit her, and she sat down as if her strings had been cut. She'd done it! She'd gotten past her fears, past Joe. Not only that, but it had been wonderful. Astonishment and exhilaration filled her. Her heart felt light enough to float.

When Kel returned a few minutes later, he wore only his jeans. Her eyes immediately latched on to the unfastened button. So sexy, she thought.

"It's late," he said. "Do you want some coffee anyway? Or something else?"

She glanced toward the digital clock on her microwave and was astonished to see it was after one. How had that happened? Hadn't they left Mahoney's shortly after eleven?

Meeting in the morning at nine. Her work mind popped up the alert as surely as a tickler on her computer. The thing was, she wanted to investigate Thunder Mountain, too, tomorrow.

Then she looked at Kel, felt everything inside her melt, and thought, what the hell. A man like this and a night like this were rarer than diamonds in her life.

"Coffee," she said, and smiled. "I'm not in any hurry to go to sleep."

His answering smile warmed her. "Me neither."

* * *

Randy sat alone in the camp on the side of Thunder Mountain, watching snowflakes begin to fall. The night sky had clouded over, and he had a well-shielded camp lantern lit. No fire, just cold fluorescent light.

The snow would help with concealment. Not that he cared at that moment. He'd been sent out here to prep for the next group of hunters, and to take out that new outfitter down below. The one whose license had been rejected but was still talking about taking some people out next week. People. Clients most likely. Why else go into outfitting except to make money? Randy had even managed to get a look at the guy at Mahoney's before racing back here. Target identified.

Now his bosses were furious with him for shooting that hunter. Sitting there in the cold, alone, he was equally furious at the bosses. The only thing he regretted was that both those men hadn't died. He'd recognized them. Sooner or later they might have remembered him.

He couldn't chance that. While his bosses remained safely ensconced on their large spreads or in their offices, he and other guides were the tip of their spear. They got paid well enough to lead these hunts, but they took a huge risk doing it.

The guides and their bosses, if caught, could face heavy fines and jail time. If one of their customers got charged with knowingly using an unlicensed outfitter, then the whole damn business would go up in smoke even if the members of the operation got away.

In short, one bit of finger-pointing at Randy could cost him everything, even if he never told them who he worked for.

Get rid of the competition in the form of that Westin

guy? Absolutely. No problem with that. But risk some-one identifying him, bringing the law's attention his way because he'd been leading horses and a pack of dogs up the mountain? Especially the dogs?

No. He might have to protect the operation, but he also had to cover his own butt. So he had. Or at least he'd tried to. He'd also been careful not to shoot at those guys for more than an hour after he had passed them. Even if they did remember him, there ought to be no connec-tion in anyone's mind.

Maybe.

He swore, not caring that he disturbed the night. Noth-ing right around here anyway that he was worried about. Anybody who happened across this camp would know that it was not on a migration path. That choice had been deliberate. The horses would get them to the good spots, well away from here.

All right, maybe shooting those guys had been a mis-take. But they weren't going to find any evidence against him unless someone identified him.

Now he wanted to know what was going on with that Westin guy. Come all the way to a place he didn't know to become a guide? And now, he was joined at the hip with the senior warden.

Westin was either very stupid or very smart. As far as Randy knew, the warden didn't like men. He figured her for liking women, but now this?

So maybe Westin had successfully dazzled her. He was new, no way to link him to any past poaching, and he probably seemed aboveboard. Honest enough to get himself in with her, anyway.

Women could be so stupid sometimes.

But having the two of them together would make his

job more difficult. He'd heard they'd teamed up when they'd responded to the shooting earlier that day. Was Westin riding shotgun with her? How the hell was Randy supposed to take him out and make it look like a hunting accident if that was the case?

This whole thing was screwed up. No reason to take the guy out. Just report him. Sure, maybe one time he could get away with convincing everyone that he hadn't been paid by these two clients. But what about the next one?

He sat up a little straighter as a thought occurred to him. What if Westin wasn't what he seemed? What if he was really looking for someone like Randy, so he could get to the whole ring?

Suddenly the picture seemed clear, his bosses didn't seem so stupid and he suspected they'd gotten intel from inside Game and Fish.

He tried to shake off the thought but couldn't. It helped him understand why they wanted Westin dead, not simply turned in. Why they'd even hinted he should take out Desi Jenks if he had a good opportunity.

Well, if that was what they wanted, he'd damn well give it to them. He didn't care if he had to take out that trouble-making warden. Randy liked his life just the way it was, and nobody was going to screw it up.

He hoped the hunter they were bringing up overnight would steer clear of everything except the game he wanted, because the hunter could face an accident, too.

Randy liked his life, all right, and he wasn't about to give it up either.

Chapter 13

Morning dawned gray, the wind still blowing hard enough to make the double-paned windows rattle. Yet it was a beautiful morning. Desi awoke surrounded by Kel's arms, by his heat and his strength, and she felt wonderful. She didn't want to move even a little bit, for fear of breaking the magic of the moment. She kept her eyes closed and relived the night before, all of it. Detail by detail, especially when they made love the second time and she hadn't feared giving him some control.

But finally she couldn't ignore the present any longer. She pried one eye open and peered at the clock. Seven fifteen. Time to rise and get ready for the meeting at nine with her fellow wardens and a couple of deputies. Time to leave magic behind and move back into harsh reality.

She sighed.

"Good morning," Kel rumbled in her ear. "Wonderful morning, in fact."

A smile creased her face and she twisted her head to see him. He pushed himself up on an elbow and sprinkled kisses on her face. "I'd eat you up right now, but I think that sigh meant you were thinking about business."

"Mostly I was thinking about you," she admitted, feeling not the least bit shy, "but there is that meeting here at nine. I've got to get ready, and have the coffee downstairs going by eight thirty because some of the guys will be early."

He smiled and gave her one more long, deep kiss. "Then let's get going."

There hadn't been much sleep last night, she thought as she rubbed her eyes. She'd gone on short sleep before when working a case, but she didn't like it. Slips of judgment were too easy to make.

Kel left the bed first, walking naked around the room without the least show of self-consciousness, to bring her her robe and slippers. "I'll go start breakfast."

Wrapped up against the chilly morning air, thinking about whether she should turn up the thermostat, instead of heading straight for the bathroom she went to look out the front window. It had snowed in the mountains last night, but not a light powdering. Solid white cloaked them.

Kel came to stand beside her. "Doesn't look like we're going up there today."

"Not likely," she agreed. "Probably just as well. Somehow I missed a lot of sleep last night, so I'd be accident-prone."

He laughed. "Go take your shower. I'll take care of everything else."

She half wished he'd follow her into the shower, but practicality reared its head. She'd scheduled a meeting. Her doing. She'd better be there.

The thought struck her as almost ridiculous. Never before had she wished she could avoid a meeting, nor had to scold herself to go. Happiness stayed with her, however, a precious flower that had blossomed inside her. She mostly enjoyed her life, but happiness like this? Very rare.

She was still smiling when she went out to breakfast wearing her flannel red shirt and jeans. Kel greeted her with a kiss and passed her a plate loaded with eggs, sausage and toast and a mug of coffee. "Eat up," he said. "Today could turn out to be long."

She looked at him and caught his wink. "Long in what sense?" she asked.

He laughed and joined her at the bar with his own plate. "I guess we'll see."

She ate, savoring the closeness she felt with Kel. Remembering how lovely it was to lie in his arms. Delighted that his size and strength no longer worried her even the least bit. She had broken the chains.

Kel spoke absently, reminiscing about a dog he'd had when he was still in school, and remarking that he'd like to have another one someday. "But dogs don't do well if they're left alone too long, so I'd need to be more settled."

"I always wanted a dog," Desi remarked. "A big one."

For some reason, that made him chuckle.

After breakfast, she glanced at her watch and said, "I need to get downstairs. Come when you're ready."

He hesitated. "Are you sure you want me to show up?"

"You were with me yesterday when we went to the shooting scene. If Jos knows it, the rest know it." She shrugged. "It doesn't matter. By now we're probably the subject of talk among any who care."

"I didn't mean to cause you problems, Desi."

She laughed. "I was the one who suggested you stay

here. From that instant, despite having a bunkhouse, the talk became inevitable. Don't worry about it. They won't give me a scarlet letter."

She tucked in the tails of her red shirt and pulled her jacket off the hook. Before darting out, she opened her laptop to the weather and looked at the forecast. "We should be able to go up the mountain tomorrow. No more snow and warmer temperatures today. By morning hiking up there shouldn't be too dangerous."

"Will we take any of your wardens with us?"

She shook her head slowly. "The whole purpose of today's meeting is to put them in the loop on the shooting and warn them to be extra careful. I definitely don't want them all working in the same small area. Leaves too much opportunity for other miscreants."

As she was about to open the door and step outside, Kel stopped her. "Desi? You gonna tell anyone about that camp up there?"

She turned, facing him squarely. "I don't believe so."

He raised both brows. "Why not? Yesterday you were talking about an overflight."

"I was. But you know, you're right. There's something fishy about the way you were sent out here and what you were supposed to do. Right now I don't feel inclined to tell anyone beyond these walls a darn thing. Not even about the possible camp."

Then, pulling up her hood against the chill, she left.

Kel didn't move for a few minutes, then slowly rose to begin cleaning up. So she'd come around to thinking there was something cockeyed about this, too.

For the very first time he cussed the military training which led him to take his orders without question. Different world, different customs, and he needed to wake his brain up, get it in gear the way he could when everything went to hell and *he* had to make up the game plan.

They'd sent him out here for a reason, but now he was wondering if it was just to get him out of the way. Why had someone submitted an application for him to get an outfitter's license? That didn't fit with the original idea of him drawing attention and learning something because the outfitter ring would get annoyed.

In fact none of it fit, and he was beginning to feel the fool. There was a story that made the rounds in the military, of a bunch of officer candidates being given a test. One of the questions was how to get a flagpole up in front of a building. Almost all the candidates went into great detail, even resorting to drawings in their directions.

They were all wrong. The proper answer was to give the order to your sergeant: "Go put up a flagpole."

Well, he'd been the sergeant. He took the orders without question, and only in the field when things started happening did he take control.

So here he was, realizing that probably the very first thing he should have done before coming out here was question his orders and get a decent explanation of what his superiors expected.

Now he was wondering what the hell they'd sent him here for, and if the rot they were trying to find might have entered the Wildlife Investigative Unit.

His suspicions were certainly amped by Desi's sudden announcement that she wasn't going to mention the camp on the mountain to anyone. Something had edged her into distrust, too.

He almost didn't want to go downstairs to the meeting. He needed to talk to Desi privately, and he didn't need a bunch of questions from her wardens. But maybe it would be more suspicious if he didn't show, when they were discussing the shooting yesterday.

Hell. Things were getting muddier by the minute. As he finished drying the dishes and putting the last of them away in her cupboard, he toyed with the idea of just setting out on his own for that campsite today, snow notwithstanding, while she had her meeting. He certainly had the training to be half a mountain goat, and the skills to protect himself from almost any threat. He could circle in surreptitiously and find out what was going on up there. Keep Desi out of harm's way.

The instant that crossed his mind, he knew he was heading for a different kind of hell. Desi wouldn't like that at all. What's more, she'd resent his male high-handedness.

And she'd have every right. She'd managed the dangers of her job without him before. And like most of the wardens she was in peak physical condition. So what argument could he offer, except that he had combat training? That probably wouldn't appease her. *She* was a law enforcement officer with a decade or more of experience.

Sighing, he dried his hands and gave up. Last night had been a wonderful experience, and if he were to be honest with himself, he didn't want to do a thing that might damage his blossoming relationship with Desi. Even if they never became more than friends, it was still a friendship to protect.

Grabbing his jacket, he headed downstairs. He'd heard the trucks pulling in, and when he arrived in the office down below, five men had gathered with Desi in the small conference room off to the side. They all looked up when he entered.

"I thought Kel should join us," Desi said from her seat at the table. "He was riding with me when we got the call from Jos, and he was the one who figured out the line of sight for the shooter. He's also a former Ranger, so he might have some insights we can use."

Nice introduction, Kel thought. He reached out to shake hands and was introduced to Fetcher, Lake, Willis, Rheingold and Logan, as well as Jos, whom he already knew. Then he took the remaining chair. The other men already had coffee in mugs that looked like they'd been used for years.

As if on cue, two sheriff's deputies arrived along with the man himself, Gage Dalton. More handshakes were exchanged, then Desi got right to the point.

"At this point," Desi said, "we can't take much action. I would agree with you all that a guy with a pack of dogs and a string of horses might be one of the poachers we're looking for. It's also possible he was the shooter. The sheriff's people are already looking into that angle."

She paused, the smiled faintly without humor. "I know we all feel the same about catching these poachers. I know we're all angry that a hunter was shot like that, deliberately. But we've got a whole lot of square miles to cover, and I need you guys out there and watchful. We can't get so focused on this incident that we leave the rest of our section open to poachers. We'd be failing our duty. So for now, at any rate, we're going to follow our standard procedures and let the sheriff do his part with regard to the shooting. If he needs our help, he'll let us know."

She looked around the table. "You are all the best wardens in Wyoming, as far as I'm concerned. I know you'll do your jobs. All I ask is that if you get wind of these criminals, call for backup before you act. Some of them aren't above killing humans."

Heads nodded around the table. Only one of the men, Fetcher, eyed Kel dubiously, and finally, when there was a silence, he spoke. "I hear you're going to be an outfitter, Kel."

"That's the plan."

"But you don't have a license yet."

Kel stiffened inwardly. He knew an inquisition when he heard it. "Not yet."

"So what's this I hear about you taking two guys out next week?"

"Friends," Kel answered. The law allowed him to guide two licensed hunters as long as he didn't accept any money for his service. Just leave it at that, Fetcher.

Fetcher looked at Desi. "You satisfied with that?"

"Yes," she answered. "If something changes, I'll know."

In his lap, Kel tried to prevent his hands from clenching. He didn't know which troubled him more, that Fetcher might interfere with the operation or that he was trying to work Desi into a bad position.

Oh, hell, who was he kidding? Paramount was that he didn't want Fetcher finding a way to damage Desi's career. Not that he could, really, because WIU had sent him and told him to get close to Desi. She was covered, and that was all he cared about. But Fetcher...the man troubled him. Did he resent Desi? Was he looking for some way to submarine her? Or did he have some other agenda?

One thing for sure: he no longer wondered about Desi's decision not to mention the campsite. They both felt something wasn't right about his assignment, and

Fetcher's questioning had put his teeth on edge, something that didn't happen often. Gut feeling. He trusted his gut feelings. Something was off.

He watched silently as new patrol routes were laid out by mutual agreement, routes that would insofar as possible keep two wardens close to each other.

"I spoke to the department this morning about all of this," Desi said as they got ready to separate. "Some biologists and others may be sent this way to pad our operations. I'll let you know when I get the word."

"We'll be okay, boss," said Lake. He patted his chest. "That's what the armor's for."

Everyone laughed, hands were shaken all around, then the room emptied. Only Gage remained to say briefly, "If you bring in more personnel, be sure to let me know."

Desi nodded. "Absolutely." Then she and Kel were alone again.

Kel waited to hear if Desi had any thoughts to share. She was rolling up a map, and gathering a couple of sheets of paper. At last she spoke. "You missed some of the meeting. And I'm sorry I didn't ask you for your thoughts on how to handle this."

"You didn't need me," he answered truthfully. "You did a great job from what I heard. What's your read on Fetcher?"

Her head snapped up from the items she was lifting from the table. "Fetcher? You mean because of his questions?"

"Yeah."

She turned and shoved the rolled map into a narrow cubby of the kind in which blueprints were often kept, also perfect for rolled maps. "I don't know," she answered honestly. "I didn't like it, but Fetcher's been a warden for a long time. A dedicated man."

"So you don't think he might be trying to make trouble for you?"

She turned. "For me?"

He didn't respond, just waited. He didn't want an automatic dismissal from her.

"I don't know," she said finally. "I wouldn't be surprised if some of the older agents resent that I became a senior warden so young, but no one's ever made an issue of it that I've heard about. Nobody's given me any trouble. As for Fetcher, he's just kind of gruff and blunt." She paused. "Did you get a different feeling?"

"You could say that. I wouldn't have asked otherwise. But I don't know the man the way you do."

She dropped back onto her chair, drummed her fingers a few times, then stared at him across the table. "If this setup gets any more troubling, I don't know what I'll do."

"Meaning?"

"You were sent out here to be a goat. I didn't like that to begin with, but the longer this has gone on the less I believe that's really what's going on. I mean, what kind of plan is that?"

"I wish I'd questioned it at the outset."

"I just assumed there were things you didn't tell me because I didn't need to know. But there weren't?"

He shook his head. "Nope. Makes me feel like a bit of a fool myself. But, as I keep reminding myself, I was trained to take my orders and deal with whatever exigencies arose. I didn't get detailed plans. I got an assignment. *Do this.* The details were mostly left to me. So it never occurred to me to question my orders. Just do it."

She sighed and closed her eyes briefly. "Don't feel

like a fool, Kel. I didn't question it either. I assumed everyone knew what they were doing. Now I'm wondering *what* they're doing."

"Same here. But we talked a bit about that, you and I. Something hinky here. That may have caused my reaction to Fetcher."

She leaned back and her chair creaked. "I'm getting more and more troubled. If they didn't expect you to draw attention and be able to give them a name to get started with, what the heck are you doing here?"

"If we could figure that out, we'd be getting somewhere. As for Fetcher…"

"As for Fetcher," she interrupted. "As for Fetcher, it's possible he checked you out and found out you don't have a license. Or it could be he heard your name before. We're not exactly the world's biggest organization. Maybe he's just trying to find out what's going on. The same as we are."

He'd have liked to believe that, but Fetcher had gotten under his skin and was already becoming an irritant. Like a warning. A lot of things had begun to act on him that way. He wondered if he just needed some sleep to clear his head because Fetcher really hadn't said all that much. Certainly not enough to accuse him of anything.

More than ever, he felt he needed to watch his back. And Desi's, too, because she'd certainly gotten tangled up with him.

"I'm getting the sense that we have things happening here on multiple levels," Desi said.

"How so?"

"Looking for the poachers is one. Not likely to happen swiftly, but still, we need to do it."

"And the other?"

"Something to do with you," she said giving him a straight look. "Either someone wanted you out of the way, or someone wanted you exposed. Got any ideas?"

He figured she was right to some extent. But there was another side to that coin. "Or maybe someone wants you exposed. I was thinking you had cover because I was told to fraternize with you, so nobody would suspect you of anything."

She nodded slowly, a frown tugging at the corners of her mouth. "But I'm hanging out with an unlicensed outfitter. If no one backs you up..." She drew her finger descriptively across her throat.

Kel didn't like the anger simmering inside him. He forced himself to speak calmly. "You got anybody upstream that you trust completely? Someone you could question about this?"

"I may, but I want to think about it before I take that risk. I'd rather have some ideas of my own to consider first."

He could definitely understand that. It would give her something against which to judge the truth of what she was told. Presently he said, "You need some sleep. You said it wouldn't be safe to head up into the mountains today, so there's no reason you can't rest."

"I should be patrolling."

He just shook his head. "You shouldn't be driving. Nor should I. Unless something comes up, call it a day off. We can leave before dawn tomorrow."

Although, honestly, he was torn. He knew they needed to be rested before they started acting like mountain goats, but he really wanted to get started. He was a man of action, and this assignment which had basically stapled him in place, forcing him to wait for he knew not how long, was irritating him as well as worrying him.

He wanted to charge ahead and *do* something. But experience had taught him that fatigue and lack of sleep could lead to thoughtless—deadly—mistakes. It was one thing if you *had* to, another if you had a chance to rest.

At the same time he wanted to take Desi to bed with him, sleep with her, hold her, make love to her. Last night had bordered on revelation for him. He'd never had an experience quite like Desi.

She sighed, and he noticed how tired she looked. Not only lack of sleep, but worry as well.

"You're right," she said finally. "I'll get a call if I'm needed. We should be fresh for tomorrow. That mountain is rugged. But I suppose you're used to that."

"Yeah. They hired mountain goats to train us."

That at least drew a quiet laugh from her. "Guess you'll have to prove it."

Upstairs he sat on the couch, unwilling to invite himself into her bed unless she indicated that she'd like that. She surprised him, though, lying on the couch with her head in his lap. A trusting gesture. He couldn't resist running his fingers through her cap of silky curls.

Her eyes closed, but he could tell she wasn't sleeping. Eventually he asked, "What are you thinking about?"

"The same thing we both are. None of this is making sense any way I look at it. Did they send you out here to get you out of the way? Why would they do that?"

"I don't know. But remember there are three other guys who got the same undercover assignment in other parts of the state."

"Maybe so. Can you be sure?"

He opened his mouth to answer, then realized he

couldn't, not really. "That was my understanding," he said finally.

"Were you getting close to something in the investigation?"

He was amazed at the way her mind worked, thinking he might have been sidelined because he was close to a discovery of some kind. That would mean that someone up the chain was involved with this stuff. "Dang, Desi."

"I know. I don't like thinking this way. But we're about to go up a remote mountainside to check on a suspicious camp, and it occurs to me we ought to be aware of all possibilities before we go, whether we can prove them or not. Could someone have enough influence in Game and Fish to get certain people sent out on a wild-goose chase? It's possible. The question is why. Or maybe some idiot really did think this scheme could work."

He mulled it over while continuing to stroke her hair slowly. "If I was getting too close to something I don't know it. A lot of us were investigating this ring."

"Then maybe the person who hatched this plan believed it might work. He might have had help reaching that conclusion. One thing for sure... If anybody wanted to keep an eye on you and the others, they know exactly where you are and what you're doing now."

"True." Passion was beginning to throb in him again, but he swept it ruthlessly aside. She was right. They needed to discuss all the possibilities. "You know, you had more trophy hunting than anyone else over the last few years."

"I know, and I'm not surprised. We have some really rich migratory routes in these mountains. Lots of animals, and excellent hunting. I'm sure I didn't stumble over a quarter of it."

"But you stumbled over enough. So I was sent this

way. That would seem to indicate that someone believed that my mere presence might make the ring nervous. Too much to lose."

"Maybe. Certainly once they found out you weren't aboveboard, the ring could offer you a piece of the action. That would be the smart thing to do."

"Exactly. Which is what everyone was hoping for."

"So it does make sense in a way." She sat up suddenly. "Then why does it feel so wrong?"

He couldn't answer that. It had been bothering him for a while now. Sensible yet somehow senseless. Putting him in the water like a baited hook? Or getting him out of the way. And why the heck had they put in a license application for him? That seemed to defy his entire purpose here, and had been the first thing to worry him.

To convince local law he was on the up-and-up? Certainly not to convince Desi since he'd been told to hook up with her and make it look like he had her in his pocket, which meant telling her what he was doing. No reason to think she'd have agreed to get closer to him without an explanation. No reason anyone should have expected that.

She sighed and once again lowered her head to his lap. "There's something we don't know."

"Obviously." He resumed stroking her hair. "I'm used to having things more straightforward than this."

"Get used to life with the wardens, Kel. People lie to us all the time when they've done something wrong." She gave a weary laugh. "I will admit this is different, though. And I hate to say it, but I'm wondering who the target really is."

"I know," he answered. "Me, you or the poaching."

"Or both of us."

* * *

Later they made slow, sweet love. Kel let Desi take the lead, and she fully enjoyed it, discovering her power over a very powerful man, enjoying his enjoyment each time he moaned or quivered. She pursued the pleasure of learning every inch of him, then opened herself to his touches in a way she never had before.

Never had she guessed there could be so much freedom in lovemaking. It was as if her lost youth blossomed once again, all the excitement, anticipation and hope. She was reclaiming part of herself, and Kel helped her each step of the way.

At last they collapsed together, sweaty despite the cool bedroom, in tangled sheets and blankets, just holding hands for the longest time.

But trouble didn't stay away for long. The phone beside her bed rang and she answered it. The sheriff spoke into her ear.

"Desi? Don woke up and gave us a pretty good description of the guy he saw before he was shot. I'm sending over the rendering now."

She sat bolt upright. "Thanks. Did he say anything else?"

"Only that the guy wasn't from around here, but he had the feeling he'd seen him in the woods before."

And we might know exactly where he is. "Thanks, Gage. I appreciate it."

When she hung up, she looked at Kel. His gaze was alert. "There's a message coming in downstairs. Don was able to give a description of the man with the dogs. I need to get the description out to all my guys and it's easier to do down there."

Kel sat up, too. "This I want to see. So Don's okay?"

"He will be."

* * *

The day had warmed enough that they didn't bother to zip their jackets as they went downstairs. Once inside the office, Desi headed to the computer behind the counter. The message was waiting already. She printed out the black-and-white drawing of a man's head and together with Kel studied it.

"I've seen him," she said. "Around. The best I can do. But he's been in this area before."

"I've seen him, too."

Desi caught her breath and looked at him. "When?"

"Around. So he's been in my corner of the state, too. Near our offices."

She looked at the drawing again. "Now, what the heck could he be up to?" But she was beginning to guess, and she didn't like what she was guessing.

Using her phone, she snapped a photo of the drawing and sent it to her wardens, telling them to keep an eye out.

Then Kel said it. "Somebody has pull in the department. Someone who is involved with this ring. I'm not saying it's one of our people. In fact, our people may not know how they're being used. But someone is manipulating us."

"Man," she breathed, "I can hardly wait to get up on that mountain tomorrow. I want answers."

"It could just be a bunch of hunting buddies setting up a camp," he reminded her.

"I know. But my gut is telling a very different story."

She closed her eyes, and although she was reluctant to let go of a single moment of her time with Kel—despite their unhappy cogitations—she felt the lack of sleep all the way to her bones. She examined every single person she knew in the department and kept running up against the inevitable wall. She didn't want to suspect anyone she knew, but there was no escaping the fact that politics always played a role. It did in every government bureaucracy. The department needed support and funding for its operations, which meant you had to be careful about the people you upset.

If someone with the pull to affect the funding—not necessarily a politician, but one on the inner circles of power—well…

Sleep caught up with her.

Kel smiled as he looked down at her and realized she'd drifted into sleep. Good. She needed it, and so did he. But his mind wasn't letting go of the impenetrable puzzle they faced. Something was wrong. Or they were looking at it from the wrong perspective. Whichever, uneasiness was riding his back like cold, wet leaves.

He let his head tip until it rested on the high back of the sofa. This was a whole new game to him. In the military, like any other organization, politics inevitably mattered: who you knew, who liked you, who was your father-in-law. Were you one of the golden boys destined for high rank? How much did you dare throw your weight around if you were?

As an enlisted man, he'd avoided most of that, although it still existed. He'd managed to get his promotions more easily than some, but he made a practice of not stepping on any toes. Pointless anyway. Why aggravate the people who were giving you your orders? You'd not only make it harder on yourself, but you might make it harder on the men under you in your unit.

But this was different. In the military, you polished the

right apples and things went smoothly. Here it was possible someone higher up the tree was polishing an invisible apple. But why? The entire department was devoted to protecting the wildlife and ecology. It was their mission. Who would want to help poachers, even indirectly?

It would require some pretty strong pressure to bend someone in WIU, or at least he believed it would. No one joined this outfit as a lark. The work was demanding, the hours long. No, it required commitment to the mission. Real commitment.

And therefore it would require some serious pressure to bend someone enough to try to protect poachers.

Not that it couldn't happen. A sigh escaped him and he glanced toward the window. The morning was slowly turning into afternoon. No calls yet. Maybe, like Desi, he could cadge whatever sleep he could. They'd need their energy and wits tomorrow for sure.

He looked down at her again and smiled. Grab it while you can was a mantra from his days in uniform. He applied it now, tipping his head back and closing his eyes. Who knew, sleep might bring something useful out of the back of his mind.

Regardless, he'd be ready tomorrow.

Chapter 14

They left at three in the morning, while darkness cloaked the world. Kel had hugged Desi all night, and they'd stolen an hour or so to make love then a little more time to eat, but rest was paramount for this expedition.

Both of them were well-prepared for the kind of hiking they planned. They wore layers of rugged clothing with heavy hiking boots, and loaded backpacks with everything from matches to flares to first aid kits and freeze-dried food. Desi remarked she had snowshoes, then looked surprised when he said he did as well.

She smiled at him, and he was glad to see her eyes dance for the first time in what seemed like ages. "Always prepared?"

He laughed. "That's the Coast Guard. But yeah, me, too. Show me a mountain and I need to hike up it."

"No Everest?"

"That thing's a tourist trap now. Covered in filth. I think not. If I want to get into that kind of mountaineering I'll try some other place."

She paused to look directly at him. "You said the mountains bothered you some, now."

"Not enough to keep me off them."

They piled everything into the back of her truck and set out. Kel felt the rush of excitement that always came to him when he knew the waiting was over. He knew full well that there were a lot of things he couldn't control. Afghanistan had taught him that lesson well. But he'd also realized that he had *some* control when he started acting, more than he had while he was sitting on his fingers waiting for others to make up their minds.

The night sky was almost painfully clear, blazing with stars. As it had been in Afghanistan, where light pollution didn't wash away the diamonds that studded the night sky. The soon-to-be hunter's moon was sinking in the west, only half visible now as the mountains claimed it.

A perfect night. He loved the night. It changed the whole world into a silvery wonderland or a darkness-drenched cavern lit only by the stars above. It sometimes concealed threat, but it also offered safety.

"How are you feeling?" he asked as they drove higher and patches of snow began to appear here and there.

"About this? Glad to be getting to it. Half hoping we find out the camp is aboveboard, half hoping we settle this problem once and for all."

He understood the mixed feelings but frankly wanted this over. Not because he wanted to leave the area, but because shadow boxing was not his style. Give him an enemy he could see.

"We're violating one of the basic principles of trekking in the wilderness," he remarked. "No one knows where we're going."

"When I get as far as I can in the car, I'm going to call the sheriff and let him know where we are, and what coordinates we're headed for. But I'm not telling anyone else."

"Okay." Good plan, especially since suspicion was digging its ugly fingers in everywhere. She had trusted the people in the department for a long time, unlike him, and this had to be painful for her. To even wonder if someone she knew was in cahoots with the poachers... well, he wouldn't care to walk in her boots right now.

As they climbed higher, he could sense the air thinning and chilling even more. Brisk, refreshing, but that cold would soon become a problem once they were out of the vehicle. Well, he'd faced that problem many times and knew the best ways to deal with it.

His thoughts turned to other matters, mainly Desi, and it occurred to him he needed to say something to her. "Desi? Once we start hiking we're not going to have a lot of breath to waste on talk. So...I want you to know that our sex meant a whole lot to me. I feel proud that you trusted me."

She glanced his way, and he was delighted to see the corners of her mouth had turned up. "It meant bunches to me, too," she said as she returned her gaze to the worsening road ahead. "It changed me. Broke some old chains. How do I thank you for that?"

"I think you already did." But his chest swelled a little anyway. That may have been one of the most important things he'd done in his life.

After that, they remained silent until the end of the road.

* * *

Ponytail man was feeling quite pleased. His shill had given the coordinates of the campsite to the damn warden. She was on her way up there with her sidekick, the wannabe outfitter. And there had not been a single quiver on his information net that she had told anyone where she was headed, only that she had logged out for the next two days.

This would be too easy. Since Randy had already blown it, he was going to get to blow it again, by blowing the two of them away. He had no doubt Randy could do it...before he died. Because Randy was a loose cannon he couldn't afford.

None of his partners knew what he planned. None of them knew that he had contacts, none of them had the least idea of what was coming down. Which was just the way he wanted it. Conspiracies involved too many mouths and no guarantee that someone wouldn't say the wrong thing.

As far as his partners were concerned, he was no different from them. If any of them talked, the worst he would get was a big fine and maybe some jail time for running an illegal outfitting company. He wasn't worried about the jail time; he had a damn good lawyer and he could take down an important man at Game and Fish if the guy didn't give him room to wiggle out of this.

But he didn't think that was going to happen. Two people were about to disappear on a mountain and no one would ever know what had happened to them. Not once the forest took care of them.

How nice that those two had become suspicious enough to keep their plan a secret from everyone. Delicious even. He'd hardly dared hope that the warden would be so stupid. But what could you expect from a woman? Ponytail man had loathed her since she took his cousin Fetcher's promotion. Fetcher should be the senior warden.

And Fetcher was on the inside of Game and Fish, not that he knew what his cousin was up to. So were a couple of others higher up who owed pontytail man favors. They'd all helped him at one time or another and they'd shut up rather than get involved in any trouble.

Fetcher would take his rightful position and life would move on, short at least one major pain in his butt, and another guy who might become one.

Not to mention Randy. That guy was going to meet with some trouble when he came down from the mountain. Ponytail had just the man lined up to do it.

Despite the early hour, he decided to indulge his secret vice: some very expensive brandy. One small snifter would make his cigar that much more enjoyable, and it wouldn't cloud his mind.

A celebration was definitely in order, and why not? His plans were working almost better than he'd dared to hope. The Westin guy was a surprise in his campaign to get rid of Desi, but a manageable one. Two birds with one stone. Lovely.

Up on the mountain Randy got the message. The warden and the other guy were on their way up to the campsite. He was to take them out. For the first time in a couple of days he actually felt good.

But his preparations were already in place. Trip wires to warn him, because he had to be prepared, not taken by surprise by anyone.

It was one of the things he was good at. Besides being

a damn good shot, he'd used trip wires to help catch trophy animals, to give hunters time to prepare their shots.

He didn't mind cheating, and evidently their clients didn't either.

It would feel so good to take out that Desi Jenks. That woman had an absolute nose for finding the remains of trophy kills. Well, that was about to end. This time she and her friend would be the trophies.

The sun wasn't up yet as the two of them left the vehicle behind and, after a call to the sheriff to tell him where they were and where they were going, began their trek into the woods. Desi felt it was safe at this point to use flashlights and he agreed. As near as he'd been able to determine from the terrain maps he'd looked at, and from the GPS on his satellite phone, they had a good five miles of hiking and climbing ahead of them.

The danger, apart from breaking a leg, would truly begin when the sun cast its first light across the world. If there were any hunters about, they could start shooting. And he honestly wasn't sure that their orange vests and caps would be enough to protect them.

Not up here. Not with what they suspected.

Desi, it appeared, was half mountain goat herself. That cute and tidy little package she came in concealed an awful lot of strength and endurance. She forged ahead tirelessly, testing her footing when she thought it necessary. To his relief the canopy was thick enough that the ground wasn't buried in snow, although chunks of it occasionally plopped down from the branches above.

The snowshoes began to seem like an unnecessary caution.

Almost as soon as he had the thought, they reached a

spacious clearing and stopped at the forest's edge. The faintest gray light had begun to appear.

"There was a fire here a few years ago," she remarked. She pulled out her binoculars from a case that had been banging against her backside, and scanned the area slowly. "It looks okay." But she handed Kel the binoculars so he could check it out, too.

"We're a ways out from the campsite yet," he remarked. He stuffed his hand into his pocket and pulled out a bottle of ibuprofen. Two fell into his hand and he took them dry, thinking *shut up, knees*.

"Which doesn't mean hunters aren't wandering around out here. Or that guides aren't keeping watch."

True. He knew better than to underestimate the enemy. The problem was, little as he truly knew, he got the feeling that the enemy in this case wasn't very bright. Shooting a couple of hunters and drawing all that heat? Stupid. But entirely possible as remote as this area was.

They walked around the clearing, wisely not edging into the open or leaving a track on the snow. Desi checked her GPS, and said, "We should be within a mile of the camp by noon."

"Eyes on," he remarked.

She gave him a half smile. "Absolutely." She hooked her radio back onto its loop on her belt and pulled her gloves back on. "Ready?"

"Always."

Kel had learned to function at two levels simultaneously. While they hiked, he could safely let his mind wander because his ears, eyes and nose would alert him if something needed his attention. So much of this was automatic to him now, after so many years of doing it.

He wondered if Desi enjoyed the same freedom, because intense concentration could eventually wear you out and make you blind to important things. A relaxed, open state of focus was most important.

She seemed to be doing fine, however, scrabbling up over loose scree easily, edging down into ravines with an instinct for the next place to put her foot.

As the day grew brighter, she used the binoculars more, and sometimes passed them to him. A couple of times, in a sheltered place, they paused to take a drink and eat power bars.

They were getting closer. He could feel it. Having surveyed the terrain maps yesterday, they were stamped on his brain like a photograph. Now he scoured the ground ahead of them looking for traps and triggers, because there was always a possibility this guy had set a perimeter.

As noon approached, the forest remained relatively quiet. A lot of wildlife had evidently moved downhill to warmer temperatures. Whatever was left was making little noise. A wind began to stir the tops of the trees, however, and wood began to creak around them as frigid tree trunks stretched unwillingly. More snow plopped from above.

Desi picked a sheltered rock, bare of snow, to perch on, and he joined her. Together they pulled out a meal of jerky and power bars.

"My kingdom for some coffee," she remarked quietly.

He grinned. "That sure sounds good."

"At this point I'd take it frozen into ice cubes."

He laughed silently, not wanting to disturb the relative silence that sheltered them.

While she gnawed on a tough piece of jerky, he said,

"I want you to keep a sharp eye out for anything out of place. Maybe I'm overly cautious from my years in the Rangers, but I want us watching for trip lines and traps."

She arched a brow. "He's not expecting us."

"Maybe not. But if he's running an illegal operation, he might want warning if anyone's approaching the camp. So he can get his clients out of the way."

She nodded slowly, chewing. "Makes sense. Well, since I'm not sure what to look for, you lead the way."

She stared off into the woods, jerky forgotten, then said, "I hope I didn't make a mistake not trusting anyone with this."

"You trusted the sheriff. And you know darn well you couldn't have mobilized a task force just because there was a large campsite up here."

"No." She sighed and looked at the jerky in her hand. "You'll never know how many times I tracked down something like this on my own. Usually individuals or families who were ignoring the law, like baiting game and so on. And every time I came out here alone, I knew the people I was looking for were armed. It's always dangerous. But when I had my evidence that something was wrong, I called for backup. Depending, two or three of us would make the approach together."

"Yeah," he agreed.

"But this is different. I don't *know* there's anything wrong. Except that Lefty didn't think it was right."

"What do you think of him?"

She half smiled. "Mostly a good guy who occasionally likes to play on the shady side, especially when it comes to fishing. But not a big problem as far as I know."

He nodded. "Well, I hope I don't offend you, but I didn't like Fetcher at all."

She sighed. "He can be hard to take, but it's gotten better. I'm pretty sure he thought he should be promoted and not me."

Kel tucked that away for future consideration. Fetcher was resentful. Could be dangerous. Lefty was shady but not bad. As far as Desi knew.

Hell. At least one person knew they were climbing this mountain in addition to the sheriff.

His guard rose another dozen notches.

The mountain grew kinder after that. Once they'd put away their lunch, such as it was, and started out again, Desi followed behind Kel and had to admit she enjoyed watching him walk.

But that was not their purpose here. They were getting closer to the camp Lefty had told them about. It might be nothing, but if it wasn't innocent, they could be heading straight into serious trouble. Especially given that Don had been shot.

She was used to walking into potentially dangerous situations. What could be more dangerous than confronting armed hunters with violations that could take away their weapons and their right to hunt for years? Fine them more than they could afford? All this time she'd been lucky. She hadn't yet met someone who thought killing a warden would be the smart response to getting caught.

This situation was different and she knew it. A whole ring of poachers, probably pulling in hundreds of thousands of dollars a year, had a lot more to lose than hunting privileges and gun. Reputations would be lost, any future chance of making that kind of money gone…and depending how many instances they could be charged with, a lot of time in prison.

In fact, it might expose some very important people.

The more she and Kel had talked about this situation, the more convinced she had grown that there were important, recognizable faces behind this operation. A politician maybe. A judge. Who knew? But someone seemed to be getting some payola to keep this under wraps and divert resources in the wrong direction.

Because this whole plan of sending Kel out here as competition had a remote chance of working, but only a remote one. How much threat could one guy pose to the ring? None, unless he discovered who some of them were. They could have safely ignored him, at least until he grew a big enough business that he was cutting in on them.

She didn't like this at all. Not at all.

And looking at Kel marching so steadily in front of her, she wondered which of them had been the target of all this. Kel hadn't been around that long. She'd been around long enough, and made enough noise, that *she* might be the real problem.

She felt sick that Kel had been dragged into this, whatever it was. She didn't want anything to happen to him. Not one little thing. He'd done his public service in the Rangers, risking everything repeatedly. Protecting wildlife shouldn't put him through the same risks all over again.

Then she shook herself and decided she was being ridiculous. Kel had volunteered for this just as she had. And depending on what they found up this mountain, they might actually do some good.

Then she heard a howl. She froze, as did Kel. Another howl joined the first, and she stood riveted by the magic of the wolves of Thunder Mountain.

Kel looked back at her and smiled, saying nothing. She gathered he enjoyed the chorus as well. Seven wolves harmonizing until they sounded like more than a dozen. A magnificent chorus, one that stirred an atavistic reaction of chills running down her spine. But not frightened chills. The kind of chills she got when a piece of music finally delivered everything it had been building toward.

Then the crack of a gun firing shattered the harmony. Silence fell.

Desi started to charge toward it but Kel caught her arm. "No."

"If that guy killed a wolf…"

"Shh. You getting dead isn't going to help the wolves."

God, she hated that he was right. Fury had risen in her, and she knew one thing: if someone had shot a wolf he was going to wish he'd never been born.

The struggle to keep this wolf pack had been extraordinary. Found on private land, they could be shot. Then the governmental protections were removed and anybody could hunt wolves in the state. Then the courts had restored the protections but that didn't mean they weren't still hunted if someone thought they could get away with it.

While she fully understood the concerns of ranchers, she was also truly aware of how important those wolves were to the overall ecology. Just one small wolf pack. A splinter group from Yellowstone. A constant tug-of-war over decades between worried ranchers and concerned conservationists.

If a wolf had been killed, the *wrong* wolf, that pack would break up and death would ensue for most of them.

She swore under her breath and resumed her trek behind Kel.

The duff was silent beneath their feet. Considering how much snow had supposedly fallen the night before last, she was surprised not to see more of it beneath the trees.

All of sudden, Kel stretched out an arm, a silent warning to stop. She halted immediately, waiting, and watched as he crouched.

"Come up beside me," he said slowly. "Carefully."

She took two steps and before she squatted she saw exactly what had him concerned: there was a thin wire stretched between the trees.

"Now look to the left and right."

"Oh my God," she whispered. The trip wire extended as far as she could see.

"It's an alarm," he said quietly. "But now we have to be careful of other kinds of traps. Anywhere the ground looks the least disturbed, avoid it."

"Okay." What were they dealing with here? But she knew. People who killed for sport and broke the law. They probably wouldn't be above killing people either.

Randy was making lunch when he heard the gunshot. Good, the damn tenderfoot had probably shot his ram. He continued cooking sausage and fried potatoes while keeping the coffee warm on the end of the cookstove. That was his other job: cook for the hunters, set up the camp, strike the camp, help carry the trophy if necessary. Might not be necessary since they'd probably only bring the head.

The only part of this damn job he didn't like was wasting the meat. He understood they couldn't risk taking it, but he was enough of a true hunter himself that he loathed the wastage.

He turned the sausages, filling the woods with good

smells, feeling perfectly safe since his trip wires had sent no warning. Whatever that damn warden and her phony friend were up to, there was no reason to think they had to arrive today.

Hell, he'd have at least expected an overflight to look for the camp. And Lefty, as far as he knew, hadn't given the most accurate directions. Those two could wander for miles without finding this place.

Smiling, he hummed an old trail song, sure that he'd be feeding two guides and one hunter before much longer.

Desi paused and touched Kel's arm, stopping him. "We're going the wrong way."

He looked at her. "The coordinates…"

She shook her head. "Use your nose. Can you smell frying sausage? It's faint but it's coming from that direction." She pointed.

He turned his head slowly, drawing short breaths through his nose, then expelling them quickly. "You're right. It's not breezy enough to deceive us."

No it wasn't, she thought. With the midday, the normally restless air had quieted, in stasis until the temperatures started to change again. Up here, calm air was rare, but they had it right now and frying food acted like a beacon.

"I don't know if they're expecting us," she said.

"They shouldn't be," he answered. "But just in case."

"Exactly. We go in as if they're waiting for us."

He looked around again. "And watch your footing. That wasn't the best trip wire job I've ever seen, but the guys who set it up may be capable of adding other surprises."

She nodded, accepting his judgment. "Should we spread out and circle in?"

"Absolutely. And keep in mind there may be more of them than us."

She turned so she looked directly at him. "I'm the warden here, Kel. I should approach them first."

She watched his face and realized that it was killing him to agree. But finally he nodded. "Consider me your sniper in the trees if you need one."

"Thanks." She meant that in more than one way. He trusted her to do her job, even if he wasn't happy about it. Well, she wasn't happy about it either, but it *was* her job as warden. She alone had the legal right to walk into that camp and demand explanations. She was glad he understood that and accepted it.

When they approached close enough to the campsite to hear voices and clattering utensils, and even a horse's whinny, they split up, circling around. With a hand signal, Kel gave her one more warning to watch out for booby traps.

She nodded and moved slowly, carrying her shotgun casually in one arm, pointed downward, as she would when approaching anyone. No reason to tell these guys she suspected them of any wrongdoing. And it was always possible this camp was innocent.

Still, tension wound her nerves tight, and she had to make an effort to keep her muscles relaxed so she didn't make a misstep. From somewhere in the depths of her mind came a line from Shakespeare:

"Once more unto the breach…"

Kel thought Desi was being entirely too sanguine about this. Yeah, he knew it had been years since a Wyoming warden had been shot on duty, but that didn't mean it couldn't happen again. He got that she was used to most people not going that far, and whatever legal penalties awaited these guys, they couldn't come close to a murder rap. But still, he'd have given anything for a few men from his unit right now. A better perimeter, more protection.

But this was just supposed to be a courtesy call, right? She'd chat them up, ask to see their permits, and if there were no evidence of any wrongdoing, she'd move on. If any evidence was in view, he'd be surprised. These guys must be more careful than that.

He couldn't have been more wrong.

Randy started serving the lunch he'd kept warm to the hunter and the two guides. He wasn't sure what they'd shot, but he had a pretty good idea from the sheer size of the tarp-wrapped bundle they'd returned with on horseback that it was a bighorn ram's head.

Dang thing was so heavy it probably weighed a third of the ram's total weight, close to a hundred pounds. Not something easy for a man to carry out and plenty of reason to be hunting with buddies. Or horses.

The dogs were swirling around, sniffing at the wrapped head, and he whistled for them, chaining them so they wouldn't tear it open.

Damn it. Those dogs were good protection, but his own skin would be worthless if he let them damage a trophy.

The two guides, Ted and Will, lounged in the folding chairs holding plates of food. Their hunter was as excited as a man could be. He wanted to keep talking about the kill.

Randy wished he'd shut up. Even though his trip wires hadn't warned him that anyone was approaching, so no one was eavesdropping, Randy hated listening to it. Something inside him rebelled at the guy's pride and boasting when Randy knew full well he'd never have bagged his trophy without the two guides sitting there and nodding quietly in response to his every comment.

Hunters like that guy were incapable of doing the job themselves. They wanted to fly in, have their hands held, be led to the game, and if necessary be assisted in the perfect shot. They'd go home with their bragging rights and their trophy and never let on that they weren't the big game hunters they claimed to be.

It was a living, Randy reminded himself. A good living, even for him. And most of the time he never saw these jackasses again. Oh, they had some repeat business, but most of the time it went to other teams for security reasons. No one should be able to easily identify anyone else.

Except the big honcho who greeted these guys at the ranch and pretended to be the man who owned the outfit. A front, a guy who could disappear in hours if necessary.

They had pretty good secrecy, Randy decided as he watched the hunter eventually settle enough to eat. A good operation. Better than some he'd worked for.

But then there were some cracking twigs. Randy stood up immediately and reached for his shotgun. So did the two guides. The hunter merely looked surprised by their reaction.

"Maybe it's one of the wolves from that pack," remarked Ted.

"It should have tripped my alarms," Randy said uneasily.

Will waved the objection aside. "They found the kill. Maybe tracked the trophy. Well, we can take care of them, too."

Randy held no great fondness for wolves, but he figured that was apt to buy a whole peck of trouble, a bigger one. "Leave the wolves," he said. "They won't come close to the dogs."

Will looked at him. "What? You a wolf lover?"

"No, but you kill a whole pack and somebody's gonna notice. No need, they won't come close to the dogs." He spoke emphatically. God, while the local wardens hated the trophy hunting, they'd go all out if their precious wolf pack disappeared.

More cracking of twigs, then a woman walked into the small clearing. Oh, for Pete's sake, the warden. No warning. How had she managed that?

"Afternoon, gentlemen," she said pleasantly. "How's the hunting?"

The hunter had apparently been warned to keep his yap shut. Will answered. "Nice to see you, Warden Jenks. We're just looking around. No hunting."

"Odd time of year to go camping," she smiled, stepping closer, shotgun casually in the crook of her arm. "What are you looking for?"

"Game," Will replied. "We're scouting for Ted here. He has a moose permit."

The warden smiled. "Hey, that's cool. Those are hard to come by. But the moose are lower down."

Everyone in the camp tensed. It was going down, thought Randy. Now. He perched on the table, hand resting on his own loaded shotgun, though he didn't lift it.

"Mind if I see that permit, Mr....?"

"Bloom," Ted answered. He reached for his wallet. A wallet that was right near his holstered pistol.

"Move slowly, please," the woman said pleasantly.

"You can understand it's a little tense dealing with so many armed people."

"Sure," said Ted, smiling. He started to pull out his wallet.

Desi watched the man pulling out his wallet, but she was horribly aware of the growing tension from the other men. She was willing to bet this guy didn't have a valid permit, but rather something he was going to try to pass off, and point out he was allowed to bring two friends with him to hunt. He was in exactly the wrong place for moose. However, over the next rise, he could find himself a bunch of bighorns who were just starting to get interested in mating. The moose usually steered clear of that display.

But here? Odd place to be no matter what was being hunted. She hadn't missed that large tarp bundle over near the horses. Nor had she failed to note that the dogs were torn between an interest in her, an interloper, and that huge ball of tarp. They smelled meat, and it wasn't her.

Ted pulled a folded paper out of his wallet, but didn't budge as he held it out. He was drawing her in. Desi lifted her shotgun a little, surreptitiously thumbed the safety off and got her finger on the trigger. The barrel still pointed down unthreateningly.

"You're kind of out of your usual way," remarked the other guy.

"This time of year there's no usual way. Gotta check everything." She forced a smile she didn't feel as she stepped forward and took the badly creased paper. It was a moose permit all right, but someone had fudged the dates. It wouldn't need a forensic specialist to see that.

"I'm going to have to ask you not to hunt," she said, and tucked the permit in her pocket.

"Why?" demanded Ted. "I've got the papers."

"It's been altered, Mr. Bloom. So I'm going to have to verify that you have a permit for this year and area."

"Damn it, I do."

"Then I'll get it sorted out quickly and you'll be able to hunt. No further problem. Your friends aren't hunting are they?"

"No. But I can bring a couple of friends with me. You know that."

"Sure. Are they licensed in the state?"

Silence answered her.

Kel watched Desi turn a little. "Mind if I see what's inside that tarp?"

"You got no right to search us."

"I have every right when I think I see a bighorn's head concealed. In fact, by law I can search this whole campsite."

Time instantly slowed for Kel. It was like watching a movie in slow motion, and none of it was unpredictable. The men had a choice. They chose the bad option. While the guy in the canvas chair gaped, three men lifted their guns and pointed at Desi.

Kel moved. While his universe seemed to have slowed down, he hadn't. He already saw the lines of fire, the vectors coming into play, already knew who he had to take down first. Old instincts and a lot of experience took over.

"You got no right," one man said.

"I have every right when I suspect wrongdoing. Even

the bed of your pickup isn't safe from me looking. Now, I suggest you gentlemen point those guns away from me. Murder is a worse crime than poaching."

"And people can disappear out here," another man said. "Done it before." He leveled his shotgun at her. "You should never have come here."

Desi, intensely focused, saw fingers twitch on triggers. She also saw Kel reach the edge of the clearing, his rifle ready.

One choice, she thought. She dropped to the ground and rolled just as the guns all fired.

Then came one unmistakable shot, hitting the ground between the men in the group, throwing up duff in a shower.

The three men froze. The guy in the canvas chair looked as if he were too terrified to even make a sound.

Kel's voice reached them. "I'm a trained sniper. Any of you want to be first? If not, drop those weapons now."

The guy at the table had his own ideas. He pivoted sharply and shot from the hip at Kel. Big mistake. An instant later he went down, holding his leg in agony.

"Do I need to repeat myself?" Kel asked.

Moving cautiously, Desi reached for her shotgun, then rose to her knees and pointed it at the nearest man. "Drop them," she barked.

But the guy who was already shot had not given up. Snatching for his gun again while howling at the same time, he pointed it at Desi. A gun fired. He shrieked even louder as his gun flew from his hands.

The other men must have decided it was pointless. One after another they dropped their rifles and sidearms.

Desi levered to her feet and Kel moved in. At rifle point, he urged the three men, including the guy who'd been practically curled up on the canvas chair, into a tight knot. "I've got 'em," he told Desi.

"I'll take care of this one then." She kicked his gun away from him, and set her own out of his reach. He was back to holding his bloody leg with both hands, one of which looked injured from the shot that had ripped his rifle away.

"What's your name," she asked as she tried to pry the guy's hands from his leg.

"None of your business."

"Let me see your wound. I've got a first aid kit."

At that he reluctantly loosened his grip.

"Well, aren't you lucky," she said. "No arteries involved. You'll live."

He spat at her but missed.

Ignoring him, wondering when all this was going to hit her, she pulled her backpack off and brought out the first aid kit. Soon she had a tight bandage on his leg. Blood still seeped, but not very much. She dressed his hand with equal efficiency then stood up.

"I've still got these three," Kel said.

She looked to where he had them at rifle point. They were all looking pretty miserable now. Without a word, she went over to the tarp-wrapped bundle that had caught her eye. The dogs were leaping toward it with excitement, but they couldn't reach it.

Moving a hundred pounds wasn't exactly easy, but she managed it. As she rolled it, a bighorn sheep's head emerged.

"That's it," she said. Then she pulled out her radio and called the sheriff. Only then did she put flex-cuffs on the other three men, including the guy who claimed he was innocent and from out of state. Squawking he'd done nothing wrong.

"You need to have a permit to hunt game in this state, sir," Desi said calmly. "You have one?"

"The outfitter…"

"The outfitter is in violation of the law if he didn't tell you that. What's more, ignorance is no excuse. You're responsible for knowing the laws before you come here to hunt. You can be charged for all of this."

At last the guy fell silent, looking horrified. But at least he had shut up.

She thumbed her radio again, and heard the sheriff answer. "We've got a wounded man. And three more in cuffs."

"We're on our way, and sending the medevac chopper."

Desi felt reaction start to hit her. Her knees felt a bit rubbery. To conceal it, she recovered her shotgun and sat on a nearby stump, surveying the scene.

It could have turned out so differently. She caught Kel looking at her, concern in his gaze, so she gave him a tight smile.

"I hope," she said, "that these birds sing."

Chapter 15

The birds sang. Well, one of them did. Faced with charges for having forged a government document, unlicensed hunting, unlicensed guiding for profit, poaching and attempted murder, Ted Wilson started talking. He didn't have all the names, but he had enough to get the ball rolling. The strands of the spider web began to be traced all over the state.

The ponytail man didn't get touched, but he had plenty of influence. Nobody heard about him because the guy who'd been doing him favors in the upper echelons of the Game and Fish Department had as much to lose as anyone. The other partners slipped away, unnamed by anyone. They'd been very careful.

Desi felt vaguely dissatisfied as the dominoes began to tumble. She and Kel sat in her living room, talking about all they had learned.

"But we didn't get the top dogs," Desi said. "They'll start in again."

"Not very soon, I'd wager."

"I still want to know if someone in the department was involved."

He turned on the sofa, laid one arm across the back and smiled faintly at her. "Probably."

"And you're okay with that?"

"I figure we'll finger him or her eventually. But how long did it take us to find bin Laden?"

That was such an odd connection to make that she laughed, and with her laughter her irritation faded. "You're right."

He set his coffee down and moved his arm from the sofa back to her shoulders. "I figure if someone in the department was involved, he's so scared right now he's paying for at least half of his sins." He tugged gently, pulling her against his side. She sighed and leaned into him.

"I just wish we could have gotten the top dogs."

"Maybe we did. We may never know exactly where it all ended, but at least we've stopped this ring. Lots of game animals are going to survive hunting season because of you."

"And you," she reminded him. "Think of it. How many unlicensed guides have we pulled in? Fifteen? Maybe more? And I'm not sure we have them all."

"That's just the guides," he reminded her. "Then there were all the other people who helped, like that Randy I shot. The support staff. Lefty, who still swears he had no idea those coordinates would lead us into a trap. I expect they'll have their own share of legal troubles. Randy worst of all because he tried to shoot you."

"They all did," she reminded him. "I'm so glad Gage

threatened them with attempted murder if they didn't cooperate. So I guess it was all worth it."

He fell silent and she tilted her head when it went on for a while. "Kel? Something wrong?"

"Not a thing," he answered.

"Then why so quiet?"

"I was just thinking about you. You really give a damn about the wildlife. To you that poaching is serious enough to put your life at risk."

"Well, yeah," she said, wondering where he was going. "Warden, remember? I wouldn't be doing this if that weren't true."

"Yeah, but…" He pulled back a little, loosening his hold on her but turning his head so they could look eye-to-eye. "I get being willing to die for a cause. Obviously. But I was sitting here thinking that no bighorn, no moose, no animal of any kind is as important to me as your life. I almost killed Randy, you know. I never wanted to kill a man again, but I'd have done it for you. I had to make a conscious decision to wing him, and I was trained never to do that. Too risky. Go for center mass. But…I'd have shot all three of them to save you."

Sorrow filled her. "Kel, I'm so sorry." She could only imagine what he must be dealing with. Memories of war must be plaguing him, all those things he'd probably be dealing with for the rest of his life. And it was her fault. She wished she had a magic eraser. "I'm sorry I got you into this. You didn't need it."

His eyes widened. "I don't recall you getting me into anything. I did just fine all on my own. I'm not blaming you for me having to make a decision. I knew when we went out there that I might have to. It's just that when I signed up for this job I didn't imagine it involving anything that extreme. Did you?"

She shook her head a little. "No, actually. I carry guns but I never expect to have to use them on people. And I never have."

"Exactly. Anyway, don't worry about it. What I'm really dealing with is you."

"Me?" Her heart skipped a beat, and she waited, feeling certain that she must have done something wrong and he was getting ready to say goodbye.

"Yes, you," he said. "You seem to have become a problem."

She drew a sharp breath. "How so?"

"When I realized I'd kill to protect you, I realized something else. I love you. Doesn't matter we're just getting to know each other…that's all mind stuff anyway. When the gut is speaking this loud, the brain should just take a hike. I love you. Deeply. And now that I've said it, I guess I should pack and go so I don't make you uncomfortable."

At once her chest tightened, as if a rope had snapped around it. Breathing became almost impossible, and the ache that filled her almost made her cry out. "No rush," she said hoarsely, all she could manage.

His eyes narrowed a little as they swept over her face. "You look like you've been wounded. I'm sorry. I should have kept my mouth shut."

With that she found air enough to cry, "No!"

He froze, just as he had been pulling his arm from her shoulders. "No? I just upset you…"

"Shut up," she ordered, her voice tight. Then before this man could say another word, she twisted, wrapped her arms around his neck and pulled him in for a long, deep kiss, the kind of kiss he had taught her.

Finally she broke to catch her breath, but now her body was humming in a whole new way. "Kel..."

But understanding had started to ease his face. The smallest of smiles tugged at the corner of his mouth. "It's okay that I love you?"

"More than okay," she said huskily. "So much more than okay. I love you, too."

He put one finger under her chin, lifting her face to study it again. "Oh, man," he breathed as he clearly began to believe her. "You, too? I mean, really? Will you marry me?"

"Yes," she said, her voice firm at last. "Absolutely yes." The last of the fear had ebbed, even the oldest of her fears, replaced by an immense joy that washed through her like the dawning of a new spring day. She felt her smile widening, widening, until her cheeks ached.

Then Kel surprised her by laughing. "I'm the world's luckiest man," he announced. Then without another word, he stood, swept her up into his arms and carried her to the bedroom.

"I won't let you go," he warned her as he laid her on the bed.

"You better not," she answered, reaching for him. "Kel?"

"Yeah?"

"It is all right to be this happy?"

"You bet," he answered before he stole her breath and her voice with a kiss and carried her to the stars.

* * * * *

MILLS & BOON®

INTRIGUE
Romantic Suspense

A SEDUCTIVE COMBINATION OF DANGER AND DESIRE

A sneak peek at next month's titles...

In stores from 12th January 2017:

- **Law and Disorder** – Heather Graham *and*
  Hot Combat – Elle James
- **Texas-Sized Trouble** – Barb Han *and*
  Mountain Witness – Lena Diaz
- **Eagle Warrior** – Jenna Kernan *and*
  Wild Montana – Danica Winters

Romantic Suspense

- **Cavanaugh in the Rough** – Marie Ferrarella
- **Her Alpha Marine** – Karen Anders

Just can't wait?
Buy our books online a month before they hit the shops!
www.millsandboon.co.uk

Also available as eBooks.

MILLS & BOON®

Why shop at millsandboon.co.uk?

Each year, thousands of romance readers find their perfect read at millsandboon.co.uk. That's because we're passionate about bringing you the very best romantic fiction. Here are some of the advantages of shopping at www.millsandboon.co.uk:

* **Get new books first**—you'll be able to buy your favourite books one month before they hit the shops

* **Get exclusive discounts**—you'll also be able to buy our specially created monthly collections, with up to 50% off the RRP

* **Find your favourite authors**—latest news, interviews and new releases for all your favourite authors and series on our website, plus ideas for what to try next

* **Join in**—once you've bought your favourite books, don't forget to register with us to rate, review and join in the discussions

Visit **www.millsandboon.co.uk**
for all this and more today!